CUP0071134

HELL iS
EMPTY

13113664

Also available from Conrad Williams and Titan Books

DUST AND DESiRE
SONATA OF THE DEAD

DEAD LETTERS: AN ANTHOLOGY

CONRAD WILLIAMS

HELL IS EMPTY

A JOEL SORRELL NOVEL

TITAN BOOKS

CARMARTHENSHIRE COUNTY COUNCIL	
13113664	
Askews & Holts	06-Dec-2016
	£7.99

Hell is Empty
Print edition ISBN: 9781783295678
E-book edition ISBN: 9781783295685

Published by Titan Books
A division of Titan Publishing Group Ltd
144 Southwark Street, London SE1 0UP

First edition: November 2016

1 2 3 4 5 6 7 8 9 10

This is a work of fiction. Names, characters, places, and incidents either are the product of the author's imagination or are used fictitiously, and any resemblance to actual persons, living or dead, business establishments, events, or locales is entirely coincidental. The publisher does not have any control over and does not assume any responsibility for author or third-party websites or their content.

Copyright © November 2016 by Conrad Williams. All rights reserved.

No part of this publication may be reproduced, stored in a retrieval system, or transmitted, in any form or by any means without the prior written permission of the publisher, nor be otherwise circulated in any form of binding or cover other than that in which it is published and without a similar condition being imposed on the subsequent purchaser.

A CIP catalogue record for this title is available from the British Library.

Printed and bound in the United States of America

For Nicholas Royle

PART ONE
KiSHi KAiSEi

1

I used to own a book of Irish jokes when I was a kid. You know, the kind of casually racist collection you'd be hard pressed to find on the shelves these days. And a good thing too. This one joke, though, has been preying on my mind.

Have you heard the one about (Paddy/Mick/Seamus) who fell down a flight of stairs while carrying a crate of Guinness but didn't spill a drop? He kept his mouth shut.

I thought of that joke while I lay there, drifting in and out of consciousness for six months, tubes in, tubes out, stapled, stitched and – in all probability – superglued. I thought how much like Declan/Ardal/Liam I was, only I had spilled plenty, and it wasn't Guinness but 'claret'. And it wasn't a crate but a body full. Two bodies full if you count the transfusions.

How did I survive?

I almost died, and I would not have been conscious to appreciate it. I was put into a medical coma. I suffered kidney failure and underwent dialysis. I lost weight. When I revived I was scared to check my body in case there were any limbs missing. All I could think about was the way Ronnie Lake's blade slid into my thigh like a rat through a shitter.

Eventually, one night, when all the lights were out and my sheets were on for a change, and not soaked through with fear sweat, I took my fingers exploring. Everything present and incorrect, as usual. Plus added bandages and splints and scar tissue. I was building up quite a collection of scar tissue. It twisted and turned under my fingers like cooled molten plastic. It was me but it was not me.

Doctor, please, tell me how I made it.

I was visited often while I was in hospital. Romy, mainly, but Lorraine Tokuzo came to say hi too, as did Henry Herschell, sort-of friend, martial arts expert, flashy dresser, doorman (which was a bit of a surprise), and even Mawker popped his head around the door on occasion, to ask me how I was doing, and to tell me how easy policing was these days with me out of action. He ducked out before I could pin him down with questions. Everyone was doing that lately. Avoiding, evading, ignoring. Why was that? Did someone else die that night? Someone that I cared about?

Nurse, I was bleeding to death... did she save me? Did my daughter—

Strength returned, incrementally. I gritted my teeth through months of physio. Apparently Lake's knife had sliced through any amount of nerves and ligaments as well as my femoral artery. Walking, I looked like newborn Bambi hobbling across hot coals while pissed. But things kind of improved. Physically, that is. I was taken off dialysis. I gained a little weight back. I found the strength in me to smile when someone displayed a kindness.

I was allowed home in December. The first thing I did was register with the supermarket and do some online grocery shopping. Here's the list I compiled:

Vodka

It turned up within a couple of hours. I signed for it and the delivery guy went off with a distasteful look on his face. *It's not as if I ordered a packet of butt plugs*, I thought, and then realised I'd answered the door wearing only a T-shirt and my woolly bobble hat.

That first drink stole away any embarrassment, and scoured my innards clean of all the overcooked vegetables and claggy desserts that I'd forced down over half a year of horizontal life. I was home. I had another drink to celebrate.

Later, half cut, I phoned up the Indian restaurant in Lisson Grove and ordered a chicken jalfrezi to be delivered. When the bell went I buzzed them in without asking and fished some notes from my wallet. But there wasn't a bag of curry and naan on the other side of the door. It was Romy. She held Mengele in her arms. He was folded over them like some big cat scarf, gazing up at me with a sanctimonious look on his face, as if to say: *This is all mine.* I made a mental note to ensure I left out a bunch of leaflets from the vets about neutering, and stalked to the kitchen.

'Do you want a drink?' I asked. 'I've only got vodka. Or water. So, you know, at least there's a choice.' I didn't want her here. I wanted her to dump Mengele and leave. I didn't like her open scrutiny of me and the way I had changed in her eyes. I felt like a new addition to the zoo. She followed me into the kitchen.

'You shouldn't be drinking,' she said.

'I shouldn't *stop* drinking,' I said.

'You've only just come off the dialysis machine. Your kidneys are weak.'

'And this vodka is strong,' I said. I chugged a couple of mouthfuls straight from the bottle and sucked in some air between my teeth to show her just how strong it was.

The look of shock on her face pierced me, but only for a second. She moved past without touching me (and that's some feat, in a kitchen where every turn is greeted by the threat of a braining from some unit or other).

'What are you—' I began, but then she started opening and slamming cupboard doors, cutting me off. I took the bottle and a glass – I'm not a total heathen – on to the balcony. Pigeon shit everywhere. A trio of the feathered dorks queued up on the roof to give me the blinking eye. I flapped at them and they flapped back. The rain would wash away the guano eventually, and Mengele's returning face at the window would keep those flying rats at a distance.

Romy came out to join me. 'I've put a tin of food in a bowl for your cat,' she said. She refused to call him by his name. 'And some water.'

'Thank you,' I said. My voice was flatter than an ironed pancake. 'Thank you for looking after him. While I was. You know. Dead to the world. Pissing through a straw.'

'What else would I do?'

I was staring at the back window of the pub opposite. A man vacuuming a bedroom. A woman on the phone flipping the pages of a newspaper. Chef in the kitchen, funnelling strained cooking oil – the colour of tea – back into the bottle. He paused for a moment and cocked his leg up, pulled his left buttock away from his right. Then he went back to his task.

I could feel the heat of her gaze. She was waiting for something I couldn't give to her. I suddenly realised where I was, and balked at the acres of nothing vaulting away from the rooftops. It was as if I could feel the weight of all those miles of nothing that reached into deep space pressing down on me like a thumb at a ball of plasticine. I moved back against the floor, flinching at the light. My eyes had been closed for too long.

'Joel?'

'You're still here?'

'Where else would I be? I'm here because I want to be here. With you. I want to help you. I thought we had something.'

'Emphasis on "had".'

'What?'

'I can't see you any more, Romy.' I moved inside. The rising panic was checked. Here was the ceiling. I was enclosed. Limited. I could no longer look at her standing outside, her eyes raptor-round. She looked too much like the shape of my dreams. Haunted and windswept. Denuded. Defeated. And it was my doing. And it had to stop. I tended to transfer any of my damage to those in my sphere of influence. If I stayed away from people no harm could be visited upon anybody. Furthermore, I wouldn't have to deal with my own wounds reflected back to me in any number of sad, sorrowful eyes.

I think she left then, but I didn't move to the living room until I'd shifted a quarter of the bottle. Christ. Half a year without booze had seriously lowered my tolerance threshold, unless they'd fortified the stuff while I was getting my cods flannelled and my kidneys jacuzzied. I sat on the sofa and Mengele yelled at me. He'd never done that before, preferring instead silent disdain, but this was a full-throated yowl, the kind of noise a witch might make as the flames lapped at her petticoat. He kept on at me. I couldn't tell if it was because he was happy to see me or disgusted by my behaviour or if there was something wrong with him.

13

My curry arrived. I paid for it and ate half of it without tasting a thing. Mengele pressed and repressed a spider into the nap of the rug, then went to the bedroom to do whatever it is cats need privacy for. To lick his nuts, or cough up something unspeakable. Not that he'd ever been shy before. Maybe he wanted to invoke Satan and give him some tips.

The curry was just getting in the way of the bottle. I put the leftovers to one side for the fridge with the fanciful notion I might reheat them for lunch in the next day or two. Then I sat in the dark by the window playing James Stewart staring out at back-yard Marylebone until I'd finished a bottle and the sense of feeling was utterly numbed.

When I went to bed, Mengele remained where he was sitting, sending me off with a baleful glare.

Sleep flashed its tits at me, that's all. I surfaced with a dream revolving around and around my head like a tornado failing to touch down. The streets were damp and my stitches and scars snarled at me when I hauled myself upright. A dull ache pulsed under the oysters of flesh at the base of my back. My kidneys complaining at the bully-boy antics of the vodka? Or humming with pleasure at being called up for duty once more? I decided to press the issue and poured another glass. Instantly it misted with cold. Vodka is lighter than water. Only marginally but there you have it. I like that, for some reason. I kid myself that I can tell, when I roll a slug of it over my tongue. I touched the glass and the chill transmitted itself to my fingers.

A spit of red light above St James's. A helicopter or a Cessna, some small aircraft flown by a sober pilot. More fool them. I tossed the vodka back and held it at the base of my throat for a moment, relishing the cold and the heat, the smooth sting of it. I watched the oily dregs settle in the drained glass.

Alcohol is a seduction. It is its own fetish. The virgin clarity. The come-hither tinkle of ice cubes. The dryness. You go through childhood sucking down sweet soft drinks, unaware of this incredible dryness that awaits you, and when you finally sample it, nothing else will do.

Most nights, if I can't sleep, I'll head out. I might drive over to Shepherd's Bush or take a walk if I've had a skinful. Now, the thought of going outside made my guts cinch tight and my forehead break out in sweat zits. I drank another shot to distract me. For some reason I was thinking of a cucumber martini I'd once enjoyed at a bar in Islington, and now I wanted one. The only green in my fridge was the kind you scrape off the Mesozoic-era cheese sitting at the back. Why was I thinking of cuketinis? And then I realised.

Romy's eyes were that shade of green. Such a paleness to them you could barely call it colour. She had a dark brown mole, just one on her body, near the nipple on her left breast. Her body was like the map of a country I'd never visited.

I had to get out of the flat. I knew that. I didn't want to become that sad, forgotten recluse who nobody sees for years and then is discovered dissolved into the sofa with the TV on and a foot of mould on every surface. But I knew I wasn't getting outside under all those billions of cubic feet of fuck all without some kind of anaesthetic. I went at the vodka like a newborn at the breast. I emptied shot after shot into my belly until the angles of the room lurched like Cubism on crack, and my brain felt as if it was surrounded by buffers of soft bubbles. I opened the door, checked I had my keys and that I was wearing something vaguely socially acceptable, and weaved downstairs. I heard Mengele miaowing and it was the ribald cackle of a Bond villain. If I went back up there he'd have a little Donald Pleasence in his claws, and he'd be stroking it with malicious glee. I didn't need to worry about him while I was out. If his Fishbitz bowl was bare, he'd eat whatever was sitting on the balcony – insect, rodent or bird – and there was always water available in the blocked guttering.

I opened the communal front door and waited for something to happen. My nerves felt knotted and tangled, like something you'd find in the fuck-ups drawer at a marionette factory. It was quiet here now, if I ignored my own little cardiac timpani orchestra. I didn't know what time it was and I couldn't sufficiently focus on my watch face to find out. I heard the soft, comforting sounds of domesticity. The murmur of a TV. The churn of a washing machine. The rhythmic clack of plates being rinsed in a sink.

I heard a door close down the street and a woman jangling her keys before slipping them in her purse. I kept my eyes on the wet, orange-blue footpaths and told myself to just make it to the corner, where Luigi's sandwich shop stood. One foot after the other. Christ. What I'd thought were a pair of trousers were actually my pyjama bottoms. Never mind. This was London. I could have worn cardboard loons and neon pasties and barely garnered a double take. At least my bollocks were covered for a change. My awkward baby steps were not solely down to the gallons of voddie I'd ingested; the countless miles of nothing on top of my head were checking my progress too. It was difficult to describe. It was like an inverted kind of vertigo, a feeling that I was untethered and that nothing so grand as gravity was going to keep me pinned to this stretch of gum-studded concrete.

I thought of Luigi while I walked (inched, actually) along Homer Street, my hand holding on to the guardrail that shielded the drop down to the basement. Luigi, who made a mean ham and cheese sandwich. He was in his late fifties and sang Frank Sinatra songs while he sliced and buttered and layered. On the walls were dozens of pictures of him crossing various half-marathon finishing lines around the world. I'd asked him once if he'd ever attempted a full marathon and he shook his head. It wasn't for lack of trying, but that he suffered from jogger's nipple if he ran too far. 'I have the man breast, no?' he said, before segueing into 'Mack the Knife'.

I was on Crawford Street without knowing it. I risked a look left, in the direction of Baker Street, and the long straight avenue of bright lights turned to fire in my mind. The sky, a deep black-blue, leapt away from me like a startled cat (I thought I saw… no, I'm sure I saw… the sky where that leap had originated stretch and begin to separate, like damp toilet tissue). I collapsed, sobbing, to the hard, gorgeous ground, close to shitting myself with fear at what such a tear might reveal.

I heard the squawk of a police siren and saw a carnival of blue and red lights chase each other across the brickwork of adjacent buildings. I struggled upright and staggered back to the flat, eager not to have to tolerate an interrogation. I shut away the screaming black acres and climbed the stairs. I felt calmer and more justified with each riser. When I got back to my rooms, I felt somewhere near normal again, although I screamed when Mengele leapt at me from the darkness of the bedroom, his claws flashing out at the belt hanging loose from my bathrobe.

2

nsistent knocking. I thought it was my booze-scarred heart for a moment, going berserk before seizing up for good. But no, it was the door. I yelled 'fuck off' until my throat was hoarse but whoever it was didn't take the subtle hint. I answered it wondering which of my cack-brained neighbours had given this knock fiend access to the building. Their lives wouldn't be worth a comma of worm shit once I was through with them.

'This had better be worth me getting vertical!' I shouted. 'If you aren't Eva Green then prepare to return to street level at a velocity much higher than the one at which you ascend— Oh, fucking Nora. Mawker. Fuck off back to your throne, King of Bellends.'

'I hardly hear this shit of yours these days, Sorrell, you do know that, right? I've assimilated it. You're like white noise. I can tune you out. You're there, but you're not there.'

'Well "hardly" works for me,' I said. 'I'll keep it up for "hardly".'

'How are you doing?' Mawker asked. He'd had a haircut. The skin around his hairline was dry and red. What a place to suffer from eczema. Unless it was something else. I wondered if perhaps Mawker was bald and that this thing on his head, this over-greased pudding of a hairstyle was, in fact, a wig. And it was chafing him. Or he was allergic to it. I imagined him at home, gingerly removing it, like Darth Vader's skull-cap, while whatever passed for his life partner cried in a corner, too horrified to watch.

I reached for my glass but it was empty.

'I'll sort us out,' Mawker said, placing a fat briefcase down by the sofa. 'I'm spitting feathers myself. I could murder a cup of builder's.'

'I don't drink tea,' I said. 'Not the sort you like at least.'

'Coffee then. Anything soft?'

'Corporation pop.'

'Water it is,' he said, clapping his hands together as if he was actually satisfied with that.

I held mine at arm's length when he got back. It looked like vodka, but it didn't have its silky allure. No oily jags on the glass. It was... heavier. I sank it though, and to give him his due, it was good. I held the empty glass out for a refill.

'Do I look like your H_2O bitch?' he asked, but he was smiling, and he fetched me another.

'What are you here for?' I asked. 'I no longer own the key to your mother's chastity belt. I raffled it off on some scuzzy MILF website.'

Mawker shrugged, mimed something going in one ear and out the other. 'When you open your mouth I think only of happy things. Gently blowing the seeds from a dandelion clock. Picking a tune out on my uke. Ethiopian coffee.'

He stood up and riffled through the paperbacks lined up on the bookcase beneath the window. 'I used to read a lot when I was younger. Before I joined up. Stopped not long after. Fiction didn't cut it for me any more. It couldn't... I don't know... keep up.'

I nodded and waited. A breath of burnt toast flew into the room. Somewhere a baby was crying. An image struck me of Sarah in her high chair, a wedge of peeled pear in one chubby fist.

'What do you like to read?' he asked.

'Obituaries. Specifically, yours. It can't be long now. Look, it's great that you've come for a visit, but I'd rather have rabies. Haven't you got a job to be getting on with?'

He looked at me as if a job was some alien thing that he didn't understand. Then he held up his forefinger. 'I do. And so do you.'

'I've got nothing on at the moment,' I said.

'You have, if you want it.'

'What's that supposed to mean?'

He opened his briefcase and dug out a wad of fat folders. The smell of age came with it. I guessed the last person to have leafed through these was now little more than a jumble of bones in an untended grave.

'Fuck off with your cold cases,' I said.

'Maybe you'll come up with something,' he said. We both had a laugh at that one. 'At the least it'll get your mind active. A way of keeping your hand in.'

'Get my mind active. Like I'm losing my marbles.'

'It'll keep you distracted.'

'From the drink?'

'Mainly, yes.'

'I'm fine,' I said.

'You're not fine. Have you seen yourself in a mirror lately? You look like hammered shit.'

21

'Five'll give you ten I got my dick sucked more recently than you did,' I said.

'When was the last time you ate something?'

'Ask your mother.'

'Joel.'

'Last night,' I said. 'I had a curry.'

He strode to the fridge and pulled out the foil cartons. 'This?' he said. He showed me the fur on it. 'This is a week old. At least.'

'So much can change in just a week,' I said. But that had rattled me. I was losing time. Great swathes of it.

'Just pull yourself together,' he said. 'There are people out there who care for you. Or they would if you'd give them a chance.'

'You need some opening-and-closing-door practice,' I said. 'Please... feel free to have a go on mine.'

He left, closing the door so ridiculously quietly that I had to get up and open it and slam it hard enough to set off a car alarm in the street. That might have been a coincidence but don't underestimate my powers as a door slammer. At least it would have given Mawker a start. If I was lucky it might have sent his syrup askew.

I picked up the folder – hating the dry, desiccated feel of it under my fingertips – and tossed it into the paper recycling box under my kitchen sink. I found some olives in the cupboard and made myself a dirty martini and it was the perfect drink, the magical drink, the impossible drink – because IT DID NOT END. And then it was dark and I'd either pissed myself or dropped a drink and I'd rather the former than to have wasted a martini to be honest. And there was a godawful banging at the door or was it in my head? Was it Mawker back already with some more dead files he'd found down the back of his onanist love seat? I got up off the floor and stepped on the martini glass. It crunched and I thought, *I'll clear that up as soon as I've hurled Mawker out of the oriel*. I didn't want Mengele hurting himself. And then I skidded on the floorboards, slick with blood, and thought, *Christ, he already did*, but then I saw I was barefoot and... you get the picture. I didn't, not immediately, because I was trousered beyond all reason. All I could think was, *Nothing good can come of that*: a scimitar of glass stuck out of the arch of my left sole.

The banging intensified. Maybe it was Mr Amorous Pants next door, whose idea of lovemaking was trying to pound his conquests through the lath and plaster and into my flat. I yanked open the door and there were Lorraine Tokuzo and Romy Toussaint. I said something but the words just tumbled from my mouth like so many dead fledglings from a frozen nest. The pair of them looked impossibly scrubbed and pink and healthy: they glowed. And they smelled terrific too, or maybe it was just that next to me, a shit-crammed pig shed on fire would have smelled attractive. Credit to them, they came in despite the miasma. As a friendly gambit I meant to say 'I suppose a threesome is out of the question', only it came out: 'Gaaah...' and there might have been some sick involved. The both of them said 'Joel' in the same way. The kind of sad, defeated way you'd say something to someone who has caused you no end of epic disappointment. There are only two syllables in Joel but this pair made my name go on all day.

I heard the bath filling; I hadn't done that. Tokuzo barged past me carrying a large bag of ice cubes from my freezer from way back when. 'They're for my martinis,' I said, only it came out: 'Dzuuuh...'

I was on the sofa and Romy had a piece of rare meat in her lap. She was assessing the blade of glass; whether it was safe to remove it. I thought: *That should be hurting more than it actually is.*

Romy said: 'Are there any major blood vessels at the bottom of the foot?'

I tried to tell her about the large saphenous veins but it came out: 'Sbmffff...'

'That would only matter if the bastard had a heart,' Tokuzo said. 'Just whip it out. If he bleeds to death then that's just lumpy gravy.'

I looked down in time to see Romy pull the glass free. There was a queasy sucking sound and it did bleed more but at least I wasn't hosing. Romy cleaned the wound and applied butterfly closures ('you really ought to have this stitched'), a wad of gauze and a sock bandage.

'It's ready,' Tokuzo said. I didn't like the words or the way she said them. She and Romy hoisted me upright and led me to the bathroom. There was more ice in the bath than had been needed to down the *Titanic*.

'Fuck *that*,' I said, but it came out: 'Krnnk...'

They stripped the robe and the pyjama bottoms off me. I heard Romy's breath hiss when she saw the map of vivid scars my body had been turned into.

Tokuzo said: 'I had no idea you were so far advanced with your sex-change plans.'

Then they tipped me in.

I thrashed about, convinced I was having a heart attack, making various noises never before heard in the animal kingdom. They pressed me back in when I scrabbled to get out. I heard a lot of 'It's for your own good' and 'You brought this upon yourself.'

After the initial shock had receded (much like my generative ganglia... probably never to be seen again) I calmed down and just lay there, teeth chattering. My head was pounding. I saw the blood that had rushed to Lorraine's face (a view that startled me; it was usually what happened to her as she reached climax) drain away. I flinched at Romy's hand on my shoulder, or rather the sudden realisation that her hand was on my shoulder; she flinched too – perhaps she'd been stroking me since I 'got into' the bath.

I was coaxed out and given a fresh towel. Now I felt pain. Romy helped me hobble towards the sofa. The broken glass and the blood and the vomit had been cleared away. The lights had been turned down. A CD was playing, too low for me to identify it, but the soft, insistent beat and shiver of strings was soothing. I sat on the sofa and Romy changed the dressing on my foot.

'You'll be lucky if you've got away without severing any nerves,' Lorraine said. 'You dippy twat.'

Romy passed me some clean clothes: jogging bottoms and a sweatshirt. I got into them in the bedroom and saw that the bed had been made with fresh sheets. What the fuck was going on? I wasn't an invalid. Not a total one, anyway.

'It's called an intervention, Joel,' Lorraine said, no doubt registering my befuddlement. 'It's what happens when idiots like you let themselves go to such staggering extremes. Friends step in and stop you maintaining levels of stupidity that ought to be criminal.'

'Thank you,' I said.

'It speaks,' Lorraine said. Something was cooking in the kitchen. It smelled great. I felt my taste buds twitch and a huge wash of saliva flooded my mouth. When had I last eaten? I must have been gnawing on something while I was three sheets. Old cheese. Breadcrumbs. Fishbitz. She eventually emerged bearing a bacon sandwich. 'You didn't have any ketchup but I've put some of chef's special sauce on there.'

I laughed at that, despite the headache, and moments later I was staring at an empty plate. I felt suddenly something approaching human again. Romy and Tokuzo moved through the flat carrying two loaded bin bags. They chinked and clinked. It sounded like a recycling plant on collection day. Lorraine caught my gaze and raised an eyebrow as if to say, *Just try to stop me.*

I sat with my empty plate until they returned.

'That was a last-time rescue,' Lorraine said. 'I'm not getting elbow deep in shit to help you out again. It's becoming a habit and I won't have that.'

She kissed me harshly on the cheek and walked to the door, giving Romy a loaded look as she did so. 'Five minutes,' she said. 'Then you make your own way home.'

She turned to me. 'Remember,' she said. 'What doesn't kill us makes us look like cunts.' And then she was gone.

Romy sat next to me. Mengele jumped up between us and started kneading her thighs, squinting up at her as if he was trying to see through fog. The slut.

'Romy,' I said.

'Leave it,' she told me. Her eyes were soft and blameless. She looked so sad. She pressed a small paper envelope into my hands. 'I don't think you should be taking these. Probably bad for you. But they'll help you to sleep.'

She gently pushed Mengele to one side and stood up. His ears went back, giving him a sudden wild look. Well, *wilder* look. It was as if he was saying, *Aw, come on, Romy, don't give me the brush-off in front of* this *prick.*

'You fancy going for lunch some time?' I said, going through the motions. I barely had any energy for myself; how could I possibly exhibit any for her? She saw it too.

'We'll see,' she said. 'We'll talk.'

'I'm sorry,' I said. 'Just a bad few days. I'll be better soon.'

'I hope so,' she said. 'Papa says hi.'

'Hi, Papa.'

After she'd gone I opened the envelope. Two big white pills. Two small yellow. And a note:

> *White = painkillers. Take now. Take the others (Valium) before bed.* Rx

I got the analgesics down me and stared out at the lowering afternoon. The sky was the colour of wet metal; it would rain soon, like a bastard.

I went to my desk. There's an old bank of index card containers I bought from a library in Friern Barnet when it closed down some years ago. I meant to use them to store the kind of things you need every day: stamps, coins, keys, travel passes, etc. But of course, I ended up filling them with shit. Receipts so old the ink had faded away. Bottle caps. Paper clips, for fuck's sake. I haven't used a paper clip in twenty years. I remembered that I also keep bottles of wine in there too. I'm not much of a wine drinker but people tend to like it with a meal so I make sure I keep some lying about. Lorraine had missed this one. A Malbec from Argentina. I set it on the table and admired its colour. In the drawer next to it was a piece of paper so creased and frayed I'd had to put it in a plastic sleeve before it disintegrated. This had been waiting for me in my PO box when I got out of hospital, along with the usual horrors (two pages from a 1999 diary with the words 'BUSY FUCKING' scribbled on each day; a small plastic ziplock bag of what looked like eyelashes; a blank cheque pinned to a note asking me to find

27

'my misssing muther plz what died two weks ago plz').

No return address on this ragged scrap. No contact details of any kind. Written in a very attractive hand. I felt some pride in that, despite the stab of the words. I'd read them so many times I knew them by heart; knew every curlicue, jot and tittle. I'd invested in it the kind of attention a palaeontologist invests in a bone sticking out of a rock in the Jurassic coast. I could have handed it over to Romy to assess, but it didn't need a genius to read between the lines. Plus, I'd already added a bunch of pathetic footnotes I didn't particularly want anybody else to see. And the whole sad eyes thing was getting a bit old.

> Dear Joel,[1]
>
> Of course, I'm grateful to you for what you did. I guess you saved my life. I just wanted to say thank you and that I'm glad you're getting better. Seeing you in hospital like that - unconscious, full of tubes and wires, it was horrible[2]. But I felt I owed you a visit. I think, maybe, we can be friends[3]. Someday. But not now. Not yet. I'm sorry. I know Mum[4] died a long time ago but it's still raw[5] for me. And I can't just forget what happened next. So, Joel, I will be in touch. Until then, take good care of yourself.
>
> Regards[6],
>
> Sarah[7]

---

[1] Joel? *Joel?* What the fuck happened to DAD?
[2] It wasn't exactly a bowl of peaches for me either, poppet.
[3] Friends? WTF?
[4] *Mum* is it? Not Rebecca?
[5] And my feelings are all so fucking well done, are they?
[6] Re-fucking-gards.
[7] And no fucking kisses. Fuck's sake.

But even though I knew it off by heart, I slid it out of the sleeve and held it like a primigravida with a newborn seconds old and I read it again, wanting to somehow feel her through the ink under my fingertips, trigger some unlikely connection. And all I could think about: the bit where there were no footnotes, no sarky comments, no snide asides.

...I will be in touch.

3

I slept well that night, for the first night in months, and I did not have anything to drink. My head thumped, with the dregs of a hangover, with the pressure to return to the bottle. But I poured the wine down the toilet. The sound of it glugging and sluicing away was like some invidious brain worm beseeching me to reconsider in a voice rich with soft plums, blackcurrants and a touch of liquorice. I did some stretching to combat the stiffness in my body where the knife wounds had healed. My physiotherapist had urged me to do this every day, and now, sweating with effort and pain, I wished I had. I felt sure that the livid snakes wound around my flesh would peel away from my body and cause me to bleed to death, but somehow I remained whole.

I showered under the hottest spray I could tolerate. I changed the dressing on my foot and was pleased to see that it wasn't as bad as my pissed brain had initially feared. As well as feeding me the previous night, Romy and Lorraine had magicked other things into my fridge and cupboards: fresh eggs, wholemeal bread, yogurt and bananas. I made breakfast from all of that and sank two very strong cups of coffee. I felt my fingertips tingling. I felt something close to human again.

I switched on the radio and listened to the news. Everything was exactly that: new. I felt like Rip Van Winkle kipping up in the hills, out of it for years. Immigrants swarming into Europe to escape the nightmare of Syria, old-age pensioners going down for planning a diamond heist, a new skyscraper nicknamed the 'Splinter' nearing completion in the Square Mile's den of architectural thuggery.

I opened all the windows; chill, clean air swept through the flat, clearing away the ghosts. I stared out at the BT tower and imagined myself standing on the top. Somehow that didn't freak me out as much as trundling around the busy, close streets in the immediate vicinity. I realised I'd been spending a lot of time thinking of height, of rare altitudes and of flying. Despite the cold air I felt sweat prickle in the lines on my forehead. I wasn't ready to go outside. Not yet.

I stalked around the flat, feeling panic thicken inside me. I had to go out. I couldn't spend the rest of my life cooped up inside. I had to work. I had to find Sarah, no matter that I was now 'Joel' to her and on a par with some old acquaintance that she might or might not look up again depending on her mood. It was no solace to me that this was a much better situation than that in which she had left me. Back then it had been for good. A permanent arrangement. The letter, though disappointing in so many ways, showed some measure of progress. I had to cling on to that.

Outside. Come on. Dip your toe. What's the worst that could happen?

Instead I went to the kitchen and retrieved the bunch of dead folders from the recycling bin. Keep your mind off. Keep your hand in. There were five folders – old manila jobs (none of this modern funky-coloured business) – stuffed to the point where the seams and folds were beginning to fail. The folders were littered with coffee rings and cigarette burns (they retained that 1980s office smell... a compost of Embassy No. 1, Shake 'n' Vac, Kiwi shoe polish).

There were adhesive labels, the gum fossilised by time, marked ACTIVE affixed to each one, although someone had slashed a black line through the word. Inside each folder was a series of sealed envelopes, only marginally less rancid than their containers. Names had been typed across the centre of these envelopes. Dates in pencil told when the files had been opened and when they had been closed. I slit open the first of the packages (there must have been around sixty or seventy of them in total) and pulled out a neatly organised sheaf of documents. Despite my initial disdain towards Mawker, I now silently thanked him. My curiosity had been piqued. And there was something about the paperwork of thirty years ago that appealed to my Luddite self: typewritten statements, carbon copies, index cards, dot matrix printouts on perforated sheets, handwritten notes (*Oi, Jenks, bet you beers that Pascoe is all over this. Pint later?*). There were photographs and negatives, long, beautifully penned letters, maps of a partially lost London that lurked just under the skin of this shining, twetny-first-century metropolis. It was like opening a time capsule. I reached out for a glass that wasn't there.

I went to make some more coffee, though I'd already had my day's ration. Something to keep me from the thought of booze, the habit of it. If anything, Mawker's files were giving me a jones for vodka, or more likely a Scotch and water... Wasn't that what all the sheepskin coat-wearing, Ford Sierra-driving coppers were drinking back in the day when these files were causing coronaries and divorces?

I sipped my coffee while I flicked through the sheets, glimpsing ghosts. Nearly known names and addresses. Tip-of-the-tongue stuff. Slant-rhymes in a dissonant memory. Many of these people dead now. Many of these addresses turned to rubble or morphed into millions of tons of gleaming glass and steel. The misdemeanours on their criminal records, some of them almost laughably old-fashioned; cute, even. Ernest Percival, fifty-two, of 6 Walmer Road, London W11 had apparently, at midnight on the night of 20th December 1961, stolen two frozen turkeys from Pyrkotis Butchers in Camden and then tried to hide them in a tree when approached by police officers.

Jesus. I trawled through three or four envelopes until I realised I was sitting in an uncomfortable position on the kitchen stool and cultivating a cricked neck. I stood up and stretched and took the pile through to the living room and stretched out on the sofa. It was old shit, but it was interesting, in the way any document from the past is interesting. A window on a world you used to know but is now so alien it seems drawn from dreams.

One envelope in particular caught my eye. The word SKYLARK was written upon it. I tore it open and out poured a glut of horror. I saw the photographs first. Large monochrome prints of what at first seemed to be pictures of carelessly spilled black paint. But paint didn't contain body parts: fingers and faces. These were bodies that had been obliterated. What could do such a thing? But I knew full well it had nothing to do with weaponry. This was catastrophic injury sustained in a fall from a great height. This was what we used to describe in the police as 'pancaking'. We had to collect what didn't stay inside the bodies with a scraper. I'd dealt with one, a couple of months before I threw my serge uniform and tit helmet at the Chief Superintendent and walked out. A Russian couple who had thrown themselves off the top of a multi-storey car park in West Kensington. They didn't look too bad, all things considered. They were lying on their backs in the snow. They were still holding hands. Blood had leaked from their ears, the only hint at fatal injury, until we tried to transfer them to the ambulance. It was like trying to heft an octopus. There was no structure to the corpses, the bones having been pulverised. It helped, in a freaky way. You could believe that what you were wadding into the body bags was anything but human. Lover's leap. Hellish romantic.

'Skylark' was apparently the nickname given to an evil bastard who'd been getting his jollies pushing construction staff from the top of skyscraper building sites in the early 1980s. London was enjoying a boom back then, and in-demand architects were sketching their erect pricks, passing them off as blueprints and pocketing acres of green. The capital was going up in the world in more ways than one. There was no obvious motive for what Skylark was doing, but there were a few theories written down on memos. *Political activist? Anti-capitalist? Protesting against the verticalisation of London? Worth looking into. Anybody on file?*

Presumably not, because nobody had ever been caught.

4

He answered and I could hear him at work, prepping something. The chunk of a knife as it blurred through onions or carrots or Jerusalem artichokes. 'You've got some nerve, calling me.'

'If I had a penny for every time someone said that to me I'd be able to buy a small packet of cheese,' I said.

'Last time I saw you, you were in my cellar, gobbing off as per.'

'Come off it, Danny,' I said. 'I was just looking for someone, *as per*. And then you started pushing buttons, trying to get me involved in one of your illegal bareknuckles.'

'And what?' he said. 'You came to arrest me? You're as much a copper as I am a dishwasher. And anyway, I've got half the Met coming to my gaff, getting involved in those "illegal" fistfights. So fuck off.'

'I'm not calling about that,' I said. 'I'm calling because of you. I need your help.'

'So fuck off,' he said again. 'I don't know x, I haven't seen y and z ran off to Gravesend with a tart.'

'I'm not after any leads,' I said.

'So what is it?' he said. He stopped prepping and I heard him put down the knife. I heard it make a metallic noise – *schrang!* – and my wounds sang in woeful recognition. 'You want me to teach you how to make pastry?'

'I need to get fit.'

'So join a gym. Go swimming. Eat kale.'

'I need a foot up my arse.'

'I can't help you,' he said. 'Do you have any idea how busy I am these days? It's not just Stodge. I've got Nom in South Ken, Nom Nom in Belsize Park and Om Nom Nom opening in Soho first quarter of next year. We're three weeks off Christmas and I've barely got time for a shit.'

'Bollocks,' I said. 'You've got an army under you. You've got no books scheduled and I've checked the *Radio Times*. No Christmas special showing plebs how to tease boiling sugar into the shape of reindeer antlers.'

'I'm off to Mexico in March to do some filming.'

'Well March is March. I'll be out of your hair after one session.'

'One session? What use is that to anyone? And anyway, I can't give you one session. I'll put you in touch with a personal trainer I know.'

'No. It has to be you.'

'Fuck's sake, Joel. Why?'

'Because I won't give up for you. I won't dare shame myself for you. Someone I know. I'll give it up and not care one fart if some faceless twonk is trying to get me to swing kettle bells.'

'There's a compliment in there somewhere, I'm guessing.'

'How do you keep yourself in shape if you haven't the time? You look like Michelangelo's *David*. Only with a smaller cock.'

He sighed; I could tell I had him. I reckoned he'd quite enjoy making me look like the gasping shamble-muppet I was. I pressed home. 'Come on, Danny. Let me shadow you. Just for one session. Just until I can breathe without fear of dying on the spot. Show me the rhythms. Teach me the rhymes. I'll owe you.'

'Big time,' he said. 'If you don't keep up, I'll drag you down to the cellar and risk ruining my hands on your dumbfuck face.'

'Deal,' I said.

I heard the scrape of the knife as he picked it up again and I had to grit my teeth. The sound of it as it went through an aubergine or a gala melon. I felt my stomach recoil.

'Be at the entrance to Hampstead Heath on Highgate Road at six a.m. tomorrow morning. If you're late by as much as one nanosecond I'll be gone.'

'I'll be there,' I said, thinking, *Fucking six a.m.?*

5

I got out of bed as soon as the alarm went off at five a.m. I had a quick shower to spray the sleep from my groggy bones and put on some sweats. Hat, gloves, fleece. Quick banana then out. I say out, but at the door I felt the familiar dark forces threatening to send me back to my cower blankets. It was too dark, too open. In the end I had to bring Sarah into it, just to help me get clear of the damned building. I turned it all into a dangerous game. It was the only way it would work, though of course playing that role again – gallant Dad coming to rescue the daughter in peril – came with its own set of peculiar risks. I stood at the end of Crawford Street and thought of Sarah just around the corner, being dragged away by Graeme Tann. I thought of all the angles of his face, the mocking smile, the deep-set eyes. The hand around her mouth. That filthy hand wreathed in its nicotine reek. Around Sarah's sweet mouth. That got me moving. Blood up, it got me around the corner. And the next. And the next. And on, until I was at Baker Street and sinking into blessed enclosure. I kept my scrutiny of my fellow passengers to a bare minimum. I didn't want to risk being recognised, or invite any kind of exchange while I was down there. Strangers make me nervous these days. I was as likely to try to pull their intestines out via their nostrils as I was to return a chirpy 'good morning'. Not that anybody ever said anything to a stranger in the Tube. I think someone might have tried in 1975 but it was later proved to be a case of mistaken identity.

I changed at King's Cross (don't we all?) and caught a Northern Line train to Hampstead. There was mist in the air. I felt the moisture of it catch in the stubble on my face. London was a bowl of green-purple shadows. I watched for a while the aircraft warning lights on the Gherkin, the Shard, Thatcher's Cock, and it was like some kind of archaic pattern just beyond my understanding. It was a pulse that spoke of the beats and secrets of altitude, a knowledge gained by those privileged to suck on that rarefied air.

'You've got the posture of a man used to sitting at a desk reading emails all day,' Danny Sweet said. He was in a vest and running shorts. His trainers looked more expensive than my car. 'You look like mashed shit. Are you ready?'

After running hard on the spot for a couple of minutes, he showed me some dynamic stretches that threatened to put me in hospital before we'd even travelled an inch. I couldn't touch my knees, let alone my toes. 'You don't just start stretching. Especially in this weather. You'll rip a hamstring or tear a calf like it was a pitta bread fresh out of the oven. You warm up to warm up.'

'So does this kind of thing help you in the kitchen?' I asked.

'Course it fucking does,' he said. Damp blond scissors of hair swung in front of his eyes. He always looked as if he was disgusted, no matter what he was doing or saying.

I wondered if he'd said 'I do' to his wife with that look on his face, as if he'd seen dog hairs in the crème anglaise. 'The levels of cretinism in some of my so-called staff are difficult to get my head around. But exercise helps to level me out. I still mete out some epic bollockings, but, you know, if I didn't have this hill here, I'd be in prison for assault.'

'*Back* in prison,' I corrected him.

He paused in the midst of a deep lunge, the muscles in his arms squirming against each other beneath the tattoos of carp and eagle. 'That part of my life is over, you twat,' he said. 'I'm a successful chef. I've got Michelin stars floating in my piss. I'm literally picking wads of cash out of the back of my sofa. I don't need to involve myself in any shit any more.'

'Apart from the illegal fisticuffs.'

Now he stood up straight and leaned in close to me. I could smell something exotic in his skin, on his breath. Remnants of his poncey breakfast, no doubt. Quinces and flaxseed and goji berries and civet crap. I don't know.

'Are we here to talk about what I might or might not be up to or are we here to get your sorry arse into shape?'

'You're right,' I said. 'I apologise. Force of habit.'

'What happened to you, anyway?' he asked, appraising me the way he might a box of rotting organic veg.

'Bad end to a bad night,' I said. 'No gossip in the kitchen?'

'We don't gossip in the kitchen,' he said. 'We fucking labour.'

'I got carved up like one of your pork loins,' I said. 'I've been out of action for months.'

'At least you won't have to worry about getting a stitch,' he said. 'You must have fucking hundreds.'

'You can have some of your own if you've got wound envy.'

'Come on,' Danny said, and took off up Parliament Hill at a speed at which a cheetah might have raised its eyebrows.

I followed as best I could but after a minute my calves felt stiff enough to split. Cramp spilled hot ants down the back of my right thigh. I looked around for the clown sawing logs at this unholy hour but it was my own breath churning in my chest. And those lights down in the urban crucible, shimmering like end-of-life coals. It really was a most distracting sight.

'What the fuck did I fucking say?' Danny demanded. He hadn't even broken a sweat. Aircraft lights stuttered above the London Eye.

'Sorry,' I said. 'I'm rusty. I'm coming back from rock bottom.'

He drew me off the path into cold, wet grass. 'Follow me,' he said. He made sure my back was to the view. We spent fifteen minutes swapping between cardio exercises – fast repetitions of squats, press-ups, planks and crunches – and, when it sounded as though I might rupture a nut, recovery spells with some deep breathing and basic yoga. He ran me ragged all over Parliament Hill, along the paths, then off road, up and down inclines, until I felt a deep burning in my thighs and calves. The cold had gone away; I felt sweat creating slick layers between my clothes. Steam radiated from me when we stopped for more exercise. I looked like a walking vent.

'I can't,' I said.

'You can,' he said. 'You will.'

There were moments on that run when I did not feel comfortable, and I'm not talking here-come-my-guts discomfort because that was pretty much a constant throughout. No. It was tied to feelings I'd experienced before, out in 'the field' as opposed to 'this field'. The tingle of pursuit, knowing someone was hot on my heels or keeping a beady one on me from a distance. I felt it now, while Danny forced me to go harder, to turn my quads, trikes and glutes into tenderised steak.

'Do you have any idea how much work you have to do to be able to survive one three-minute round in the ring?'

'Three minutes?'

'You fucking joke. Long, intensive sessions with the big bag.'

'I bet. I bet you spend hours pummelling your big bag. If you're not getting your dishwasher to do it for you.'

'It's not rocket science, Joel. You have to put in more than you take out. Same with everything.'

'Suet pudding?' I asked. 'Anal sex?'

'So push yourself now and you'll suffer tomorrow but the day after your body will thank you.'

'It won't.'

'It will. Now come on.'

I put my head down and set off at a gentle trot. I made sure Danny's expensive running shoes remained visible, but credit to him – he'd cut his pace significantly to allow me to match him. That was all I saw. My toes and his heels and their monotonous tread on the glistening path across the Heath. But then another pair of shoes joined us to my right. I looked up and there was a lean, wolfish guy with a bald head and week-old stubble keeping pace with me. He didn't meet my gaze. Nor did the guy who ghosted in on my left. Shorter, stockier, wearing a bobble hat and a snood that concealed the lower part of his face. We looked like a sweatier, slower version of the Red Arrows.

I heard the slap of a foot behind me and there, not two

feet away from my sluggish arse, was a loping beard and dreadlocks, dressed in neoprene so tight it might need scalpels to get it off him.

But even with three guys tracking me, the tingle, the not-rightness, was still there and my nervy little glances left and right went further afield than my companions, though they probably thought otherwise. I couldn't see anything though. Which meant they were very good at concealing themselves, or my watch-it gland had crashed and burned.

'What the fuck is this?' I called out to Danny. 'Synchronised cunts?'

Danny stopped and I ran into the back of him.

'Fifty press-ups,' he said. 'Last one to finish gets a leathering.'

I was taken by surprise; the others were already four or five in. 'What do you mean, "leathering"?' I asked, as I got down to it. I hadn't done press-ups since the last year of high school. And sex didn't count, apparently.

Nobody responded. I was in the late thirties, convinced I could feel the connective tissue around my wounds beginning to separate, when the others finished and rose, sedately, to their feet.

'How do you keep it together in the last few rounds when your body is willing you to throw in the towel but you can't because to do that is to lose. What do you do, Joel?'

One of them threw a punch at me but it was telegraphed and it was easy to dodge. I moved my hands out in front of me low, fearful of a blow that might unwrap me where I was weakest. The other one launched a kick and it wasn't hard but it caught me right in the back of my knee, causing my leg to buckle. Off balance, I put out a hand and gibbon no. 1 caught it, hoisted it north and punched me hard in the face. I felt it in the marrow. Blood began leaking down the back of my throat.

'We're not in the ring,' I said. 'I'm never likely to be in the fucking ring.' Blood sprayed. I was like a porpoise with a ruptured blowhole.

'Everyone's in the fucking ring,' he said. 'You're born into the fucking ring. And every day you either win or lose.'

'Fuck off, Danny,' I said. 'I asked for help because I'm weaker than a vegan's handshake. I don't want to go back to hospital.'

He came up to me and planted his gorgeous trainer right up my bum bone. It felt as if my spine was going to pop out between my teeth. Danny remained close enough for me to suspect he'd got his foot stuck, but it was only so he could ladle on the theatre.

'It's all tied together. The fitness. The fight. You know that. And that's why you came to me, rather than Johnny Gym Kit. You need to rediscover the bloodlust. Because without it, you're finished.'

I knelt there feeling pain – proper, unregulated, unnamed raw pain – jogging through my meat and bones and it felt real. It felt good. I felt myself unwind into the moment, and into the spaces that the others populated. I ended up with a cut above my eye, and I'd have some bruising on the arms and chest, but all things considered I felt okay. *Better than these clowns*, I thought. I'd given each of them something to remember me by. Now my only problem was Danny Sweet, who was capable of boxing me until my pips flew out. But if he was miffed that I'd doled out some thrashings to his lieutenants, he wasn't letting on.

'They're bottom-feeders,' he said, when I asked him what he thought of my moves. 'I've seen blind people move faster than those puddings.'

'Still…' I said.

'I picked them so you'd get a workout without cracking a nail. You were okay, but I'd leave puffing your chest out for another day.'

'So what now?' I said.

'You'll be fine,' he said. 'Stop looking for brownie points and get on with it. Keep the exercise up, but you need to load up on calories too. You run, you burn more. And because you've been on your arse for weeks without proper fuel, you're skinnier than a supermodel's fart.'

'I appreciate this,' I said.

'I look forward to the favour being returned some day. And if you want a sterner test, you know where to come.'

We traipsed back to the park entrance. Mud on my legs was drying to a thick glaze that tightened the skin. I smelled sweaty, rank. I felt great.

He slid behind the wheel of his Bentley. 'I'd give you a lift,' he said, 'but I don't want Sorrell juice all over my leather.' Then he was gone.

I walked down to Kentish Town and in a greasy spoon ate a massive breakfast that didn't even touch the sides. I bought a couple of pastries to go – the waitress looking at me as if I was a trencherman in training, or more likely someone with a serious tapeworm problem – and caught a Tube home before I realised what I was doing.

I bumped into an off-duty copper down there who gave me a wet wipe and advised me to dab off the blood on my face – *that* had been why the waitress was giving me odd looks – and I thanked her and bit down on the rejoinder I was about to let loose, something about what was life like when you had a few hours free from Mawker's ring piece.

When I got back I crashed out on the sofa and slept until dusk. I stripped and showered and dressed in my date-presentable wardrobe: jeans, unironed (but fairly high quality) shirt, Chelsea boots and the envy leather. Best knickers and socks, obvs. I stopped short of talcing my cods but consented to a cheeky dab of come-hither fluid at the back of each ear. I headed out and though it was hard to get over the threshold, I was thinking HOME>OUTSIDE rather than SAFE>BALLS-OUT DANGER. It was okay. I could do this. I'd broken the back of this particular monkey.

Agoraphobia: ✓

Alcohol: ✓

Romy: ?

By the time I got to the house in Islington, my legs and arms were stiffening. My chest pinged with little agonies every time I shifted position. But it was an agreeable range of discomforts, the kind of self-righteous pain that tells you you've worked hard, you've earned it.

In a strange way, though, I also felt looser than I had for a while. I felt as though I was moving much like I used to before the attack, although the carvings in my flesh still felt tight and inflexible, like veins of gristle in an otherwise tender sirloin steak.

I prevaricated outside the door for a while, as I knew I would, but once I realised what I was doing, I rang the bell and wished I'd bought some posh chocolates or a bunch of flowers. I had half a pack of Wrigley's in my pocket and that might have worked in an ironic way once upon a time. But it would likely get me a slapped face or at best a look to shrivel any skin that wasn't still clinging on tightly.

She opened the door. She didn't say anything. She left the door open. She went back inside.

I left it a moment and then followed. I suddenly felt as vulnerable and on edge as I had when I entered the old

Southwark factory a fit man and came out wanting for a shroud. It struck me that this might well be as much of a Damascene moment, albeit with slightly less bloodshed.

She was in the living room. The TV was on; she was watching a film, but she'd hit the pause button. Al Pacino was caught in the moment of destroying a TV of his own.

'Good film,' I said. 'But not your thing, I'd have thought.'

'Don't presume to—'

'I'm sorry,' I said. 'You're right.'

She sighed. Worry or doubt or a combination of the two were dragging at her features and I moved fast to stay them.

'I made mistakes,' I said. 'I won't make any more.'

'I want to believe you,' she said. 'Watching this film, how close to danger they skate every day. The wife at home whose place is always second. Second to his job, second to the evil scum he's trying to put behind bars. I don't know if... I don't know how anybody...' Her fingers toyed with the buttons on the remote. 'Would you like a glass of... oh, shit. I'm sorry.'

I smiled. 'You see? How easy it is to fall into traps? I do it all the time.'

'It's not a trap, Joel. It's something normal people do. It's a social thing. But now I can't do that. Because you can't do that.'

'You can. I'm not an alcoholic.'

'Which is the first thing an alcoholic says.'

'I don't care about that. I'm not. I think I might be forgiven if I was.'

She seemed shocked by that, or maybe that was just her default look these days.

'I don't like the life that's gathered around me,' she said.

Pincers of guilt, but I had to stop beating myself up. I'd

done my best not to bring her into the line of fire. I'd not made the mistakes I'd made with Melanie. I told her as much.

'No,' she said. 'That's not the issue. I can take care of myself. I'm talking about you. The fallout from you. The blood and the knife wounds. The coma. The stitches. I don't want to face each day not knowing whether you'll still be alive at the end of it.'

'This was an isolated incident,' I lied. 'Things very rarely get as serious as this.' Another lie, but a white one.

'And so you can walk,' she said. 'And fight again. And use that filthy, smart mouth of yours to get you in and get you out of trouble. All is well. But next time. And next time. If it's not death it might be something worse.'

'I'll tell you now,' I said, 'if it *is* worse, then I don't want to live through it. If I'm paralysed, or in a coma, I'm giving you permission to turn off the—'

'I don't ever want to be in that position,' she said. 'You make it sound so easy. But it's not you standing there looking down at whatever's left in the hospital bed. It's not you staring at the coffin.'

'I've been there,' I said. 'I know.'

'I DON'T!' She sighed and clapped her hands to her face as if shocked or disgusted by her outcry.

'Then walk away.'

'I can't,' she said. 'But I won't do what I did again. I won't come and see you in pieces in hospital.'

'Okay,' I said. 'It's a deal.'

'So now what?'

'Are you hungry?'

'Kind of.'

'Joel… that filthy mouth of yours.'

'Let me show you just how filthy it can be,' I said.

There was still anger in her eyes when she approached me. I felt the edge of teeth in her kiss.

Later, in her bed, when the breathing had calmed down and the sweat was cooling against my skin, I reached out and cupped her warm breasts in my hands, felt the dance of her heart inside. I kissed the inside of her thigh and smelled fresh seed and the hot, incredible musk of her sex.

A muscle in my calf sang where I had pulled it as I reached my climax. She was on the edge of sleep.

I said: 'What if it's you who puts me in hospital?'

6

It was that same tweaked muscle in my leg that wakened me, a few hours later. It was the middle of the night, or early morning, however you like to frame it. A.m., anyway, with a very low number in front. I hobbled out of the room, careful not to rouse Romy, and found a tube of Deep Heat in her bathroom cabinet. I slathered it onto my calf, working it until the burn had all but camouflaged the pain.

I only meant to go for a stroll around the block, but once it became clear that the pain had not been caused by a tear, and was easing somewhat with my perambulations, I kept moving and found myself gravitating towards that square mile crowded with all the big stuff. The Splinter beyond the protective construction boards gleamed like something shaved and showered, ready for a night of hot, rampant skyscraping.

Not thinking too hard about what I was doing, I moved to the half-built skyscraper opposite and padded down the side of the boards until I found a lamppost I could shin up. When I was level with the barrier top, I paused and checked for cameras and motion alarms. It looked clear. Maybe they weren't as security conscious as they might have been.

Maybe they hadn't been installed yet – I mean, what are you going to break into a building site for unless it's to play in the sand? At least there was a stairwell. I wouldn't have to climb up the scaffolding. I had no idea whether that was normal. I had no idea how you built a sandcastle, never mind a high rise. What went in first? The toilets? So I skipped up the first few flights but after ten minutes of stairs I found myself wishing that they put the lifts in first. Was that unreasonable? And then, just add rooms and walls around it. How hard could it be?

A bit higher and the stairwell changed. The walls disappeared and London took over. I felt a squirming in my guts, my groin and my knees. Worms of ice. Strike that. Ice fucking snakes. So much space. So much height. I remember in the distant past, when I used to own a TV, never being able to not look when there was a documentary on about rock-climbing or mountaineering, even though it felt as though I'd sunk my junk into a pit of fire ants. I've got a 'friend' who likes to send me YouTube links on the laptop. I can't help but click, even though I know it'll be some sweaty palm viewing up a ravine or on a cliff edge. Mental Eastern Europeans dangling off bridges and cranes. Like a big bag of sweets I'd wolf it all down and then feel sick afterwards. *Man on Wire*. I went to see it the day it was released. And that epically grim documentary about people who throw themselves off the Golden Gate Bridge. I've woken up drenched in sweat thinking of a walk I made around the perimeter of a crumbling old tower, death hovering by the edge of my left foot at every step.

I continued to climb. I heard the squawk and chatter of a radio and footsteps clanging on metal – gangway perhaps, or metal rungs on a ladder. Here was the reason for no technological defences. They had human security. I waited on the concrete steps listening hard for the guard's intentions. I heard the crack of the radio broadcast button and a clear voice: 'It's colder than a nun's quim up here,' he said. Something unintelligible crackled the other way. Laughter. Another shot of white noise. Then footsteps fading.

I left it a bit longer and proceeded up the steps. I was beginning to understand the language of the tower, its peculiar phrases. The way the wind caught in the brick netting secured to the scaffold. The distant skirl of cement dust as it played around the foundations. The metallic shiver in the girders as they incrementally relaxed and realigned.

A stiff breeze, riddled with winter, tore through the exposed bones of the building. There were other giants rising in concert with this one. London, irked by the knowledge that it was a global shortarse, had decided to tilt for the heavens. Across the way the Splinter was nearing completion. Nearly 800 metres of glass and steel fitted together with the kind of top-level engineer-fu that ensured there were no visible joins. There seemed to be no window frames, just a uniform smoked-glass look throughout, as if it had been fashioned from one stupendous layer. It was beautiful and terrifying and it felt as though I could just reach out from where I was standing to touch its gleaming, polished shoulder. The summit of the Splinter would be a jagged thrust of reinforced glass. Something playful the architect had come up with, to offset the dreary pursuit of money that would go on in all the floors beneath it. He wanted to replicate the shattering of some boiled sweet or other that had caused him to lose a tooth. Work was ongoing; the building was due to open officially in the first quarter of the New Year.

I admired it for a while and then tried to imagine a

struggle and a person being thrown over the edge. Was there any chance, I wondered, that the Skylark had finally lost one of these skirmishes and plummeted to his death instead of his intended target? I made a mental note to check the details of the final victim, thinking that whoever had been in charge of the investigation back then ought to have done so as a matter of course.

I got so high that I ran out of building. Steel rods reached up from concrete cores. A guy stood there, slouched against them, observing my trespass. My heart pounced but it was just a hi-vis gilet and a hard hat jammed on a strut. Christ it was cold. Wind buffeted the heights – it probably did so most of the time, no matter if it was completely still at street level. I was about to go – cursing myself for not rocking up in hat and gloves – anxious that Walkie-Talkie Man was going to be back up here before long, when I saw light on the uppermost levels of the Splinter.

I might not have been so surprised at that of course, in this metropolis of megawattage, but for the way the light arrived, and the nature of it. It bloomed into being and was softer, a buttery light next to the harsh burn of the halogen. It flickered and leaned as it was moved across the floors. A security guard whose torch had let him down, relying on a candle? Highly unlikely. Kids then. BASE jump researchers. I kept my eyes on the flame. Now it ascended. When it had risen as far as it was able I thought I saw something just beyond its reach: the pale round of a face most likely, looking out, as I was, on the yawning muddle of roads and buildings that meant home. I fancied, with a chill of recognition, that he, or she, was looking straight at me, though surely I was concealed by the dark. It didn't stop me from moving back into deeper shadow, or whomever it was from suddenly extinguishing the flame.

* * *

It was there again, that weird feeling of invasion, the tingle I'd known when I'd gone to meet Danny Sweet, as soon as I'd vaulted the fence back on to Bishopsgate. I couldn't spend enough time trying to understand it, or the direction from which it was coming, because already that agoraphobic press was recurring and I felt the urge to retreat. Every car on the road was a blunt-nosed trauma delivery device. Every person carried with them an arsenal. There were fingernails sharpened and shaped into scimitars. Watch straps that could be reversed and made into knuckledusters. Windsor knot garrottes. Engagement ring gougers. All these ugly faces of intent. There was grim potential in every one; and I felt eminently targeted.

I leapt into a taxi on London Wall and was back home before I realised I was supposed to be spending the night with Romy. I sent her a text describing the agonies I was suffering and that I didn't want to keep her up all night, ruined old man that I'd become.

I took the radio through to the bathroom and languished in water slightly cooler than that needed to poach an egg. Mengele sat on the toilet lid and gazed, rapt, at the patterns the reflected light made on the wall. For a smart-looking cat he behaved sometimes as if the space between his ears was filled with nothing more substantial than pickled shit.

After twenty or so minutes of meandering tunes by chilled Scands that sounded as if they'd been composed on a frozen xylophone in a cathedral of ancient ice, I noticed the letters that had been shoved out of the way by the door as I'd entered the flat. I don't often get anything delivered directly but since being out of action and newly afraid of open spaces I'd asked Jimmy Two to pick up any mail for me and drop it off before he went off to fix my car or attend his twerking workshops or whatever it is he does to keep out of trouble.

I got out of the bath and dried myself on a towel that was so rough it snagged on the various fissures and creases of my skin. I looked up to see a framed photograph of Becs when we first started seeing each other. I wondered what she'd make of my body now, if she could see it. Probably nothing. I ought to know for sure, but I don't. You get married, you spend all that time together, you think you know a person inside out, but there's always that capacity for surprise, isn't there? No, I didn't know her completely. She knew me better than I know myself.

I raised my hand to my face and smelled traces of a variety of Romy perfumes on my fingers. For a moment I was back in her bedroom, watching her take her clothes off, feeling various parts of her fill my hands, listening to her breath catch and fall against my throat. The heat of her.

We are in this game for one throw of the dice. You have to play it as best you can, even if you don't know the rules. No time for regret. I wish I could latch on to that and relax. Forget. Live a little.

I picked up the post from the mat and leafed through it. One letter was addressed by hand. And I realised straight away that I knew its author.

7

I remembered the handwriting, that was the strange thing. Well, another strange thing, given the content of the letter. I thought about it for a while and a face lifted from the internal directory. I saw it as I last had, twenty-five years or so ago. Fresh, attractive, dark brown hair in bunches. Dark brown eyes. We called her Spanish because she holidayed in Marbella every year with her family without fail... What about a name then?

Little circles over every 'i' and 'j'. Every 'O' contained a smiley face. You'd think you'd grow out of that shit. Given the content, you'd maybe call it a day. Bottle-green jumper. Grey A-line skirt.

Karen Leonard.

I said her name aloud. We'd had a bit of a thing for each other, in as much as two thirteen–year-olds can have a thing. We'd snogged at a Golden Oldies school disco. Christ. 'I Got You' by Split Enz. 'Baggy Trousers'. 'Geno'. I remember she kept her eyes open. A couple of years later, after O levels, she and her family moved away. I don't remember where or why or even if she told me; it happened fast. Maybe it was

Marbella. She was back now though. And impatient.

Hiya Joel.

Blast from the past, hey? Wish there was a better time to say hi but needs must. I'm in a spot of bother. Basically need to bend your ear for half an hour if poss. I'll be at the Beehive on Homer Street every nite from 7-8. Come and have a drink with me. Just like old times down the Brooklands, hey? You on a pint of Foster's and me - the usual - half a Ginnis and black. Good times. Yeah, well not any more.

Joel. Thing is, my baby boy was kidnaped yesterday. Help an old freind out? Deets at the B'hive.

Kaz x
(Karen Leonard - remember me?)

I folded the note and put it in my pocket. I spent most of the day reading and rereading it, and remembering the author. I lost hours to reminiscences about old friends, and teachers, and school corridors we had walked. The people we were. The people we leave behind. The people we become. I thought of Sarah, and all the relationships – short-term and enduring – that she must have nurtured in the years since she left home.

I could see The Beehive from my bedroom window; it spooked me a little to think that she'd chosen a meeting place so close to where I lived. The letter was dated yesterday, which meant that this 'baby boy' had been gone forty-eight hours at least. But surely she'd been to the police. Surely he'd have been reunited with her by now? *Of course. Surely.* Those words spent scant time in my vocabulary before being replaced by 'oh shit' and 'bollocks' and 'fuck me'.

I checked my watch. An hour until I needed to be where she threatened to be. I looked around the flat and wondered if I should bring her back, away from the optics and the taps. But no. Too much water under the bridge, most of it polluted.

It didn't stop me from putting a bit of effort into what I chose to wear. An old flame always carried a little heat; we'd liked each other back in the day. A lot, as I recalled – at least on my part – but then I was and still am a sucker for anything even halfway female.

I ironed a shirt. I put on clean socks. I didn't polish my boots but at least I kind of thought about it. I was at The Beehive at seven on the dot and spotted her straight away, mainly because The Beehive is a tiny boozer and there was nobody else in there. She was Karen Leonard all right, but then she kind of wasn't either. And it hurt because it reminded me that I didn't look as lean or as carefree as I might once have done, and that if you saw time caught up in the hair of a contemporary, then you could be painfully certain that it was caught up in your own as well.

Perhaps she saw some of that disappointment in my face and shook hands with some of her own, or was it that she thought I looked like so much backcombed shit? It was conceivable that I always had and that's why she legged it when we were young.

Maybe that night of the Golden Oldies school disco she only kissed me because she mistook me for Snogger Jackson, who was just like me but with added looks, charm and muscles.

'Sp-aren,' I said, hoping she hadn't noticed. Spanish was hardly a pejorative nickname, but I never knew if it irritated her so better to play safe.

61

'Soz,' she said. Her hair was short now, and shot through with threads of grey that she'd dyed at some point in recent weeks but now the colour, a red of some sort, was growing out. She wore a scuffed biker jacket over a *Star Wars* T-shirt and skin-tight jeans. There was a dusting of make-up on her but it was slapdash, as if it was something she didn't do too often, if at all.

'I got your letter,' I said.

'Well, yeah.' Something was in her, gnawing at her. It wasn't the loss of gloss, or the accretion of years that was dragging her down. And it wasn't this business of the child. You don't look like this in twenty-four hours. It was something else. Drugs. Drink. Instant coffee. I don't know.

'Something about a boy,' I said. 'Something about a kidnap.'

'Something about *my* boy,' she said.

'What's going on? You reported this to the police, didn't you?' Knowing full well...

'I can't report it to the police, Soz,' she said. 'I'm not supposed to have a baby.'

'I don't follow.'

She sipped from her glass. Not Guinness and black. Gold Label barley wine. *Strong as a double Scotch, less than half the price*, as the old ad used to go.

'I was on the run with Simon because he was going to be taken away from me.'

'So you're on the run... and he's been taken away from you anyway.'

'Kidnapped,' she said. 'There's a difference. If I'd stayed where I was staying then social services would have had him.'

'Maybe it's social services who took him now,' I said.

'Don't be a jerk, Soz. That's not how it works, and you know it.'

'Where were you staying?'

'I was living in a B&B in Mablethorpe,' she said. 'Scrounging as many benefits as I could.'

'How refreshingly honest,' I said.

'It was just me and Simon. Olly had done a bunk. Cliché dad who wants his freedom after chucking his muck.'

'So what happened with social services?'

'I took Simon to the GP. He was crying and wouldn't sleep. Feverish. He had swellings on his wrists and ankles. I had to take him for X-rays and they found multiple fractures. They were there within minutes, like fucking vultures, waiting to whisk him off.'

'And you legged it?'

'Too fucking right. I never did nothing. I read up on it. It was my fault, kind of, but not because I smacked him or anything like that. I breastfed him.'

'And your enormous norks crushed his tiny limbs to bone dust.'

'Funny. Apparently there isn't much vitamin D in breast milk—'

'What about vitamin double-D?'

'Soz, this isn't a joke. My little boy… he had rickets.'

'I'm sorry, Karen, but my bullshit monitor is flashing red at the moment. We're sitting here in the pub and your baby boy is God knows where and you look about as frantic as a sloth on tranqs.'

'I *am* on tranqs,' she said. 'I took fifteen milligrams of diazepam this morning and this is my second beer. I look like I couldn't give a shit but inside I'm ripped apart. If I wasn't taking the edge off I'd be climbing the walls.'

'So who's got him? And why?'

'I don't know. That's why I came to you.'

'You think it might be this Olly?'

'It could be,' she said, but she had seized upon the answer as if it had never occurred to her before, which it must have.

'Even though he'd never shown any interest before? He left when? When you told him you were pregnant?'

'No. After he'd knobbed me. He fucked off to Aberdeen to find work on the rigs.'

'So he didn't even know you were pregnant?'

'Not that I know of.'

'Doesn't sound promising, does it? Who else? Any grudges?'

'Does the Pope shit in the woods?'

'Make me a list,' I said, and handed her my notebook. 'Addresses would be helpful. While I get you another drink.'

I stood at the bar and shook my head when the landlord, a guy called Mike who wore waistcoats, made to pour me a Kronenbourg.

'I'm off the pop, mate,' I said.

'Course you are,' he said.

'No, really, I am,' I said.

'That's what I said,' he said.

'Pour me one for my friend,' I told him. 'But not another can of falling-over juice. Make it half a shandy.'

'It'll be like piss after what she's been supping,' he warned me, but he poured the drink and I paid and I left him with a hard stare.

She'd written me a list. It was long. I went through it with her and crossed off the names of those who she hadn't seen for over two years or those who had families. In my experience, any level of 'settled down' has a dissipating effect on the red mist. There were five names left.

'Right,' I said. 'This is more manageable. Who is Tommy Hulce?'

'He's an old trick,' she said. 'I did him out of a ton one night.'

'He local?'

'He was. He died last year. Motorbike accident.'

I looked at her. 'So we could probably cross him off the list?'

'I guess so.'

'Anybody else you fear might be harassing you from beyond the grave?'

'Soz, I know you think I'm just a stupid junk-head, but my head's been scrambled by this. I'm fucked up. I don't know what to do.'

'Okay. Anyone else we can lose?'

'Jeff Grealish,' she said. 'He died of cancer in 2012. Sorry. Not thinking straight.'

'And then there were three.'

She told me about the names that remained. Two of them – Toby Fletcher and Imran Raza – were a couple of pissheads who'd recently suffered the same trick as the late Mr Hulce; she'd lifted their wallets while they lay comatose after a night of Drambuie and doggy style. She didn't know anything about their domestic lives. Benjie Weston had been 'the one' for her, she told me. She'd been serious about him and to show her devotion hadn't taken any of his money. But he was definitely married. She'd put pressure on him for a while to leave his wife and two sons and move in with her. When he told her to leave him alone she saw it as a challenge and intensified her pursuit of him.

I stared at the names and tried to drum up some enthusiasm but it was difficult. I couldn't make the mental leap required to swallow any of this. I wondered if I was meant to be the next sting on her rota, that this was just a part of her act to soften me up. Karen Leonard's UK tour of gullible contacts.

'I got in touch because you're an old friend and I'm all out of old friends,' she said, as if she were reading my mind. 'I trust you. But I don't have any money.'

'Hey, come on,' I said, thinking, *Fuck's sake*. 'Old friends don't do it for the money.'

8

So I looked into these gullible prongs Karen had been shafting. Imran Raza lived in a small flat near Highbury, within the shadow of the Emirates Stadium. A Tottenham Hotspur football club flag was pinned defiantly to an upper window. I sat in the car watching, waiting. There was precious little else to do. I imagined Sarah sitting in a room somewhere, gnawing at her nails, wrestling with the urge to call me, to do the right thing, to help me apply the glue to the crack that separated us.

Do it, I thought. And took my phone out, anticipating the call.

At that moment, Raza appeared at the communal doorway. He was dressed in sweatshirt and jogging bottoms, spattered with old paint. He held a lunch box in his fist. A woman in a dressing gown clutched a baby to her waist and gave him a kiss goodbye. She looked frazzled, head nodding on the block wishing the sleep guillotine to fall. *Money tight in that domicile*, I thought. Rents here were high and there were mouths to feed.

I put myself in Raza's position. Would I go to the trouble

of trying to shake down an ex-fuck because she fiddled me out of the thin wedge in my wallet? With a wife at home? I'd stand to lose everything. Unless the wife was in on it too and that nipper she was dandling turned out to be Karen's child. I'd paint my bollocks with meat sauce and squat over the piranha pond if it was. He was heading along Drayton Park towards Arsenal Tube station. A day's hard graft, providing for his family. I sauntered after him thinking no, this guy's just glad to have got away with it. He'll think twice before the knickers come off in future. Lesson learned.

I watched him until we got to the station then mentally crossed him off my list. He wasn't a kidnapper.

An hour later and I'd found Toby Fletcher. He worked in an office in Pimlico. I sat in the coffee shop across the way on Belgrave Road, a busy little joint run by garrulous Italians who didn't have a clue about decor but made a great cup of coffee. The breakfast crowd were in, ordering paninis and croissants. Fletcher came in an hour later to order a round of coffees. Again, I was unconvinced. He looked like someone who was mildly disgruntled by the fact that he'd been sent out on a beverage run. I squeezed past him. He was playing *Plants vs. Zombies* on his phone. I didn't get the vibe from him – and I've felt it so many times – that he was blackmailing anybody. But unlike Raza, I hadn't seen him with his family. That might be an indicator of his potential.

But I waited until he had his hands full of cardboard and coffee before I challenged him about it.

'You what?' he said. He didn't have a very pleasant mouth. His teeth were yellowish and furred, his tongue squirmed between them, grey and dry like a regurgitated chunk of meat.

'I said, "Have you kidnapped any young children lately?"'

He wore an expression that sat unhappily on his face, midway between bemusement – as if at some moment a camera would emerge from a hiding place to show he was the focus of an elaborate prank – and open hostility.

'You fucking what?'

Froth oozed from the holes in his plastic lids as if agitated by his rising temper.

I'd already decided he was thicker than bull semen but I decided to see if he'd go for the hat trick. I asked him again.

'Who are you?' he said.

Disappointed that he'd changed tack, but he still hadn't answered me, I decided to change tack too. I slammed my hand up into the tray of coffees and launched them into the air.

He cried out and stepped back, lost his footing and went down on his arse. The drinks followed, an all-out macchiato attack. I offered him a pocket tissue but he was looking at me as if I was threatening to set off a nail bomb.

I withdrew my phone and found the photograph of Karen I'd taken in The Beehive the previous evening.

'What can you tell me about this woman?' I said, fully expecting another question in return.

His astonishment intensified under his mask of caffeinated milk and hot water.

'You know her,' I said. 'I know her. I know what she did, I know what she's capable of. What are you capable of?'

'She fucked me over,' he said. 'Played me like a muppet. Pocketed the best part of a hundred quid.'

'While you were sleeping?'

He was opening up now; I think he thought I was a copper. All of the fight had, literally, puddled out of him.

'Yeah,' he said. 'She spiked my drinks. I'm sure of it. She said she was on cider but I reckon she was swigging Appletiser.'

'That'll teach you to not buy the drinks,' I said.

'So what's all this about? You going to get my ton back and lock the slag up?'

'Not on my to-do list, no,' I said. 'I'm helping her out.'

'Helping her? That cunt? Why?'

'Someone kidnapped her little boy,' I said.

'Good,' he snapped. And then he thought better of it. Thick as bull semen, but there was some compassion running through his veins. 'I mean... tough on the kid... Hang on, you think I had something to do with this?'

'Like one of your airborne lattes, it crossed my mind,' I said.

'Why are you helping her? She's fucking poison.'

'Old friend. What can you do?'

'Loyalty means nothing to some people.' He said it sadly, slowly, as if speaking from bitter experience. 'She'll fuck you over too. That kind of person can't help themselves. It's in the blood.'

'You married?'

'On the verge.'

'Kids?'

'She's pregnant. Six months.'

'What were you thinking?'

He looked utterly miserable, as if he'd walked into the room marked MEATY FLAPS only to find an overweight crow trying to take off. I almost felt sorry for dumping coffee on him.

'What does anybody think, faced with the old life sentence? I panicked. I wanted one last roll in the hay.'

I believed him. I told him so. I told him I wouldn't bother him again, but to not push it about getting his money back, to consider it a shot across the bows.

Before he went off to find some paper towels and a story

that wouldn't make him a laughing stock with his work colleagues, I asked him if there had been anything odd that struck him about Karen.

'You mean other than the fact she's a jackal in human form?'

'Anything you saw, something she said, anything that happened that made you feel, I don't know, that it was out of whack, that she was up to something.'

'No,' he said. 'I mean… hindsight and all that, but at the time no. I did it, didn't I? I didn't walk away. If there was anything, I guess it was that she wanted to go to the bar all the time. She was utterly cool and calm and in control. It was like she was working to a script.'

'Maybe she was.'

'Maybe. This was obviously nothing new to her.'

I drove to the Tube station and dumped the car. I fed enough coins for a couple of hours' parking into the meter and texted Jimmy Two to pick her up before lunch and that he could have his wicked way with the old girl for the rest of the day. He texted back to say in that case he was going to visit his ageing mum out in Tooting and take her to Wimbledon Common for the afternoon. The car would be back on my road with a full tank by breakfast. Why can't there be more people like Jimmy Two in the world?

I caught a Tube train to Richmond where this special guy Karen had met was living. 'The One'. I wasn't expecting to see him – Karen said he worked long hours in the City – I just wanted to get a sense of who he was from the house he lived in. And it was a big house with a lush garden, a driveway spacious enough for three cars. There was evidence – in the plastic toys scattered around the front lawn – of children. And so, again, I just couldn't see the motivation. The risks of kidnapping someone else's child – a screaming, teary toddler at that – outweighed any rewards. Benjie Weston, if I were to meet him now, would be just how I imagined him to be: he'd deny it at first, then he'd regret it when I proved to him what I knew. He'd beg me to keep quiet. And he wouldn't have a clue about any kidnapped boy.

She was pissing me about. It struck me that her proximity to me was no fluke: she wanted to meet me at The Beehive because she knew I lived on Homer Street and that maybe it was a way of pinpointing my exact address. She could be in my flat now, rifling the drawers, pocketing any number of treasures. Not that there was anything worth taking.

I had to get back. I had to—

My phone rang. It was Karen. She was screaming into the receiver. I wondered if she'd tried to steal some of Mengele's Fishbitz and he was now hanging off her, having driven his claws two inches into her flesh. I pleaded with her to take it easy, that I couldn't understand her, but she would not be mollified. So I put the phone down on her. When she called again she'd managed to put a lid on it to some degree but hysteria simmered just beneath the surface.

'Just count to ten,' I said, 'take a deep breath and tell me what happened.'

I heard a rush of air and she said: 'I got a phone call. From Benjie. He's got Simon—'

'You're kidding. I'm standing outside his house right now. It must be worth four and a half mil.'

'What's your point?'

'Why would he do this? That's my point. His wife will leave him. He'll lose his kids. He's likely to go to prison.

And for what? He isn't getting any money out of you.'

'Principle.'

'*Principle?*'

'What does it fucking matter?' she screamed. 'Maybe his wife has left him already. Maybe his kids despise him. He might have lost his job. He's behind on his mortgage repayments. He's gone stark, raving bonkers. What does it matter? All that matters is that *he has got Simon*.'

'What does he want?'

'He didn't say. He told me to sit tight, that Simon was safe and well, and that he would call again later with his demands.'

'When?'

'Nine o'clock. On the button, he said.'

I checked my watch. It was coming up to quarter to four.

'We can get you to Scotland Yard,' I said. 'I know someone there who will sort this out. He can get a trace set—'

'No,' she said. 'No trace. No police. Just me and you.'

'Karen, I'm not tried in negotiations. I get into a tizz if someone asks me what kind of sauce I want on my bacon roll.'

'I can't do this on my own. And I can't do this with the police.'

'You can. They'll help you. There's a kid involved, for Christ's sake. We can't fuck about.'

'I won't do this with the police involved,' she said. And now all traces of the panic were gone. Her voice was cold, flat, inanimate. It was like listening to a Conservative frontbencher. She thought Benjie Weston had cashed his mental chips; I thought she had. Pull back to reveal me sitting in my own waste wearing my underpants for a turban.

'Okay,' I said. 'Where are you now?'

'Chinatown. I'm in a restaurant on Gerrard Street,' she said. She told me its name. 'I'm drinking free green tea.

There's a phone box across the way. He told me he'd call it at nine.'

'No mobiles?'

'Apparently not, no.'

'Okay,' I said. 'It's his party. I'll be over there by eight thirty.'

'Please,' she said, and the line went dead.

Benjie Weston. Who the fuck are you? Other than someone with a dog's name.

I approached the house. No cars. No signs of life. I peered through the front window into a large sitting room containing an upright piano and three guitars in stands. There was a plant in rude health on the windowsill. If the house was vacant, it probably hadn't been vacated too long ago.

I took a quick glance up and down the street before vaulting the fence and hurrying down the side of the house. The garden went on and on, bordered on either side by neatly trimmed leylandii. A large trampoline stood within their shadow. There was a suite of garden furniture under tarpaulin. French windows separated me from a living room containing a plasma screen as big as a goalmouth. Neutral colours. A huge sofa. A tartan cat basket. Nobody inside.

I didn't have time to do any background checks on Weston and find out how fruity loops he was at work or the pub or the gym. And it didn't matter. At nine o'clock he'd show us just how balls-out bat crackers he was.

I hopped on the Tube and got off at Cannon Street thinking about Weston's kids. They couldn't have been much older than five judging by the size and type of the toys lying around the garden. An age when your parents are like gods;

you look for them, you call for them, you want to be with them all the time. Sarah had been just the same. Seeking my hand with hers on even the shortest walks, homing in on me at any moment of stress or pain. It had been my side of the bed she came to after a nightmare or during a bout of sickness. The pictures she drew – I have them all in a big plastic tub at Keepsies, the storage place – are invariably of me and her. Which is not to say she didn't have a good relationship with her mum, of course she did. But Rebecca will say it's because I was her mental equivalent at the time. I was a goofy dad, she was a daddy's girl.

There are some things it's impossible to imagine; stuff so dark the mind recoils from it. It censors you, and a good thing too. How bad would things have to have become before I held the blade to my daughter's throat? The person with sleepy eyes who had reached out for me at the start of every day. I was the patient in her clinic (her notes on my clipboard: *you just need a medisan*), the customer in her restaurant (*soop – £15*), the visitor to her beauty salon (*yes, you can paint my nails but no photos or I'll tickle you squitless*).

I couldn't harm my girl. I'd sooner die. And yet many apparently loving fathers had crossed that line. Smothered, strangled, stabbed. Children so small. Voices of confusion and hurt. Tiny hands latticed with defence wounds.

Jesus fucking Christ.

I thought of Karen and again I began judging her. Wasn't she the kidnapper, technically, if she was keeping Simon out of the hands of the authorities, who presumably believed him to be at risk if he stayed with her? And the level of calm she was exuding. All right, she'd been blazing at me on the phone, but the sudden switch to ice maiden suggested she was strung out on some form of medication, legally acquired or otherwise. Should I judge her for coping like that, when I was guilty of keeping any number of distilleries in business? She cared, obviously, or she wouldn't have asked for my help. She wouldn't be necking green tea by the potful, waiting for the phone to ring.

I meandered and fulminated until the sky turned dark and I found myself down by the river at Upper Thames Street. To the east, monsters reared. Great cranes adorned with festive lights reached like children on tip-toe trying to drape tinsel around the Christmas tree. I peered at the summit of the Splinter for soft, uncertain light but either I was too far away or the mystery inhabitants were abroad.

I turned to stare along the grey ribbon of Southwark Bridge Road and without thinking I was halfway across it. Exposed, the wind plucked at me and it felt like the little black beaks of memory opening me up all over, urging me to revisit that night again. I was about a mile away from where I almost died. It took me fifteen minutes to reach Silex Street. New padlocks had been placed on the doors but no such attention had been paid to the upper windows, which sagged open like aghast mouths. Around the back I found a plank of wood I could wedge between the perimeter fence and the underside of a first-floor window frame. I was up and in before I'd thought that the wood might be old and waterlogged and full of rot. I stood there in the cold, still air of dead rooms and felt about in my jacket pocket for the little LED torch I carry with me. The night sprang back from it, so physical, so solid, that I tensed up, believing it must have been a person.

I saw in the beam evidence of the forensic team's presence, after I had been shuttled to A&E. A latex glove. A length of yellow tape snarled in spider webs and dust. All of Sarah's things were gone – her blankets and books – but I couldn't know if she'd taken them herself or Mawker's unit had seized them for study back at the lab, thinking they belonged to Ronnie Lake.

Here was blood. And here. And here. It was dark, drained into the old wooden floorboards like mahogany stain. Ronnie's or mine? A bit of both, I'd have thought. A lot of both. I don't know why I'd come here. Time to kill I could have killed in a coffee house or a bookshop or a bar. Sarah wouldn't have stuck around in a place meant to be her grave, a place that must have smelled like a butcher's display after I'd mopped myself all over it. All I'd done was reopen wounds that my mind had been working hard to sew shut behind the scenes, while my body fought to heal itself.

Disgusted, I made to leave and the torch picked out an edge of clean orange. I swept the beam back the way it had come: there, near the area where Sarah's den had been arranged, something sticking out of the cracks in the floor. I teased it out: a discarded train ticket.

It suggested travel between Blackfriars and Bedford stations. The date of issue was this March, one month before I broke into this building. Off-peak day return: £15. It could have belonged to anyone, but Sarah had been here at the time and it had been bought in conjunction with a young person's railcard.

Bedford? The only thing I knew about Bedford was something my geography teacher mentioned at school, that it was home to a lot of people of Italian descent. That and... vans, I guess.

I dug around in the cracks in case there was any other booty to be found, while inwardly rehearsing the putdowns I'd volley Mawker's way for missing this piece of evidence.

Okay, it wasn't crucial, but it could help me in my search for Sarah, even if she'd made it clear she didn't want me to come looking for her any more.

I checked the time and swore. I'd spent two hours in this dive. I got out and hailed a cab on Webber Street. Twenty minutes later I got the driver to drop me on Shaftesbury Avenue and I walked down to Chinatown. I was feeling a little ill after being in the Silex Street factory and the taxi back was too hot, driven by a guy whose No Smoking sign was meant for everybody else but him.

An old Chinese man raised his hand to me as I entered the restaurant. It was pretty busy but he knew who I was here for; he led me to a table by the entrance littered with torn tissues and a green teapot.

'She gone piss,' the old guy said, and asked if I wanted a menu. I shook my head and sat down. It was quarter to nine. I guessed Karen had chosen this spot because you could see the telephone box across the way. YOU CAN EMAIL FROM HERE a sign said, but clearly nobody had, perhaps ever. I'd been mildly surprised to see the phone box at all. They seemed out of place, out of time. They were the kind of endangered species your eye tended to dismiss these days. Unless you were desperate for a slash. It had ever been so. They stank of stale urine and stale cigarette smoke when I was a kid, nipping in to see if there was any forgotten change in the coin return slot.

The only time I'd used a phone box as an adult had been during a trip to Bristol, what... ten years ago? I forget my reasons for being there, but I was staying at a friend's house in Cotham. We'd gone out for a night in the city centre and, true to form, reduced ourselves to a state of utter paralysis on pints of Directors and, as I remember, a huge bottle of pineapple dessert wine.

We became separated at some point, and I was so wankered I didn't remember anything until I came to at four in the morning walking on a street I didn't recognise. Which wasn't difficult considering I didn't live in Bristol. I'd misplaced my phone and my wallet and had to call an operator to say I was lost and how the hell did I get back to Aberdeen Road?

Karen looked tired and used up, like a tissue. Nothing would rescue her from the creases and wrinkles worming through her skin. They were soul deep. She was like milk, or meat, on the turn. She must have been reading my mind.

'You look like barbecued shit,' she said.

'Don't say it too loud,' I said. 'I might end up on the menu.'

'Do you want a hit of whizz?' she asked. 'It might be a late one. What do you think?'

'One of us had best keep a clean head, and a foot on the brake. It's nearly time.'

She picked up her clay cup then put it back down. Her jaws were clenching like those of a snake trying to swallow something way too big for its mouth. 'I don't even fucking *like* green tea,' she said.

'You know, when I was a kid living up north, I had a friend who used to go down to London a lot to visit relatives. They didn't have a phone down there, either that or they didn't allow him to use it. So he'd call me from a phone box. This is back in the day when you could make a call for two pence. But he didn't even have that. If you called someone, there would be a second, a split second, where you get through before you hear the tone and you have to feed the coins in. He shouted my name into that gap and put the phone down. And he called again. Shouted his name just in time before the pips went. Then he called again, a dozen times, to give me – piecemeal – the number of the phone box he was calling from. So then I could call him and we'd have our chat. Ingenious, really.'

She seemed a little disgusted with me. Disgust did wonders for her face, actually; it gave it a lift. 'Is that story meant to cheer me up? Put me at ease? Because it did fucking neither.'

We both raised our heads at the strident sounds of the phone ringing. And then she looked at me and her face had changed again. It was haunted, pale. Tears quivered, on the edge of release. It was an expression that stayed with me, long after she had gone and I had learned the terrible truth.

9

We hurried across the way where a guy was staring at the phone box as if it were an alien come down to Earth. 'It's for her,' I said to him as he reached out a hand to answer. I picked up the receiver and passed it to Karen. She didn't say hello. All she said was four words over the course of about twenty seconds:

'Where?'

[beat]

'When?'

[beat]

'Why?'

[beat]

'Okay.'

And then she was walking west, towards the heart of Soho.

'Where are we going?' I asked. 'What are we doing?'

'We've been given another location. Another phone box. In Ladbroke Grove.'

'Fuck off,' I said, and stopped walking. A woman with a shopping trolley knocked against my thighs, hissed the word 'spastic' and marched by, glaring at me. 'Did he say "Simon Says"?'

'What?'

'What is this? A fucking game? Was it Benjie Weston?'

'I think so, yes.'

'You *think* so?'

'Well it didn't sound much like him.'

'We go to the police,' I said. 'Now.'

'I told you, I can't. The police get involved, I'm finished. I'll never see Simon again.'

'What the fuck is he playing at?' I said. 'What does he stand to gain from sending us halfway across sodding London?'

'Maybe it's to make sure the police aren't involved,' she said. 'He could be keeping tabs on me.'

'In which case he's not going to be too happy if he sees me ferrying you around town.'

'He knows I've got a driver,' she said. 'I told him I'd wrap the car around a tree if it was just me. My nerves are shot. I almost took the thing up on to the kerb just getting here.'

She was parked in the NCP in Brewer Street. I paid the parking charge and we went to her car.

'Christ,' I said. 'I wish I hadn't given up my car earlier.'

'What?'

'A fucking Mini,' I said. I was broadsided by how tiny it was. The Minis on the road these days don't warrant the name. 'How old is this thing?'

'I don't know,' she said. 'What does it matter?'

'S reg. What was that? Seventies? I think I was at primary school when this rolled off the production line. I've sat in baths bigger than this.'

'I'm sorry,' she said. 'The Jag is being serviced today.'

We got in and there was a smell of mildew and petrol.

'Look,' I said. 'That stuff looks like rust there. It's not rust, it's liver spots.'

'Shut up, Joel. Fucking drive.'

We got in and I got it going, momentarily puzzled by the presence of a choke, and the rampant, skeletal gear stick. 'Add water and clothes and this is a washing machine,' I said. The sound of the engine was like a wasp trapped in a jar.

'We have to be in Ladbroke Grove by nine thirty. Do you think you can manage that?'

'It would be quicker to walk,' I said. 'Backwards.'

'Joel.'

I drove through Paddington and up through Little Venice. Karen fiddled with the radio but would not rest on a station. She moved on before a sentence was finished or a chord completed so it was impossible to tell what was being talked about, or what was being played.

I pushed that grunting Tonka toy through the traffic and road works. It was more Bean than Bourne. The wheels were too soft and the suspension too hard. I felt every crease in the road and by the time we turned on to Cambridge Gardens I had a headache and arseache and my ankle was pounding from too much heavy-duty clutch dipping.

'Are you sure this is the right road?' Karen asked, swaying her head this way and that in a bid to see a likely telephone box. I looked too, but the windows were more befitting a doll's house. Plus, they were permanently foggy, no matter how much cold air or hot air I aimed their way. Well, I say 'hot air' but it was no hotter than the burp of a polar bear after it's been at the chilled contents of an igloo. 'There it is,' I said, guessing wildly. It could have been a portly tall guy in a big red coat, but no, it was a telephone kiosk and it was ringing.

'We're early,' I complained, and not without some surprise, as I pulled up alongside it.

Karen was scrabbling at the door handle and trying to unbuckle her seat belt at the same time.

'Relax,' I said. 'Wait until nine thirty.'

'But it's ringing now,' she said.

'We're early,' I said again. 'Let the fucker sweat. Let him not keep to the clock. It says something about him.'

'What does it say about him?'

'It tells me he's nervous. That he's impatient. Maybe he's under pressure.'

'So what if he is?'

'It might be something we can use. It might mean he makes a mistake.'

'What if his clock is fast? What if it's just that?'

I shrugged. 'He was right on the button at Gerrard Street.'

Karen sighed noisily and stared at the red blur. I thought I could hear the ticking of my watch over the air con and the endless drone of cars.

9.26.

The phone stopped ringing.

'Fuck,' Karen said.

'It probably wasn't even him,' I said. 'Wrong number. Happens all the time.'

'What if your watch is slow?' she said.

'It's not,' I said. 'He'll call back.' But already I was thinking about what we might do if he didn't. Maybe he was under pressure and had cracked, thinking we weren't playing his game any more. Maybe he was using a different timer, one that was inaccurate. I'd played poker and lost.

At 9.30 the phone rang again and I tried a told-you-so smile but it crumpled on my face under the weight of relief.

She caught that. I kept forgetting she knew me. Aeons had passed, but she had buttonholed me as the cocksure gimp I'd always been. I went with her. We squeezed into the box.

She picked up on the fourth ring.

'Where?'

[beat]

'When?'

[beat]

'Let me speak to him.'

[beat]

'Okay… Okay.'

She put the phone down in the cradle and turned to me. She was searching my face as if it had been me on the other end of the phone, somehow ventriloquising.

'What now?' I asked.

'Ealing.'

I looked behind us, towards the heart of London. Romy was that way, and Sarah too, somewhere. I knew that he was there too. I knew this was bullshit. Perhaps Karen caught on to that as well because suddenly her hand (dry skin, ragged fingernails) was around mine and she was tugging at me to return to the car.

'Please, Joel,' she said.

'Ealing,' I said. 'By ten, I'm guessing.'

She nodded.

'What did he say when you asked to speak to Simon?'

'He said: "It's late. He's asleep. Little boys need a lot of sleep."'

I didn't like the sound of that. It sounded like a threat. Where was he sending us? Who was at the end of the road? We sat in the car and I stared at the white spots on the bonnet where filler made ugly scars against the, arguably, even uglier pale-blue paint. I didn't want to get us going just yet but I knew I'd have to or Karen would whinge and my headache wasn't up to it. And anyway, we were going to struggle to make it to Ealing in thirty minutes, even if it was clear roads all the way. The engine started – I didn't want to worry Karen by asking what we'd do if it didn't – and though it sounded like a washing machine full of bricks, it got us on to the Westway and it got us off at Acton where I found Noel Road and though we cut it fine we made it to Mattock Lane and the phone box and more meaningful looks, and more unanswered questions and another order to get us further away from where I believed we really needed to be.

10

The darkness seemed too big for the car. It felt, sometimes, as we hugged the hard shoulder on the M4 heading west, that were we to open the windows by even a crack, the enormity of the sky would simply pour in on us like oil and smother us in our seats. The time he was giving us to get to these more and more remote phone boxes stretched out like old barbed wire. Thirty minutes to get to the airport hotel in West Drayton; forty minutes to get to Station Hill in Reading; ninety minutes to get to the Marriott in Bristol; then it was Paignton in Devon.

That last shift was a killer. It was getting on for three in the morning and by the time we arrived we almost messed up. By 'we', I mean 'I', obviously. Karen had fallen asleep.

I tooled around the streets looking for Torbay Road, but we had plenty of time and once I'd located the kiosk I set a timer on my phone to go off after fifteen minutes. Then I closed my eyes. And almost immediately opened them again to find that it was five minutes past when he should have called and my timer had not worked because my battery had run out of juice. I felt my gut squirm with chains of ice and got out of the car as quietly as I could. My breath churned around my head: chains made real. I closed my eyes and rubbed my face until it was warmer. I couldn't feel my feet. All of the houses along the road were ink stencils, copies of copies, dark, asleep. Just looking at them made me feel tired to the chambers of my heart. I went to the phone and picked it up thinking, hoping crazily, that I was not too late and that maybe the bell wasn't working and it was ringing silently but when I put that cold curve of plastic to my ear there was only the purr of the line's potential. I put it back down and it rang immediately. I picked up, glancing at Karen to check she had not been wakened. Her face was grey behind a caul of frost spreading leisurely across the passenger-side window. She looked dead: deep shadows where her eyes and mouth were situated. Hollows beneath her cheekbones.

A voice said: 'Who the fuck are you?'

I didn't like the snarl in it; the assumption of control.

I said: 'The VD clinic. Your tests came back negative. You've got to stop shoving chickens up your arse.'

'Put Karen on.'

'Karen's off duty,' I said. 'It's me you should be talking to anyway. I'm the one ferrying her all over the country in a death trap. Can I bill you for petrol expenses?'

'You answered late.'

'I know. I'm sorry. I dozed off. It won't happen again.'

'Maybe it's too late for "sorry". Maybe it's time, instead, for funeral hymns.'

'There'll be hymns aplenty,' I said, 'for you if you hurt that child.'

'You're in no position to make threats.'

'It isn't a threat. It's a promise.' I strained hard to hear something in the background that might give away his location, but there was nothing. He was being careful. There was no hint of any stress in his voice either, which put paid to any suspicions I had that he might be malleable. 'If you're late one more time, it's the end.'

I bit my lip and checked my watch. How much more of this? 'Let's call it the end now,' I said. 'I'm tired and bored. Karen's fallen asleep she's so tired and bored.'

'I don't advise –'

'Fuck what you advise. I want to hear that child now. I want to talk to Simon. Otherwise I'm ditching this car and booking into a hotel for what's left of the night.'

There was such a seamless silence at the other end that I wondered if he'd killed the line while I was mid-rant. But then I heard snuffling and shuffling and soft, murmured words in the background – of encouragement, perhaps – and a boy's voice, full of sleep, said: 'Mum?'

'Simon?'

'That's all you're getting.' Snarl was back.

'What about you?' I said. 'What are you getting? Why are you doing this? When are we going to get a list of your tedious demands?'

'Here's a tedious demand,' he said. 'Land's End, by ten a.m. tomorrow. Plenty of time. Going soft on you in my old age. No more mistakes.'

'Which phone box?'

'Use your imagination,' he said.

'You're in London,' I said. 'I know it. What's your fucking game?'

But now he had killed the link and I slapped the phone back half a dozen times before it docked and I didn't care who I woke up.

I trudged to the car and got in. Cold was scraping its nails up and down my back. The eyes that gazed at me from the rear-view mirror looked like black scrawls scribbled onto a special effects head. Karen had managed to remain asleep. I heard an electric motor on a milk float somewhere beyond these houses and I remembered breakfasts in our kitchen in Lime Grove, bright winter sunshine lancing the table while Sarah messily consumed her boiled egg or her Ready Brek, nose glued to a copy of *Twinkle*.

It wasn't Twinkle.

It fucking well was *Twinkle*. I should know. I paid the subscription on it for God knows how many years.

It was The Beano. Twinkle *died a righteous death some time in the nineties and a good thing too.*

Because *The Beano* is a bastion of all that is good in the world.

Nobody became a serial killer because of a few jokes about farts and bogies.

Define 'joke'.

Let's see… how about you, naked, giving me your 'come hither' look?

I thought I always looked dashing.

Interesting you should use the word 'dashing' because that's what I was always doing when you got naked – 'dashing'. In the direction of 'away'.

As much as I wanted to wake Karen up and tell her the situation I left her to slumber. Letting her know I'd fucked up wasn't a good idea. The quiet was nice, anyway, once you blanked the wasp-playing-a-kazoo-in-a-tin-can noise created by the Mini's engine.

I drove as hard as I could though the time restrictions were gone. I wanted to exorcise that snarl from my thoughts and ninety in a death trap seemed a valid way of going about it. But then I saw a sign for Salcombe and my foot came off the accelerator as though raised by some invisible puppeteer. Salcombe was home to Melanie Henriksen now. There was the information but so what? I was twenty miles away from where she stuck her finger up schnauzers' arses and sold ridiculously expensive kidney tablets for old cats and – quite possibly – went home to a nice guy who looked after her and did not place her in danger.

You never meant to do that.

No. But it happened.

Yes. And I died. Do you blame yourself for that as well?

Of course I do. I should have been home. But I was out, wasn't I? Drinking. It's what I'm best at.

Oh, I don't know. You've quite a nice line in self-pity.

Fuck off, Becs.

I would leave Melanie alone because she left London. She went away because of what happened. She went away because I remained there.

I steered hard left on to the slip road that would take me into the town itself. It was late. I didn't want to stand over her while she slept. I just wanted to see her place, and maybe the house where she lived. I just wanted to close the chapter by crystallising all of that in my mind.

I found it pretty quickly. It was set away from the centre, on a quiet lane with a view of the sea and the harbour. There was a pale blue awning: *Henriksen's Veterinary Services, since 1958.* There was a brass plaque on the door in the shape of an Airedale terrier. I've never understood the appeal of such dogs. I thought the point of a cat or a dog was to have something that felt calming and agreeable when you stroked it. I imagined stroking an Airedale would be akin to stroking a tramp's matted beard.

The impulse to ring the bell was very strong.

Everything dark. I got out and peered through the window but could see only vague outlines: plastic chairs, shelves with pale things on them, pet food, I imagined. A counter. Cards and photographs on the wall behind. I stood back and gazed up at the windows above the surgery. Did she live on the premises? I couldn't remember the setup, or whether she'd gone into such detail. Probably not, since the last time I'd seen her everything about her was full of goodbye.

I was backing off, getting ready to return to the driver's seat – marginally less comfortable, I'd imagine, than an electric chair – when a light came on in the vet's office. And she was there, moving behind the counter, wearing a ridiculously thick woollen jumper. Her hair was longer than it had been in London, but in the way she walked I could see how she was recovered. A strong woman who had managed to draw a line under a bad episode and was not looking back.

I caught myself reaching out to tap on the glass but even if she looked up, the light from inside meant that she would not see me. But I stayed my hand because me here meant memories and I had no right to just come wandering back into her life. She didn't deserve that kind of upheaval. I'd had my chance and it had not worked out. Complaining that it was circumstances or bad luck wasn't going to cut it.

I moved away from the window; she retreated from the counter. The door closed. The light went off.

Karen woke up as I was slowing down along the A30, the sea writhing beyond the edge of the land. I was remembering Melanie, a figure in a doorway in Maida Vale, a moment of warmth on a cold, dangerous night.

'I dreamed we stopped,' Karen said.

'We stopped,' I said. 'A toddler would need to stop regularly to stretch his legs in this thing.'

'I slept okay.'

'You are obviously half cat. We've been ordered to Land's End, by the way,' I said.

'What time is it?'

'It's early. Six-ish. Sun's coming up.'

'Do you think it might stop here? Do you think it will end today?'

'It would be fitting, wouldn't it? Land's End? Better than Fiddler's Ferry. Or Wetwang.' Something was bothering me but I couldn't get it to put out; it flirted instead, maddening, beyond the reach of fingertips.

'Are you okay?' she asked.

'Tired,' I said. It wasn't anything to do with Melanie, although I thought, maybe, somehow, it was. I chased the tail of it for a few seconds until I realised Karen was expecting me to say more. I let it go. 'Hungry too,' I said. 'I could eat a baby through a colander.'

'We should find this phone box,' she said.

I was beginning to apologise; why did I think a joke about a baby would be a good idea while with someone whose only child had been kidnapped? But she either hadn't heard or was paying me no notice. I pulled up in the car park next to a couple of tennis courts. There was a phone box outside a pub nearby, its door hanging askew in the frame.

'Shit,' Karen said.

'Yep.' The phone's guts were hanging out and the receiver was gone. Spray paint and beer cans and condoms inside.

I got out for a closer look just for something to do. There was a piece of paper, nice paper, neatly folded and pinned to what remained of the kiosk. And I thought of Melanie again. How I was hidden from her, but in plain sight. And of course he knew where we were and what we were doing. Of course he wasn't in London. I looked behind me at the other cars in the car park.

'What is it?' Karen asked.

I plucked the note from the booth and handed it to her.

'Fuck you,' she read.

'He asked me who I was,' I said. 'Before I'd said a word.'

'I don't understand.'

'You were asleep. I should have realised immediately. He's been watching us every step of the way.'

She walked away from me towards the tennis courts. She let the paper fall from her fingers. 'So what now?' she asked. The skyline beyond her was thickening with ash-grey cloud. My stomach rumbled again, but this time the noise came from somewhere inside that weather.

'We go back,' I said. 'We've been led a merry dance for some reason. Hopefully it was all just a cruel prank and when we get you back to Leonard Mansion Simon will be waiting for you. And lesson learned.'

'We should eat first,' she said. 'I don't want you fainting on the motorway.'

I nodded and we got back in the Mini. I couldn't remember passing any shops since we'd come off the main road, certainly nothing that would be open at this hour. We could always drive off road and try to hit a sheep and then fry it on the Mini's overheating bonnet.

I was weary and in dire need of a shower. I got my wish, sooner than expected, as the rain came spearing down within minutes and the road vanished, turning to a vague blur from the torrent and the resultant spray rising beneath it. That and the perpetual mist of the glass made it impossible to see anything more than about one millimetre in front of the windscreen wipers, which were flailing about ineffectually like the world's worst semaphorist signalling for help while drowning.

'Christ,' I said, unhelpfully, as I righted the car after veering on to the other side of a road filled with headlights. 'We can't drive in this.'

We got off on to a track and followed it for a mile or so. Rain was dripping into the car now. My seat was filling with its own puddle of rusted water. 'Did you actually buy this car or was it bequeathed to you by your great-great-great-great-great-great-great-great grandbastard?'

'Over there,' Karen said.

She was pointing at something to our left, a series of farm buildings emerging from the maelstrom. No lights. The windows looked like holes in a street fighter's mouth. I pulled up outside and we ran to the door.

'It's open,' she said.

'That's because nobody lives here. The place is a wreck.'

'Should we move on?'

'No,' I said. 'It's either this place or sitting in the Mini till it blows over and I'd rather sit in a hammock of sick than spend another minute in your so-called car.'

We got inside but there was only so much of it still benefiting from a roof so we were still outside, technically. Old dead rooms, anonymous, all of them larded with muck and bird shit and drifts of litter. We found a tent in a back room full of rusted pieces of machinery: a lathe, a circular saw, all of it beyond function, corroded to brown flaking lumps. The roof was on in here but water drizzled down the walls anyway. Someone had barbecued something in the grass collector of a lawn mower. The cold, sour smell of ancient charcoal hung in the air like a threat. I checked inside the tent. A couple of gossip magazines from months back. An empty packet of Walker's cheese and onion crisps. Nothing else.

'It's mostly dry,' I said. 'We can sit in here. Keep it warm for the serial killers until they get back from doing some serial killing.'

'Don't—' Karen said. One of her eyes was bloodshot. Fatigue was bowing her mouth, her shoulders. She looked at the very edge of tolerance, sanity, understanding. But then she smiled and lifted up two bottles, one of vodka, one of Coca-Cola. 'Rescued from the car,' she said. 'My "in case of emergency" stash. And I think you'll agree we've reached that point and gone beyond it.'

'Not for me,' I said, but my voice wouldn't back up the meaning in the words.

'Fuck off,' she said, and a harsh bark of thunder underlined her opprobrium. 'When I drink, I never drink alone. And I'm going to have a drink. Gird your fucking loins.'

'I'm off the sauce,' I said. 'Things got nasty. I got nasty. The booze got nastier. I'm out.'

'You said it but your eyes haven't come off this bottle since I whipped it out.'

'So I'm a looker these days. I'm not a drinker.'

'You want a drink. You could *murder* one. And you deserve it.'

'I just want to go to sleep,' I said. 'I've been on the go since forever. Vodka's just going to complicate matters.'

'I won't make any moves on you, if that's what you're worried about.'

It wasn't. It was the moves the drink was making. The crack of the seal was like the shush of nylons being removed in a girlfriend's room.

'What happened to you, after you left school? Where did you go? Marbella?'

'Christ, no,' she said. 'My dad lost his job and, like a good boy, did what he was told. He got on his bike and looked for another one. We ended up in Walsall. And stop changing the subject.'

'I'm not changing the subject,' I said. 'You *are* the subject.'

'Well if you want to talk about the past, you drink with me. Just one. It's all I'm having.'

'Right,' I said. 'We don't have any glasses.'

'Where we're going, we don't need glasses.'

I laughed. She laughed. The laughter was all wrong. It spiked and jagged and rebounded in the cold, sour room where meat had been cooked. Where magazines had been read. It was the laughter of lost people.

She necked the vodka and took a hit of Coke. She handed the bottle to me. I hefted the vodka in my hand. It had weight; the glass was smooth and curved. It fit my hand like the warm thigh of someone giving herself to me gladly, utterly.

'One,' I said.

'May the devil make a ladder of your backbone,' she said. 'And pluck apples in the gardens of hell.'

I raised the neck to my mouth and let the rim dimple my lips. I caught that clean alcohol vapour at the back of my throat. A shitty day. A shitty job. Fuck it. I tipped the bottle and welcomed her home. I pushed away the Coke when she offered it. 'One drink,' I said. 'I didn't want an emetic.'

'You've a gag for every occasion, haven't you?' she said. 'And all of them slightly less funny than a kiddies' cancer ward on fire.'

'Like the vodka,' I said, 'that's a bit harsh.'

'So what's your story?' she asked. 'What are you going to do when you grow up?'

'I got married. I had a daughter. My wife died.'

'Oh shit, Joel,' she said. 'I'm sorry.'

'Forget it,' I said. 'It's life, isn't it? We all hang on this threescore years and ten business but I've known people who checked out in their twenties who lived richer lives than those who lasted four times as long.'

I took the bottle when she offered it again, and eyed it warily. I didn't recognise the label. I imagined someone whose only involvement with Russia was invading it during a game of Risk peeling potatoes in some shabby homemade distillery in Lewisham.

'"Excelsior vodka",' I read. 'Well, at least they tried.'

I took another swallow. As always, with cheap booze, the second swig isn't so bad, mainly because the first has destroyed your nerve endings and taste buds.

'I know a guy who collected rare bottles of single malt whisky,' I said. 'He was surrounded by it, thousands of pounds of the stuff. Twenty-litre bottles of smooth ambrosia laying in their own wooden racks. But he never touched any of it. He poured himself a glass of Bell's or Teacher's, a blend, so he'd know he'd had a drink.'

'I can't tell the difference,' she said. 'So I buy shit. And anyway, you drink to get drunk. Well, I do. What's the point of blowing your wad on something full of butterscotch notes, or whatever? It's all just puke and headaches in the morning.'

Rough or not, it was giving me a buzz. And I'd missed it. We talked about school for a while; people we remembered – the staff mainly: Mrs Ness, the English teacher, known as Sea Monster. Mr Biggins, the woodwork teacher, known as

Bilbo. Mr Fives, the PE teacher, known as Bunchof. We were such an inventive lot.

'I fell in with a bad crowd in Walsall. Weed, whizz, pints of snakebite for breakfast. I'd had three abortions by the age of sixteen, before I had Simon. I thought I'd never have kids. Clock was ticking so loud you could have used me as an egg timer. I wasn't what you'd call mothering material. Sleeping rough. Crack. There was a guy said he'd put a roof over my head and three square meals in my belly if I went on the game but I had enough about me to not get involved in any of that.'

'Your mum and dad still around?'

'Died when I was in my twenties. Probably relieved to see the back of me. Nobody else to turn to. Shouldn't really have had Simon but what can you do? You can't prepare for how you're going to feel. And I loved him from the moment I found out. Poor little fucker. I'm the worst thing that ever happened to him.'

'Don't speak like that,' I said, going through the motions because I kind of agreed with her. 'You're doing your best, aren't you? You're here at least. Looking for him.'

She was crying. She was silent. Her face hadn't changed. It was as if she wasn't even aware of it, as if it was something she'd done so often it had become second nature, like breathing.

Within the hour the bottle was done and I was moving through the farm buildings convinced there was a chicken we could cook while Karen sung hymns we'd been taught at school. She had a high, quavering voice that threatened to ascend into dog-only frequencies whenever she was low on breath.

Every step of the way, I was thinking, while I chased the chicken's shadow. He was with us every step of the way.

Rebecca/Romy would be so disappointed with me now. Tokuzo would stare and nod, hands on hips, and say, 'UNSUR-FUCKING-PRISING.' In an upstairs room I found a sofa wrapped in polythene. Brand new. I laughed out loud and collapsed on to it. An epiphany: there was no chicken.

> *Wherever you travel I'll be there, I'll be there,*
> *Wherever you travel I'll be there.*
> *And the creed and the colour and the name won't matter,*
> *I'll be there.*

Religion, I thought. *Not too creepy.*
Every step of the way. And I blacked out.

I woke up and thought: *Karen.*

I checked my phone. No signal. Because no juice. It didn't feel like I'd been out long though. I moved off the sofa – not brand new at all. Not covered in polythene. It was rat-chewed and sodden. I was soaked too and smelling like something scraped out of the bottom of a fishmonger's hopper. I squelched downstairs. How I hadn't killed myself was some mystery: gaping holes in the stairs, beams and girders hanging out of the walls, fangs of broken glass. Slow combers of nausea rolled through me. My head felt as though it had been used for the past twelve hours by the drummer in a band called One Hundred Percent Drums.

'Karen?' I called out. My mouth felt as though it had been filled with glue and fur. She wasn't in the tent. The vodka bottle pointed at me as if waiting to decide Truth or Dare. *Truth: I'm a cunt.*

The car was gone too. I sat on the doorstep and tried

to understand what was going on but it was like trying to undo knots in spaghetti.

I stood up, determined to propel myself into some kind of positive action without knowing what it was I meant to do. I was still pissed. *That is in my favour*, I thought. So I crammed my fingers into my mouth and tickled the flood button at the back of my throat. A few minutes later, a few pounds lighter, the decor of the farm buildings enriched, I staggered up to the main road, eyes streaming, nose running – but feeling a whole lot better – and tried to get a grip on where the hell I was.

You are in... hang on, let me just check the map... yes, here we are... THE MIDDLE OF FUCKING NOWHERE.

Thanks for that, Bear Grylls. I need a comfy hotel. And a massage.

Don't we all? Just start marching, boyo. If I'd known you were going to be such a thundertwunt with your life I'd have taken you with me.

That's nice of you to say. How would you have done it? Suffocated me with your boobs?

How long would it take for you to die if I was just kicking you constantly up the arse?

A very long time, I'd imagine.

That then. Up the arse with my boot.

I set off with the road we'd travelled in order to get to the farmhouse at my back. The sky was a washed-out colour, like semi-cooked egg whites. It was sulking and miserable after the epic spanking the weather had given it. But it was cold and fresh and I needed that. I felt grimmer than a pan of overcooked cocks, but I'd nipped the vodka in the bud while it was still stewing inside me, which gave me a strangely heroic feeling. This brisk walk would drum some more of it out of me too.

I lucked into a ride soon; a guy in a lorry who let me sit in the bed. He'd been filling in potholes in Mousehole, or mouseholes in Pothole, and his lorry was empty but for a bucket, some shovels and the faint smell of hot bitumen. He dropped me off in Falmouth and I went straight to a pharmacy where I bought disposable razors, a toothbrush and a box of co-codamol. There was a nice-looking hotel near Gylly Beach and I went in and booked a room, apologising to the receptionist, explaining I'd been the victim of a particularly vicious and unfunny stag prank and that I needed to be in London looking vaguely human by that evening or my wife-to-be would rearrange my internal organs. She put me in a room with a sea view and told me to leave my clothes in the laundry bag outside and they'd be express laundered and pressed within the hour.

I showered and shaved and knocked back four painkillers after they'd dissolved in a glass of water. Then I ordered a full English and a pot of super-strength coffee. Soon I was back in my clothes – clean, fragrant, almost fully functional – and brimming with spunk, vigour and righteous fury. Someone was going to have a head ripped off today, and it wouldn't be mine.

My phone was still out of commission; but I stuck it on charge while I used the phone in my room instead, and started the laborious process of getting through the bland, automated voices at Scotland Yard in order to talk to someone with even less personality.

'Mawker,' he droned, eventually.

'It's Joel,' I said.

'Up and about? At this time of the day? You don't *sound* pissed.'

'Fuck off, Ian,' I said. 'There's no need to get clever. I'm off the soup. What's your big achievement? Opposable thumbs yet?'

'If you listen very carefully you can hear the water slipping from the duck's back.'

'I didn't call you for all this phone sex,' I said. 'This is important.'

'It's nothing to do with you, no matter how much you think it is.'

'What? How do you know about it?'

'It's all over the fucking news, Joel. And I'm telling you to keep out of it.'

'I'm in it up to my fucking neck, you mumbling cunt,' I said. 'I just spent all sodding night driving her around the south-west in a fucking Strepsils tin.'

'Christ, you *are* pissed,' he said. 'I have no idea what you are blathering on about.'

'Karen Leonard,' I said. 'Benjie Weston.'

'I don't know those names. If you've been in a threesome then congratulations but you'll put me off my afternoon snack. I *was* going to have a cheese scone.'

'Benjie Weston kidnapped Simon. Son of Karen Leonard. I spent last night helping her track them down.'

'And did you?'

'No. It was a wild goose chase.'

The line went quiet for a moment and I thought he'd gone. But then he said, 'I'll look into it. You should have reported this yesterday.'

'*She* should have reported it the day before yesterday,' I said. 'But she was bricking it over social services. That's why she came to me.'

'So you haven't seen the news then?'

'What are you talking about?'

'Where are you?'

'Fucking Falmouth.'

'Stay there for a bit,' he said. 'Go crabbing. Eat a cream tea.'

'What's going on?'

'Call me when you get back,' he said. 'I've got to go.'

He put the phone down and I realised I was holding the receiver as if it was keeping me alive.

PART TWO
GUNSELS

11

I turned on the TV and was presented with a vision of hell. It took a while for the penny to drop but when it did I had to cling to the bed for fear of falling off it. Cold Quay was in flames. Red Row – I felt it was a somewhat theatrical and bad taste nickname given to the high-security division of the prison which harboured the hard nuts and psychos, including Graeme Tann – had been breached; seven convicts had escaped. There were no details yet as to who had broken out. Most of the other inmates had been rounded up and were in the process of being transferred to temporary accommodation, although there were a few stalwarts sitting on the roof, throwing tiles at the police and demanding prison reform.

I tried calling Mawker again but the fucker had gone out. I thought of calling Cold Quay but all the phones would be shapeless lumps of molten plastic judging by the pictures. I caught myself hoping Tann had been trapped in a cell when the fire reached him but I knew that wasn't the case. I knew he was one of the seven. I knew he was behind all of this. Luckily for him I had been out of the picture while he fiddled with his box of Swan Vestas. I'd have been up there like a shot as soon as the inmates started kicking over their slop buckets, and he knew it.

He knew it.

I switched the TV off and stared out of the window. Sweat was a tickle in the small of my back. I pulled my boots on. My breath was coming in hot, short stabs. Impatience crawled under my skin.

I checked out, expecting to pay a heavy surcharge but the receptionist – an engagement ring on her finger – let me off and wished me a happy wedding day. I gestured at her rock and said the same thing. Then I ran to the station and caught a train to Paddington. I had to change at Truro. Five and a half fucking hours. I wanted to tear my hair out and my skin off every minute of the journey. I managed to steer clear of the service car and topped up only on painkillers to stem the thud of post-drink fear shaking my core. I splurged on a taxi to take me the half mile back home but once there I resisted the temptation to go charging in. I checked out the entrance and the cars in the street and waited a good quarter of an hour. Nobody went in. Nobody came out. I was cautious going up and quieter than a ninja's fart when I opened my door. Nothing.

I fended off Mengele with my leather-jacketed arm while pouring Fishbitz into his empty bowl. 'Miaow' can mean *I love you*. But it can also mean – and it does, usually, where I'm concerned – *I'd rip your throat out if my paw was just a little bit bigger, you bipedal shit-gannet.*

I got outside again quick. Late afternoon. I'd been away from London too long, but not long enough for him to have discovered where I lived. I took Mengele around to Keepsies where I dropped him off with Keith. He's always happy to see Mengele, putting him on mousing duties. Mengele was happy too because Keith rewards him with titbits from his packed lunch.

I took the opportunity to open the safe in my cubicle – as I usually did whenever I was in a pickle – and agonised over whether to take the gun. I hate guns. People invariably die when they are in the vicinity. That is, after all, their raison d'être: taking life. You can get cute little pistols with pretty pearl grips to fit inside a purse. You can get high-powered rifles described as sports models. This is all camouflage to deflect people from the thought that what they hold in their fists are extreme blood-letting death devices. I never met a person – a right-thinking person – who shot someone with a gun and kept their weapon. If you see what a bullet can do up close and then choose to use it again you are every shade of shit known to man.

I shot someone once. And it led to death. Not something I'm proud of. I don't ever want to do it again. But this city. These times. It scares me to think of society falling one day. Eco-catastrophe; class war; a meteorite crashing into the heart of London; North Korea emptying its nuclear load all over the face of the capitalist planet. The people with the immediate advantage will be those with a gun tucked into the waistband of their pants. The criminal minority will hold sway. Who gets the food when food becomes a scarcity? Is it divvied up by a committee or does the guy with the cocked Heckler take it all?

A bit dramatic. A bit J.G. Ballard. But I think about it a lot. It's bad enough now. It could easily get a lot worse.

I took the gun and put it in my jacket pocket. If Tann was out (if... oh, he's out all right) then I wasn't taking any chances. It might increase the likelihood of my own body becoming riddled with holes but it did his too, and that sounded like a good trade-off to me.

I checked Google to see if Karen Leonard's name was listed but if she was there, she was buried among about a bzillion other Karen Leonards. She hadn't given me her address and her phone went straight to voicemail. She'd vanished for the second time in my life. I tried Mawker again and he answered around a mouthful of food.

'You noshing off the Superintendent again?' I said.

'Only if he's turned himself into a cheese bap,' he said.

'Karen Leonard. Tell me you've put the word around.'

'Her and the other one. Chap with a dog's name.'

'Benjie,' I said. 'Benjie Weston.'

'Yes. A big fat fuck-all for both of them.'

'What about the car? Mini. Old and ruined like your penis. UEK 603S. Same colour as the panda cars you used to frot against when you were a nipper.'

'Hang on, give us that reg again.'

I headed towards the Tube, phone clamped to my ear. I was almost at Edgware Road when he got back to me.

'Okay, we've got a name, but it isn't Leonard. It's Leslie. Jeff Leslie. Car's registered under his name. He lives in Lee. SE12.'

'Address?'

'You really ought to back off, Joel.'

'I'll back off if you fuck off. Address.'

Within the hour I was getting off a train in Lee, one of those conurbations south of the river that grew out of the presence of the railways. It was the kind of inoffensive suburb I'd driven through on any number of occasions without it ever registering on my radar. Karen Leonard seemed to live in a place off St Mildreds Road, which forms part of the

110

South Circular, the lucky thing. I got to the street and stood in front of the house, a rough-around-the-edges semi with a front garden containing dead or dying plants in the borders. The balding lawn was littered with dog turds.

I knocked on the door and felt my hands tightening to fists. No answer. A car roared past in the street behind me, the driver leaving it as long as he could before changing gear. I waited until I could no longer hear the protesting engine and then I walked around to the back of the house and put a brick through the kitchen window. I hadn't even got the latch open when I felt bad news pouring out through the hole I'd made.

I jack-knifed over the edge of the kitchen worktop and peered around in the gloom. A streetlight just outside just about let me see okay. No body here; no signs of struggle. The kitchens tended to be the war zones, I found, after years of call and response. People brained with cast-iron skillets. Sliced open with broken crystal champagne flutes. Skewered with expensive Japanese knives. Most of it from the wedding gift lists. Not that there was any of that stuff here. It was basics, if that. Paper plates. Instant noodles. Half a jar of fossilised Nescafé. More dog shit in a corner, stiff and furred with mould.

I moved through to the hallway. Nude walls stained with water leaks. Bare bulbs dangled from a peeling ceiling. Bills scattered on the floor. Nothing to suggest a family lived here, or a woman in the process of trying to find her little one. In the living room I found a wastepaper basket filled with empty cans of strong beer as well as twists of kitchen foil scarred with burns. Delivery pizza boxes freckled with grease. A big TV and a PlayStation. GTA. CoD. Excelsior vodka. *Spiritus Sanctus*.

I went upstairs. *May the devil make a ladder of your backbone.* Karen was in the bathroom. She was on her knees, her head back, resting on the edge of the bath. She was stiff as a bull in a cowshed; she'd been killed hours ago. Her mouth was open wide and a meniscus of blood quivered within, poised to roll over the Plimsoll line of her lips. Her expression reminded me of someone at the shadow zone between confusion and sudden understanding.

I sat down on the floor opposite her and thought about her and I thought about the house. I pulled out a handkerchief and used it as a barrier when I touched her, turning her fingers so that I might see if there was anything under the nails. Only deeply packed filth. It had been under her nails when we shared our Cornish jaunt. Perhaps she'd brought some south-west grit back with her too. No blood. No skin. No hair.

I rubbed my face and thought about her and me and what friendship meant to desperate people who needed the money. She'd stitched me up. It had to be about cash; I'd done nothing to cause her to harbour a grudge. I'd have liked to have known how much she'd been paid. I wondered if she'd followed the news stories about me and Becs and put two and two together. When the moths started flying out of her purse maybe she'd visited Graeme Tann at Cold Quay. I would have liked to have heard the conversation she had with him. His promises. And her, thinking she had an escape route. A chance to start again when all roads were destined to lead her back to this eternity of cold dark. As if they were going to pay her anyway.

All of the shampoo bottles and deodorant cans were neatly placed on the surfaces. No sign of struggle here. Unless the killer had a touch of the OCD about him and tidied up after himself, which was unlikely. And why leave the body?

As a message, maybe? As a warning. *I did this.*

There was a passive spot of blood to my right, near the threshold of the door. There was another one, also passive, on the skirting board on the landing. I got up and had a look. I didn't know what I was looking at or what to deduce from it. But I didn't think they belonged to Karen. There were two bedrooms up here. Both of their doors were closed. Was that a good thing? If it was, my heart wasn't buying into it.

I pressed my hand against the gun in my jacket pocket. It didn't reassure me in the slightest.

I opened the bedroom door nearest the blood stain and went in. The master bedroom, if you lodged your tongue in your cheek. Barely enough room around the bed at the centre to walk freely. Anybody with over-developed calves would be struggling. No wardrobe, just an extendable pole jammed between the walls. Plastic hangers. Clothes that smelled faintly of mildew. Second-hand stuff. Cast-offs for a castaway. Dead girl's clothes for a dead girl. I had a quick look in the bedside table. No photographs. No pictures drawn for Mum. Maybe this Jeff Leslie didn't like having kids' stuff knocking around.

Who are you, Jeff Leslie? I thought. *And where the fuck are you?*

I went back to the landing. The door to the other bedroom was now slightly open. Fuck. This. I pulled out the gun and edged towards it. I had my hand on the wood, was about to push when it burst open in my face and I went backwards, pinwheeling, the gun flying from my hand, and I went down the stairs to the half-landing, closing my eyes against the crack I knew I was going to get on my head. It wasn't too bad; I'd twisted slightly so I was able to get a hand under me and soften the blow somewhat, but I still saw stars. The doorway widened and he came out and he had a claw sticking out of the middle of his hand. He was smiling down at me. His hair was the colour of ash and it was long and lank and hung in his eyes. He was wearing a vest. His arms swarmed with tattoos. His nails were painted black. He was wiry. His face was filled with hollows and shadows. He looked hungry as fuck.

'Leslie?' I said. My voice was clenched with fear. In those momentary interstices of shadow whenever I blinked, I saw knives slicing into me in the old newspaper factory on Silex Street; I felt pieces of me disengage.

'I'm Paul,' he said. 'I'll be your killer today.'

The claw was no such thing of course. It was a curved knife. I know a little about knives. Being opened up by one gives you that kind of focus. It was a *karambit*. It had a finger guard, which meant it would be difficult to knock it from his hand. He held it with a hammer grip. He looked as if he knew what to do with the thing. As if he'd had plenty of practice. He was looking to get a bit more.

'How do you know me? Why do you want me dead? What have I done to you?'

'Ask me no questions I'll tell you no lies.' He was at the top of the stairs, his boots lipping the edge of the riser. I recognised his voice. He'd been the guy on the end of the phone, sending us deep into the West Country. I wondered briefly who the kid had been, but it could have been anybody. *Say 'Mum' and I'll give you a bar of chocolate.* What did it matter now? I smelled tobacco on him, and leather. Blood had dried on his nostrils. Maybe she'd cracked him one before he delivered the *coup de grâce*. Maybe he had a coke habit. What did it matter? There was nothing I could use.

'What difference does it make?' I asked. 'Give me a reason, at least. What does it matter if I'm dead? Don't let me die not knowing. How shitty is that?'

He wasn't playing ball.

I'd landed in an awkward position. My back was crunkled into the corner and one leg was folded underneath me. I was worried I might have done some medial ligament damage there, but really that was the least of my problems, all things considered. I moved my head away from the wall, convinced that half of my brains would unravel from the fracture the collision had undoubtedly caused, but my skull was sound. I saw the gun immediately. It had fallen to my right; it was two feet away, that was all. I almost laughed out loud.

'Hang on,' I said. I reached out and picked it up. He yelled something incoherent and launched himself at me. I slipped the safety off. I levelled the gun at him and shot him in the jaw. There was a weird splintering impact that reminded me of someone hitting a stick of rock with a toffee hammer. His mouth dropped and bloody teeth spilled as if I'd just hit the jackpot on the one-armed tooth bandit. He looked both mildly disgusted and vaguely distracted. It was an expression that followed him into death as he buckled and fell headfirst towards me.

'For someone who doesn't like guns,' I said to him, 'I don't half relish pulling the trigger sometimes.'

I checked his pockets. A couple of tenners. A free IKEA pencil. Juicy Fruit. I disentangled the knife from his finger and pocketed it. I edged past him and went up to the second bedroom. I felt the familiar push-me-pull-you of adrenaline and lactic acid meeting each other head-on. I felt as if I wanted to run a marathon at full speed (including a lap of honour) and simultaneously go to sleep for ten years. I was sick to the core but ravenous too.

Here I found a handbag. Karen's presumably. And that was confirmed by the presence of her passport. Now there were photographs. Men. Pictures of her in bars partying hard. More men. And here a photograph of a baby swaddled in blankets. Asleep, it seemed. Dead, in actuality. On the back she'd written the words *My Si. RIP.*

Simon.

There had been no Simon. Well, maybe for a heartbeat or two. She'd used a dead baby as bait to get me out of the city. She and 'Benjie' – whoever the fuck he was – had given me the runaround. I left the room and stared down at 'Paul'. I had a feeling he was a jailbird, recently freed. Everything was pointing towards Cold Quay. I reckoned I could trace Paul back there. I reckoned I could trace Karen to Paul, or maybe even to Graeme Tann. While he was in prison he held sway; now he was out, imagine the clout he could wield. I was a sitting, shitting duck.

I was on the phone to Mawker again, booking it back to central London. I told him about the assassin and Karen's involvement and subsequent forced retirement. He swore at me for the best part of a minute and told me he was sending a squad car to pick me up from Charing Cross. It was too dangerous for me to go home, he said. I had to spend some time hiding in the long grass, like a zebra, he said. Until Tann was caught. I didn't argue with him; I knew I was vulnerable. The next Paul who came my way wouldn't enjoy the same kind of theatre. He'd get up close to me in the street and tear my neck open without any fancy introductions, or he'd put a bullet through my face from distance. Seven had scarpered from Cold Quay. If Paul was one of them – one of a cadre close to Tann, committed to him, under his spell – then there were conceivably five left who might be keen to do his bidding.

Was this the same guy I'd put away? A pathetic, weak, snivelling Peeping Tom? I'd visited him a while ago and he'd put me on my arse, but he was still half a pint of semi-skimmed milk to my pot of extra-thick double cream.

True to Mawker's word there was a police car at Charing Cross. Some of Mawker's cronies were at the ticket barrier and they ushered me into the back of it. A woman was waiting for me.

'Carla Kemme,' she said.

'What's that, German?'

'Yes, top marks. My father was from Potsdam. I'm here to help you, Joel. We have to move quickly.'

'I think I'm being followed.'

'We've sent out a few decoys already. And our drivers are good. Fast. We'll get you away without any dramas.'

The car nosed out on to The Strand and we turned east. I felt myself pressed back into the seat as the driver floored it. His eyes flashed to the mirror every three or four seconds.

'Any word on who this guy Leslie is? Was?'

'We traced him to a hotel in Luton. He's at some conference, blissfully unaware of the fun and games going down at his pad. Karen Leonard was related to him. Niece. Stole his car.'

'Where are we going?' I asked.

'Safe house. You've been classified as being in considerable danger.'

'Graeme Tann?'

'Graeme Tann.'

'So he did get out?'

'Yes. We're hoping we can have him back behind bars

117

within the next twenty-four hours.'

'Anybody caught yet?'

'No. Unless you want to count Paul Kearney.'

'The guy in Lee?'

'He was in Cold Quay with Tann. One of the rogues' gallery. Lifer. Long criminal record. Murder at the top of it.'

Kemme was inspecting her nails. Her fingers were extraordinarily long. She wore her hair in a fiercely angular bob, which looked as if it had been cut by mathematicians rather than hairdressers. Her glasses seemed too narrow to be of any use.

'What do you do with Mawker?' I asked.

'As little as possible, although we share a wedge of grey space on the Met's Venn diagram.'

'You're in the police?'

'I work for Protection Command,' she said. 'Specifically SO1. We provide specialist protection, usually for heads of state, government ministers, VIPs.'

'But you're slumming it for Sorrell.'

'You said it, not me.'

'Where are we going?'

'Crouch End,' she said. She had the air of someone who had been in the job for so long that she could perform her duties without even thinking about them. It was like listening to someone recite a script. I wondered about that. At least the driver looked as if he was on point. He drove down a one-way street and swung us into Gray's Inn Road, going north.

'How we doing, Dev?' asked Kemme.

'All clear, far as I can see. I can spin us around one more time if you'd rather?'

'I trust you. Let's crack on.'

We flew up York Way and angled east, through Holloway

towards N8. On Weston Park Dev stopped the car and got out. He spoke into his lapel. Within a minute I'd been ushered into a spacious house on the south side. It was frugally decorated. Policemen stood in the kitchen drinking tea and leafing through newspapers. There were bursts of radio static. Dev went to the blinds in the living room and checked the road. I stood at the threshold feeling like a spare cock at an orgy.

'This way,' said Kemme. She led me upstairs and into one of the back bedrooms. There was a bed and a chair and a table. There was a lamp on it. That was all.

'There'll be someone in the building with you at all times,' she said. 'Feel free to move around the house all you like, but do not go into the garden and do not go into the street. If you have any dietary requirements, someone will see to them for you. Ditto reading materials.'

'How long am I here for?' I asked.

'Until we round them up.'

'I'm not sure about this. I can look after myself.'

'Maybe. Personally I'd have you as bait in your own flat with a unit ready to move. Mawker wants you protected. He says you need a break.'

'He needs a break,' I said. 'In the neck area.'

'Right,' she said, breezily. 'I can't stand here chit-chatting all day. I've got a life outside to grab by the balls.'

'You'll be back?'

'At some point, yes. There are forms to fill in and I don't trust those idiots downstairs to put their underwear on the right way round, so yes, I'll be back. But don't miss me too much, will you?'

She called out for Dev and then they were gone. I heard laughter immediately from the serge-bots in the kitchen.

Someone turned a radio on and a song came on from my youth. I listened to it as I stared out across the leafy hamlet-of-yore. I felt hemmed in and not merely because Crouch End didn't have a Tube within walking distance. My mood worsened when the DJ described the song when it finished as a Golden Oldie.

I went downstairs and made a cup of tea and the two police officers there didn't talk to me and I didn't talk to them. They looked like adverts for the police from the 1970s. Moustaches. Beer-bellies. Brylcreem. All that was missing were the mutton-chop whiskers and the Ford Cortina.

I went back up to the room, drank some tea and sat on the bed. It all caught up with me and when I was aware again it was gone midnight. My legs were aching where I'd fought against the stiff pedals in Karen Leonard's Mini. The tea was cold but I drank it anyway. I could hear someone downstairs peeling cards from a deck and patting them on the kitchen table, and the Golden Oldies kept coming. The Lotus Eaters. Scritti Politti. The Icicle Works.

I swung my legs off the bed and tried to open the window. Of course it was sealed shut. The radio clicked off and then there were footsteps on the stairs. He switched the light on and stood at the door. His tongue poked around his mouth for stray morsels of Pot Noodle or whatever the fuck cliché copper food he'd been eating.

'It's sealed shut,' he said. 'And it would make my job so much easier if you didn't try to leave.'

'I just wanted some air in here,' I said.

He looked at me as if I was a cheeky monkey in an infant class.

'Get you anything?' he said.

'Fancy a pint?' I said.

'Not on duty. But I can arrange for a range of beers or lagers to be delivered to your suite.'

'Never mind. What's your name?'

'I'm Officer Towne,' he said. 'Officer Moore will be taking over later. You should get some sleep.'

'I've had some sleep. I want to go walking.'

'Yes, and I want Charlize Theron to give me a full body massage but it ain't happening any time soon.'

'The fuck is this?' I said. 'Graeme Tann goes free and I get banged up. It's beyond irony.'

'It's for your safety,' he said.

'He's coming for me at home. If he doesn't know I'm in Crouch End then surely I can go for a walk around here. Just for an hour. Jesus.'

'Sorry,' he said, in predictably flat, police tones. 'There's no guarantee he didn't have you tracked. I can protect you in here. I can't protect you out there.'

'You don't look as if you could protect the skin on a rice pudding. No offence.'

'I'm a fully trained police officer, sir,' he said, putting a bit of spice on the 'sir'. 'I can handle myself.'

But he was looking at me as if to say 'I could handle you'. Part of me really wanted to test that, but it would only piss Mawker off, and his heart was in the right place. Well, I say 'right place'. The right place for Mawker's heart was actually Mengele's food bowl.

'Fuck it,' I said. 'Go back to your cards and lard.' And then I thought of something.

'Hang on,' I said.

'Sir?' He might as well have said 'Turd?'

'There is something I could do with, if I'm going to be

stuck here for a while. The cold case files Mawker brought over to my place.'

'I'll have someone pick them up,' he said. 'Anything else?'

'No, that's it. Thanks.'

'Can I go back to my cards and lard now?'

'Knock yourself out.'

I dreamed Karen was with me in the Mini, but the car was filled with water and she was drowning. I thought I would drown too, but every time I opened my mouth to pull in that final, liquid breath, Sarah finned up out of the darkness to pass the oxygen from her lungs into mine.

I woke up gasping, disoriented. It was night time again, four a.m. according to my watch. At least I was catching up on my sleep. I got up and managed fifty press-ups and went in search of the shower. After ten minutes under water as hot as I could get it, I returned to find that one of the face furniture brothers had left a tray of sandwiches and a steaming mug of tea on the table. The case files were stacked alongside.

I called out a thank you from the top of the stairs and a voice with Welsh depth to it said, '*De nada.*'

I dressed and bolted the food, then stretched out with the case files and took restorative sips of tea. The bare bulb was of high wattage and its light cast strong, enormous shadows against the angles of the room. But it also picked out the subtle shadows on the folder I'd just cast aside. One of my most prized possessions – and I store it at Keepsies because I'm scared it will get lost or destroyed – is a vinyl copy of John Lennon's compilation album *Shaved Fish*, given to me by Rebecca on our fifth anniversary. I've long misplaced the card that accompanied it (it's around somewhere, tucked inside a book most probably) but its message to me remains, because she must have written it leaning on the album. The words have indented on the cover, and you can see them if you tilt the sleeve in a particular way against the light.

Here's to another five... and maybe more, Faceache. I love you, R xxx

The ghost words on the cardboard were undoubtedly in Mawker's hand because they were capitalised and abbreviated.

DO NOT LET ON TO JS ABT GT VSTS!

What was that supposed to mean? JS was me, presumably. GT: Graeme Tann. What visits? Had he been let out of prison for some reason? I tried Mawker on the phone but he wasn't answering this early. I took the folder down to the kitchen. My bodyguard was sitting with his feet up on the table rubbing at something with a scrap of sandpaper. On a small TV, a nature programme depicted something big with lots of teeth creeping up on something small with big eyes.

'Moore, isn't it?'

'Chris Moore, yes.' He swung his feet away from the table and sat up.

'You know Ian Mawker.'

'I do.'

'Any idea what he means by this?'

I had to get a piece of paper and shade with a pencil the area containing the words so that they would transfer and be more legible in the softer lighting down here.

'No idea,' he said, once he'd read it. 'What's that? Vests?'

'Never mind,' I said. 'Does Towne come back later?'

'He does,' Moore said, returning to his sandpaper. When

he noticed me watching he held up a piece of wood. 'Pawn,' he said. 'I'm slowly making a chess set for my nephew.'

I went back upstairs and leafed through the pages, looking for something to alleviate the boredom. I read some more about the mythical beast that was the Skylark. The speculation. The list of possible perpetrators, many of which would no doubt be dead now. He had to be athletic, they reckoned. He was getting in and out of these construction sites at speed. Up and down stairs like greased shit. No working lifts. And he was strong too. Able to overpower his victims and, in some cases, heave them over railings. You couldn't do that if you were five foot nothing and built like a streak of piss. So many blank spaces in these files. So many question marks. It really was a cold case.

How many crimes went unpunished around the world? The number of people who got away with it. All those victims, some of them never found.

Click.

I put down the pages and looked up at the wall. A sound. A different sound. It hadn't come from this room and it hadn't come from just outside it. It hadn't originated in the kitchen either, where Moore was sitting, buffing his chess piece: I could just hear the faint *skrit* of sandpaper. I thought about it, and listened some more. Nothing. Could be any number of things. I didn't know this house. I didn't know this neighbourhood. I was just jumpy and on the lookout for not-rightness. And—

And *click.*

Followed by a faint scraping sound. Metal on glass. Someone was trying to get in.

I got off the bed and stole to the window. Nobody there,

but it was too dark to see anything in the garden below. Coming up to five a.m.

On the landing I could no longer hear Moore's woodworking, and I hoped that was because he'd heard the noises too and was now doing his job, hopefully with a fully loaded gun in his hand. I slipped down to the final half a dozen stairs and strained for shadows and sound. Either Moore had left the building, or someone had come in; fresh night air laced the stale. I did not want to call him and give away my position.

All of the lights went out.

Now I couldn't hear anything because my heart was thrashing in its bone cage like a frightened bird, filling my ears with the thud of hot blood. All that rolled around my mind were the words *safe house/shit house* over and over.

I edged along the wall to the corner of the hallway and glanced around it towards the kitchen. In the diffuse light from the street I could just see Moore's legs stretched out from the chair in which he was sitting. The rest of him was obscured by the wall. One of his legs was twitching around, the shoe on occasion tapping out a tattoo against the table. He wasn't describing the beat of a song he liked; I knew he was dead, or well on the road towards it.

I backed off, keeping my eyes on the doorway, waiting for someone to advance, but he never came. I felt my neck prickling, but there could not be anybody behind me. Entry was forced via the kitchen. In the end, fear turned my head. Just as I thought: *The door shut. Nobody there.*

When I turned back, a figure stood in the hallway, about six feet away from me. I almost moaned. I almost dropped to my knees and begged him to do it, to finish it, because I couldn't cope with the stress of it all. The not knowing where or when. By whose hand. By what method. It ate into me like an aggressive cancer. Death would be a release from it. A flash of light. A sting of pain. Insensate eternity.

But then: Sarah. But then: Rebecca. You bend but you don't buckle. You falter, but you do not fall. He moved towards me and I braced myself. Another game of death. Another few scar cards to add to this livid deck. He got to the newel post at the foot of the stairs and I stared in wonderment as he turned and glided up them, his head back, eyes trained on the landing above for what might be waiting for him. He hadn't seen me. The shadows too dark; the spill of streetlights through the casement just a little too bright in his eyes.

I didn't breathe.

Once he'd vanished from sight I got myself moving. It would be seconds before he realised there was nobody up there. I swept through to the kitchen and, careful not to tread in the fan of blood widening under Moore's chair, got myself through the door the killer had so expertly broken open and I was over fences and down back alleys and through hedges until I was covered in scratches and I couldn't see any more for the sweat and blood filling my eyes.

12

Mawker met me by the water at the Millennium Bridge. I'd been skulking around on buses for a couple of hours, unable to go home, and reluctant to seek refuge with any of my friends in case I put them in jeopardy. In fact, I'd just finished texting Lorraine Tokuzo and Romy Toussaint to suggest they get out of London for a while, just in case. I huddled into my coat and stared up at the skyscrapers. They were calming, somehow. Maybe because they promised a way out if things became too gnarly. Romy sent me a message imploring me to come to her father's house. Tokuzo sent me a gif of a face being repeatedly slapped above the words 'FUCK YOU'.

For some reason Mawker's voice was making me think of ancient, blind goats stumbling on rocks and falling to their deaths down steep faces of scree. I was quite enjoying the imagery. But he was haranguing me now about the intruder, why I hadn't stuck around to at least identify him if not incapacitate him.

'Ian,' I said, 'correct me if I'm wrong but the idea behind a safe house is to ensure that its inhabitants don't come into contact with anyone dangerous. There's a level of protection involved. You know, I think the clue might well be in the name.'

'Agreed,' he said, 'but seeing as though the opportunity presented itself…'

'How did he find us?' I asked.

Mawker blew out his cheeks. 'Who's to know?' he said. 'Could have been a tail after those cold cases were picked up for you.'

'So it's my fault, is what you're saying?'

'Or it could have been someone was on you every step of the way.'

'Maybe an insider,' I said. 'Someone who'd like to see me on Clarkey's gurney. Someone with shit taste in coats and haircuts.'

'I can't say I've not been tempted in the past to turn the nation's killers your way, but I'm sorry to disappoint you. My unit's integrity is squeaky. As is mine.'

I let that slide without comment but the idea of a tail was, anyway, much more feasible.

'Any names yet?' I asked. 'Other than Tann. And this Paul guy in Lee?'

'Paul Kearney. Nurtured on violence. He stabbed a teacher in the arm with a screwdriver when he was six.'

'Nasty,' I said. 'Still, credit where it's due, he did introduce himself politely. Impeccable manners. What about the creep at your so-called safe house?'

'Jon Les,' he said. 'We caught him… well… he's dead. Shoot-out at a gastropub on Broadway Parade.'

'Shootout? In Crouch End? Jesus.'

'What can you do? It didn't take long. He's a knifer, by trade. He held that Brocock as if it was a dick he didn't recognise. We gave him every chance.'

'Did you have to kill him, Ian? We need a live one. We need to get some information out of the bastards.'

'We shot him through the leg. Fucker had a heart attack. You can't legislate for that.'

'Anything on him? Any leads?'

'Nothing useful.' Mawker pressed a folder into my hands. 'Here are the others. You can keep it,' he said. 'I printed it off for you myself. Bit of homework. You'll be hoping there's no test off the back of it.'

I opened it and looked inside. A list of names, Kearney and Les among them. A bunch of photographs. Bullet heads. Prognathous jaws. DIY tattoos. Scars. Trophies.

'Lovely,' I said. 'Thanks.'

The Thames blew us a kiss: there were the ghosts of diesel and death on it. The corpse of a bird drifted by. A helicopter swept over the Tate Modern. I stared up at the Splinter, and the lights reflecting off its glass skin. I thought I'd rather be up there. I'd be safe up there. Tann wouldn't dream of it.

'So we've got another place, in south Tottenham,' Mawker was saying. 'We'll double the security. We'll make sure—'

'No,' I said.

'Then go home. We'll have officers stationed all along your street. If he makes his move—'

'No,' I said.

'What are you going to do?'

The look on his face told me he knew exactly what I was going to do. I confirmed it for him.

'That would be a mistake,' he said. 'I couldn't allow it.'

'It's why you gave me the folder, you tit,' I said. 'You either want me to be bait or you want me to do your dirty work for you. Well I'd rather be out here than trapped under a roof with your so-called professionals.'

'I can't be seen to be helping you.'

'Why change the habit of a lifetime?' I said. 'I prefer to be on my own. I might have a chance of living through this.'

'You know my number, if you want to talk,' he said. 'And if you're caught with that folder, I had nothing to do with it.'

I wanted to ask him what it was he did all day. But there were other, more pressing questions. What was it about Tann that evinced this extraordinary loyalty in the relatively short time he'd spent in prison? Where did I turn to next? And never mind these snivelling little henchmen, where was *he*? I'd been watching the news since it happened – in hotel bars, in the windows of high-street TV shops, on my own phone as I took buses from one place to another, trying to shake off would-be pursuers, trying to force some anonymity into my weary bones.

The blaze at Cold Quay was under control, but four of the six remaining escapees were still at large. Their mug shots stared grimly out from the screens as if they were auditioning for parts in *Neanderthal! The Musical*. All except Tann, who looked fit and lean and piercingly intelligent. *One of the largest manhunts in history*, squealed the headlines.

We will not rest until they are behind bars.

A combined prison sentence of 267 years.

They are likely to be armed and are considered extremely dangerous.

Do not approach them, under any circumstances.

Their names seemed to contain fragments of the aggro in their faces: George Carney. Vic Bledsoe. Lenny Bates. Leo Brand. I stuffed the folder into a jacket pocket and asked Mawker if there would be anything else.

'We're trying to find these fuckers,' he said. 'We will find these fuckers. This is an island. There's a limit to the number of places where they can hide out. All the airports and seaports are on high alert. You really don't have to do this.'

'Airports,' I scoffed. 'They aren't going to leg it. Not until I'm on the barbecue coated in my formaldehyde marinade. I can't just sit around waiting for them to pop up,' I said. 'And there's Sarah to think of. She's still out there somewhere. Tann knows that. I have to be proactive.'

'You sound like the training videos we used to watch at Bruche.'

'And as ever, you sound like a cunt. Go home to your Vaseline and your microwaved pumpkin.'

'Whatever that means.'

'See you,' I said. It was cold, getting colder. I needed to get warm. I set off marching, expecting some final attempt at smart-arsery, but then I remembered something and turned back.

'On the cold case folder,' I said. 'There was some handwriting. Well, the indentation of it. Your handwriting.'

'Go on.'

'It said something like "don't let on to JS about GT" something or other... "V-S-T-S".'

'I don't know,' he said, way too quickly for my liking. 'I don't remember.'

'Come on, Ian,' I said. 'JS is me. GT is Graeme Tann. What the fuck is V-S-T-S. Visits? Were you letting him out?'

'I wasn't letting him do anything. Not my say-so. If he was going anywhere it was down to the Home Office.'

'Then why your handwriting?'

'Who says it was my handwriting?'

'I do.'

'I can't be the only person in the world with shit handwriting,' he said.

I stared at him. 'Fine,' I said. 'Play your games. But if I find out—'

'You find out what? And then you'll do what? Come on, I'm aching to hear some more of your empty threats.'

'Don't fuck with me, Ian.'

'Tell you what,' he said. 'Piss off back to your grief pit, or some shit-stained bedsit somewhere, or go vagabond and walk holes into your shoes. I couldn't give a tinker's cuss. I've just about had it up to here with your constant yapping. Nothing but your worries is the important thing. Everyone else's plight isn't worth the candle. Well, I'm sick of it. You're a one-story scream queen and I've heard it too many times. Good-fucking-night, you arsehole.'

He stormed off in the direction of Blackfriars, if indeed it is at all possible for a man with a side-parting, an iron-free shirt and slip-on shoes to do anything quite so dramatic.

I headed east, towards vertical London. The towers and cranes. It was getting dangerously close to up-tools hour but I needed to get some height in my veins.

An hour it took, to steal through those shadows, to hide from the overweight waddling serge-muppets with their crackling walkie-talkies, to creep up the steps and shuffle along gangways and duckboards where the shiver of brick netting and the creak of scaffolding was like fear given a voice.

I got to the top and stood looking down at the river, like a black split in the earth. All the teeming lights, gradually shutting off now as dawn streaked the sky with pink and puce. Tann among them. Tann and his cronies, tightening the net, or making it bigger. How could you conduct a search when so many people were looking for you? How could he be so single-minded? So driven? Or maybe I shouldn't gild what he was doing with such positive terms. *Monomaniacal.* There, that was better. That's what fuckheads with a purpose were. I was asking myself the question, but didn't I already know the answer? I understood that level of commitment; I'd lived it – I was living it – hunting for Sarah.

Another helicopter swooped by and I flinched, discomfited by its appearance below me as it swept west following the wind of the river, and watched until its lights were lost to the glittering backdrop.

'Pretty, isn't it?'

I flinched again. The words had been spoken less than a foot from my left ear. I stepped back, conscious that there was no barrier between me and a thousand feet of screaming death.

'You could say that,' I said. I'd been caught trespassing. I didn't know what that meant – caution? fine? something more serious in these times of suicide bombs? – but it couldn't be good. 'You don't look like security.'

'What does security look like?'

'Uniforms. Hang-dog expressions.'

I had my fist tucked up tight on my hip. I was going to *gyaku tsuki* the crap out of him the moment he took one step nearer. It was difficult to make out his features in this rarefied altitude; none of the ambient light from the lower reaches was finding its way up here. But he didn't strike me as Tann-related. And if he was, he'd had his chance to heave me over the side rather than chew the fat.

'So you're construction?' I said. He shook his head.

'Tell you the truth,' I said. 'I'm fed up of playing twenty questions. I couldn't give a watery shit who you are. I was just after some "me" time.'

'Me time,' he said. 'Up a skyscraper.'

'Yes.'

'I hear you. It's why I'm here too.'

'Well two "me"s make an "us". And I don't want "us" time. So could you kindly…' I indicated the wide-open space before us and while my unspoken invitation to enter wasn't explicit, I wasn't going to complain if he took the hint.

'I was here first,' he said.

'Okay. You want to play territory games. Stay here. I'll go and find another floor.'

'Everywhere you go from here is down,' he said. I couldn't be sure if that was some kind of veiled threat or an existential slight.

He was right, though. Here was the eyrie. Top of the heap. Everything else was little people.

'I built this,' he said.

'You just said—'

'I don't mean I got my hands dirty. I mean I designed it.'

'Really?' I said. 'That's impressive, I guess.'

'Thank you.'

'So you're what? An architect?'

'Yes,' he said. 'Let's say that.'

I wasn't happy about the way I was still standing between him and the great blue bye-bye, but when I moved to rectify that, he moved too.

'What are you doing?' I asked.

'We've talked about me. Now let's talk about you.'

'Let's not,' I said.

'You're trespassing,' he said. 'One phone call and there'll be a bunch of security guards on the ground floor ready to fill your face in.'

'Do what you fucking want,' I said, tired of all the vocal tennis I had to put up with all the time. 'Just get out of my face. Give me ten minutes, please.'

'Rough day?'

I nodded. 'Rough fucking week, actually. And you're not making it any easier.'

'Define "rough".'

'Seriously? Why does it matter how rough "rough" is for me? I've got a hang-nail. My wife won't blow me any more. My local supermarket doesn't stock dried blueberries.'

'It's a bit worse than that, isn't it? I mean, why else would you be here?'

Now I could make out some detail – my eyes growing used to the gloom. He was in his sixties. Maybe older. But he dressed like someone much younger. He wore jeans and a zip-up hoodie. He wore hiking boots with thick rubber soles. All the better to grip these dodgy boards.

'I'm not here to kill myself if that's what you mean.'

'Famous last words.'

'Like you said,' I said. 'Rough day. Let's leave it at that.'

'I spend most of my time here.' He walked to the very edge of the duckboards.

'Hey!' I said. I had been convinced he was going to walk straight off the edge of the building but he stood there, toes overhanging, hands in pockets as if it was the most natural position in the world. I closed my eyes and tried to ward off the visions of falling. I felt my groin and hips and knees do that weird jelly thing as my nerves sizzled like fury. He didn't seem fazed at all by the brutal height and the vicious winds churning around us.

'It helps level me out,' he said.

'What about your designing?' I asked. 'Does it make things difficult for you? Shouldn't you be at floor level to get a better perspective?'

'All my best work has been done with my head in the clouds.'

I felt suddenly tired. I don't know if it was because of the time I'd spent in hospital – I was sure my body was still some way off making a full recovery – but I was finding it hard to burn the midnight oil these days. Maybe it was injury, or fear, or just age, that great reducer.

'I was spending a lot of time feeling as though I was up against everyone in the world and that I had to fight for breathing space,' he said. 'I couldn't find the centre of me. I felt as if I was searching constantly, that it was overtaking my life. I couldn't rest for the fear that I was losing myself to these blueprints. That they were taking me over.'

'But no more, presumably?' I asked.

'God no. I'm talking about my time back in the eighties and nineties, when I was young. When I was working sixteen-hour days and then getting shit-faced and coming straight in from the bar to do another sixteen-hour day. I never felt it when I was young, but I was building up quite some wall of debt. The kind of debt you can't see until you hit a certain age and everything catches up with you.'

It wasn't so bad, having some company. Someone who didn't judge you or advise you. Once we'd got past that cautious stage of introductions I saw how he was quite affable, perhaps as starved of decent companionship as I was. He was entertaining, smart, inquisitive – the conversation didn't always circle back to him – but I played his questions about me with a straight bat. Neutral all the way. Because you never knew. It wasn't in my nature to trust. Not any more.

He pulled out a candle and sat cross-legged on the deck. I sat down too. All the tension and fear relaxed with me. He lit the wick and his face shivered orange above it, creased and stubbled, the eyes kindly, wrinkled, an unholy blue.

'I saw you the other night,' I said. 'I was over there.' I pointed at the jagged stack of the other tower, its cranes and rods like broken bones sticking out of the end of a ruined limb. 'I saw candlelight.'

'Well, no electricity up here. And torches are too bright. I want to be able to see the beam of the guards before they're on top of me.'

'But you designed the place.'

'Kind of,' he said.

'You did or you didn't.'

'It was a project that was taken out of my hands at a somewhat advanced stage,' he said.

'So you're here because what? You want to sabotage it?'

'Nothing so dramatic,' he said. 'I just come here to think about what might have been, and for inspiration. A different perspective.'

I must have dozed off. When I awoke the light had changed again – weak winter sun dribbling like liquid flame along the edges of all the glass buildings; orange everywhere – there was a note tucked into my jacket.

Come to my office any time you want to talk, it said.

I got down to ground level as the construction crews turned up to the site. I skipped out of sight while they stared after me, none of them willing to part with the bacon rolls sticking out of their fists to play the hero. I spent the next hour or so sheltering in back streets by skips filled with restaurant waste. The sun went in, as it so often does in this mulchy, mushroomy country. A light rain began to fall. I played spotting games in the rush hour that I had not played since I was a kid in the back of my parents' car on trips to the seaside. Keep my mind off the cold. Ten red cars. Ten

BMWs. Ten buses. Ten twats crossing the road with their faces in their iPhones. I called Jimmy Two. When a barber's opened I went and had my head shaved. I bought some reading glasses from the pharmacy and poked the lenses out, then grabbed some breakfast in Waterloo and caught a Tube to Mornington Crescent to pick up the car where Jimmy had left it, in a pay and display space on Chalton Street. Half an hour later I was on the A1 heading north.

13

I parked the car next to a small wood, not far from where I'd played a game of chicken on the motorway six months previously. I opened the window and sucked in some of the brittle winter air and sat there for a while, rubbing my hand back and forth across the brutal new landscape of my head. Farm smells. Something cloacal hanging about in the shadows between the wet, dark trees. The faint rumble of motorway traffic.

I liked it here, away from the city. I could feel the vampire of London unhooking its fangs from my neck, bit by bit. A little green. A little quiet. I could hear myself think. I could feel the tension unravelling from muscles that seemed to be coiled too tightly whenever I was out on the streets. Fresh air. Christ. I should do more of this. Get in a car and drive away from the madness for a while, preferably with nobody mad in the seat next to mine. Preferably in a car larger than something made in Lilliput.

I got out and walked through the woods in a roughly north-westerly direction. I enjoyed the feel of the damp air in my lungs, and the exertion as I stepped over felled branches and brackish puddles. Looking up, I could see the sun, or the area it inhabited behind the thin, hazy cloud through the criss-cross naked canopy. Back home, if I looked up, there'd be the dizzy-making towers, or acid rain, or a wad of pigeon shit on its way down to meet me.

Didn't we used to do a lot more of this, back in the day? Me and you and Sas?

Yes, and you complained before, during and after.

Did I? Are you sure? I like a good hike though. Get some mud on my boots. Scour my lungs out.

I remember one day we drove out to Ashridge because Sas wanted to see the deer and the bluebells and you told me you'd rather stick your penis in the shredder.

Yes, but the sentiment was well meant, no?

Enjoy your walk, Yul Brynner. I hope your legs fall off tomorrow.

I smelled the prison before I saw it. That cold, charred smell, a nauseating odour of incinerated wood and plastic that feels as though it's clogging up your airways, layer upon layer. I thought I could still see remnants of the previous day's fire in the carbon colours of the clouds, all ash and charcoal. I got to the edge of the trees and stared down at what remained of Cold Quay.

Bedlam, more like. I'd seen some pictures on TV but this was much worse. The full extent of the damage was shocking. I could see the roofs of the units and dormitories and they were all collapsed. Nothing had escaped the flames; everything was coated with ash and soot. Wood was mackerel-striped where the fire had gnawed through it. Steel girders had swooned in the heat; one building leaned as if demonstrating the effects of being blown over by high winds. Debris littered the areas between the buildings, perhaps dragged out by firefighters trying to control the blaze: charred mattresses, melted plastic stretchers, piles of clothes. All the windows had shattered in the heat. Things fluttered, trapped in tree branches or the links of the fences surrounding the perimeter: latex gloves, documents, newspapers.

Other fences had been hastily constructed around the perimeter, which I thought was a bit odd. The prison was already contained by a fence. Security guards roamed the interstitial areas, some with dogs. I saw one area in the car park cluttered with bulging black bin bags. Styrofoam cups spilled out. Maybe where the TV crews had gathered. Nobody here now. Dead news. The story had scarpered, on the heels of the escaped inmates.

I wanted to take a closer look, but I was sure I would get no joy from the security guards. I sauntered down anyway, wishing I had a dog of my own so I could pretend I was just taking it for a walk.

I saw heads turning my way pretty much as soon as I broke the shelter of the trees. I walked with my hands in my pockets, staring at my boots, trying to appear as if I was lost in my own thoughts. I got as far as the south-east corner when the security guard ostentatiously rapped on one of the metal posts supporting the chain-link fence with a truncheon.

'No further for you today, chucklehead,' he said.

'The land around here doesn't belong to the prison,' I said, with conviction, not knowing whether that was true.

'I don't care,' he said. 'We're in the middle of a serious jail breakout. We can't take any risks.'

'I'm walking off a hangover,' I said. 'Where's the risk? It looks as though the horse already bolted on that one anyway.'

'Funny fellow,' he said. He had a face like a blind

carpenter's workbench: acne scars peppered his skin and he had a nose that looked as if it had been torn off and reattached upside down; it was more of a snout, really. His jacket was a size too large and his trousers a size too big. 'But you go no further, otherwise I go to town on your wagging jaw with this.' He brandished the night stick and his face split under the weight of a smile.

I stopped and considered the repercussions were I to argue the toss with this one-brain-cell freak. Hardly worth it. Stick v hand? The stick always wins. Plus, extra sticks because of the serge backup he could rely on. I wasn't going to kick up a fuss by getting the gun out here. I'd be arrested within the hour. That serge backup was gravitating towards him now, more meat-heads than you'd find at a brawn festival.

I held my hands up and turned away, headed back to the woods, gritting my teeth against the laughter and the whispered invective. Before I reached the trees it had begun to rain again, the same thin veils. It soaked you with stealth, this rain, and I was shivering by the time I made it back to the car. I turned the engine on and whacked the heating up. Thankfully it didn't take too long to kick in. I rubbed my hands and thought about what to do. I was hungry and tired, but I didn't want to go back to London without having had a proper look around that prison.

I got back on the motorway and drove to the services at Newport Pagnell. I ate fish and chips and checked into the motel where I took a shower and got my head down. I slept dreamlessly for ten hours and woke up in darkness. I dressed and checked out, picking up a sandwich and a coffee on the way. I ate as I drove, and listened to a delicate Chopin prelude on Radio 3.

It was still raining. I reached the spot where I'd parked

earlier and switched off the engine.

I got out and jogged down to the vantage point at the edge of the wood. A single torch beam cut through the darkness down in the shattered prison complex. A subtler light spilled from a Portakabin set back from the ruins. I wondered if the same number of security guards would be on site now. Maybe they were down to two: one on patrol, another in the Portakabin, playing cards or shuffling through a well-thumbed copy of *Reader's Wives*. Maybe even just one guy. It didn't matter. I didn't intend to engage in any banter this time.

The only sound was the soft hiss of rain on the nude branches and my jacket as I broke cover and followed the route down to the fence I'd taken earlier. The cloud cover was good, and there was no light beyond what the guard was producing.

I got to the fence knowing that the guard was moving away on the eastern side. I just wanted a quick look at the top end, in case there was anything to give me a clue about where Tann was heading. I didn't expect it. The police would have picked this place over like a baboon on its flea break; if they hadn't found anything, why should I?

That thought didn't deter me. Mainly because I'm a stubborn bastard, but also because I suspected the police weren't necessarily going to be interested in the things that caught my eye. Dangerous men were out and about. There wasn't much detective work needed in such a situation. Maybe if there was a map on a wall with big red arrows and a note saying: LET'S HEAD FOR THIS PLACE, CHAPS. But that was extremely unlikely. Everything interesting was away from here now, hence the absence of boys in blue. Security guards didn't count. The police were into damage limitation. This was politics as well as policing. Reputations were at stake.

I hunkered down behind a mass of metal bed frames that had warped in the immense heat. No sign of life. Up ahead, the uniform shape of the fence had failed; presumably this was where everyone had got out. I reached it and saw shreds of clothing caught on the barbed wire. I got my torch out and risked exposing myself for a few seconds of illumination. Yes, there had been a grand old scuffle here. Part of the prison wall had collapsed, bringing down the perimeter fence. Broken glass, spilled blood. I was tempted to go inside and have a mooch around, but it would be a waste of time. The prison had been overcrowded and underfunded. It was antiquated – one of the last in the country to continue with that happy practice known as 'slopping out' – and had been dogged with rumours of brutality over the century or so it had harboured convicts at Her Majesty's pleasure.

I heard a scuff of a boot on concrete. The guard wasn't one of those people who liked to do circuits. He'd cut back instead of going all the way around. Maybe he was on his way to the cabin for a cup of tea and a shufty at Suki from Hemel Hempstead. Maybe he'd heard me or seen the flash of my mini torch. I hoped volcano face was still on duty. I'd have that night stick halfway up his magma chamber before you could say 'topical application'.

I waited but there was nothing else. I waited some more, just because I'm cautious like that, and then kept going along the shattered perimeter until I reached the far corner. I looked around me at the likely route the escapees had taken. Presumably Forensics had been out here to take boot casts, or whatever juju those white gods get up to, and I did see some evidence of plaster, but they'd obviously been more interested in the interior of the prison than the exterior. I'd have to rely on scraps.

I headed in the direction of another line of trees. If I was legging it from a prison, trees would be my shelter of choice, especially when the alternative was miles of open countryside. But I didn't get anywhere near them. My foot went straight through the ground up to my thigh and I went over. The pain was immense, and for a sickening few seconds I thought I'd broken my femur. I was either going to pass out or scream the remaining bricks down at Cold Quay. Either way I was dead in the water. But it quickly transpired that the pain was only muscular – I'd perhaps pulled a hamstring; it didn't help that it was so cold – and that what I'd fallen into wasn't, as I'd suspected, a rabbit hole or some other such death-trap. It was a tunnel.

I checked the surroundings and got the torch on again. Yes, a tunnel. But nothing so grand as an escape tunnel dug out of the earth with a teaspoon over the course of decades. This was some kind of service tunnel, it seemed: careful scraping about revealed rails sunk into the earth.

It seemed to go towards the trees. There was a sleeping bag in there, chewed to bits by rats or foxes, and some cold drinks cans, a small hill of cigarette ends. I don't know what that meant. Maybe someone keeping tabs on the prison. Maybe a place to keep warm while they made a drop or expected something in return. I found the entrance to the tunnel covered with stones and pieces of brick. Beneath that was a section of plastic sheeting, presumably to keep the worst of the moisture out and prevent collapse. There were some containers inside resting on what looked like radio-controlled carts. The containers were varied in size and shape. Some were plastic pods sealed with gaffer tape, some Tupperware boxes, some just wraps of tin foil. Most were empty but I found one stuffed with shivs. Another contained a bag of weed. One of the tubs was dusted with remnants of coke. Goodies bound for clink that never arrived because of the riot. It looked as if I'd discovered some method for transporting contraband in or out of the prison.

I wondered whether I should get this stuff back to Mawker, but what good would it do? Perhaps there were others stalled mid-journey that might offer a lead in my search for Tann, but I doubted any of them would give me co-ordinates leading me right to his door. He was far away. He wasn't stupid. If they couldn't catch him within the first twelve hours of his escape, then he could be anywhere. Someone could be hiding him in an attic or a cellar. He could be out in the wilds. He could be across the Channel and sunning himself in Puerto Banús by now.

But I guessed he was still in the country. There was the small matter of me to deal with, and I didn't think he'd give up the opportunity to do so. He knew I stood between him and any chance he had of a long, peaceful exile.

I watched the long, slow beam of the security guard's torch as he came back and wondered why this broken-down doss hole needed any kind of protection. Maybe the prison service was so strapped for cash that they wanted to make sure nobody came to strip the lead from the windows, or made off with the copper wiring. I supposed there might be some salvageable stuff in the canteens and workshops. And at the very least, they didn't want kids getting on the site and doing themselves a terrible injury on the broken glass and weakened masonry.

I headed back to the car, having wiped off the canisters and returned them to the tunnel. If I got caught with any of that shit I'd be liable for a bed in Cold Quay's replacement. Gone two a.m. I felt as if my internal clock had been overwound and dropped on the floor and kicked against a wall a few times. I wasn't even sure what day it was. Only the Christmas lights shining in the houses parted by the M1 gave me any kind of clue as to where we all were.

I thought of wrapping presents on Christmas Eve with Rebecca and trying, and failing, every year to get her to do it in the nude. While wearing a Santa hat. I would always write a letter from Father Christmas to Sarah after I'd had a few Bristol Creams, disguising my handwriting best I could. *You've been very good this year. You know that Mummy and Daddy love you very much. Maybe next year you can sit on Rudolph... I've been very busy, you know.* And then I'd scarf the mince pie and toss back the glass of brandy and put the carrot back in the salad crisper.

I might *have wrapped presents with you in the nude if you didn't get so piss-pants drunk.*

It's Christmas Eve. What else are you supposed to do?

But that's your excuse for everything. Christmas Day. New Year's Eve. New Year's Day. The first daffodil of spring. Having a shave.

You're being dramatic. And more than a bit unfair.

Just think on the number of times you could have spent truffle time with my magnificent norks. But you forwent that because you had your gob around a bottle neck.

That was then, Becs.

Yeah, well, I was then, too.

Becs. Please.

The wipers keeping beat to the sad song that always played. The rain. The splintering of all those red lights on wet tarmac. So much blood. There had been so much blood. The amount we carry in these fragile vessels. And it had all flowed so feverishly for me, as mine had for her,

147

all those years ago. Now it felt like cold porridge in my veins. What was left of hers was soaked into the fibres of the floorboards on Lime Grove or turned to ash by the flames at the crematorium.

One thousand degrees Celsius.

You always said I was hot stuff.

14

It isn't difficult to find information about ex-cons. Maybe the nasty ones. The ones who've spilled blood to a point where life stops. The sex deviants. The kind of people who raise tempers. You don't want public lynchings on the streets. But it gets a little easier if you trip down to the next zone down on the old 'naughty pyramid'. The bank robbers. The organised crime heads. The serial, serious burglars. The ones who, in contrast to the killers and rapists and kiddy-fiddlers, sometimes find a weird kind of celebrity among the populace. Murder a policeman in the line of duty and you're a bad boy. Break into his house while he's at work and you're a cheeky chappie. It gets a little bit more onerous to find the few prisoners who have been granted release from Cold Quay, and it's nigh-on impossible to find anybody who once walked the corridors of Red Row, mainly because they're either dead or still there… well, they would be if it was still standing. What I'm getting at is this: you don't get released from Red Row.

Except, someone did, once.

Frank Pastor. You might recall the name. It was all over the papers.

Pastor was from Norfolk. King's Lynn, specifically. He ran a farm park near Methwold. You know the kind of thing. Paddocks and ponds filled with animals. The kids can get up close to the rabbits and chickens, feed the goats, then the parents are bled dry at the gift shop and cafeteria. Frank was arrested for murder in 1999 when an eight-year-old girl, Lucy Leigh, was found strangled in a field a mile south of the farm. Strands of Pastor's hair were found on Lucy's clothing. A fortnight later Pastor's wife, Carmen, and most of the animals, died when the farm was set on fire by arsonists who'd already decided Pastor was guilty of his crime. It was an ugly mess. Pastor was sentenced to life imprisonment and bundled off to Cold Quay. Six years later another body was found in the same location as Lucy. But this was a grown man who had committed suicide. Russell MacLeish. There was a letter in his pocket, confessing to Lucy's murder and admitting that he had framed Pastor because he had been in love with Carmen. That he was indirectly responsible for her death had become a burden too many for him to bear.

So Pastor was released in 2005 and given a considerable amount of compensation. He gave it all away to charity and shunned the offer of a new identity. He wasn't ashamed of who he was; he had done nothing wrong. He might have changed his mind if he'd known the amount of bother he'd receive from the papers wanting to tell his story; he was hounded for months. But eventually that all tailed off and, apart from the odd cowardly attack from those who thought there was no smoke without fire (no pun intended) – bricks through his window, car tyres slashed – he was left alone to stew in his own juices.

He still lived in Norfolk, but had moved to a little

place called Honing in the north-east of the county. There he rented a small barn that had been converted into a bungalow. I found it round six in the morning, after a lot of roaming around back roads and getting lost. It was very plain, very easy to miss. It was as if the tragedy of his story had imbued it with grey, as if the stones that surrounded it were incrementally pulling the barn down to be back among them again.

Early, but fuck it. I knocked on the door and a dog barked. Deep bark. Big dog. A face appeared at the window to my left. He didn't open it. He just stared at me. I'd worked it out that he was in his mid-fifties, but he looked much older. Who wouldn't after the kind of mill he'd been fed through? His hair, grey and unkempt, was in need of a wash and a cut. Deep channels had forged ways through his skin, making his face look as if it had ambitions to be a slot machine. His eyes were blue and damp and haunted. He didn't look as if he'd been to bed.

He came to the door and opened it. Smells flew at me. Dog shit and dog food and wet dog. The dog flew at me too. I didn't know the breed but it was large and furious and filled with teeth.

I stepped back, but Pastor had grabbed the beast by the collar. I stood there looking at the cords leaping out of his forearm as he barely prevented it from turning me into Sorrell mince.

'Mr Pastor?' I tried to say, but all that came out was fear-spittle and air.

'What do you want?'

'My name's Joel Sorrell,' I said, pulling myself together. 'I'm looking for my daughter. Her mother was killed by a man who has escaped from Cold Quay.'

'I know you. I read about you. And what? You think I'm the go-to guy when women get killed?'

'You were proved innocent,' I said. 'You know why I'm here.'

'So I was at Cold Quay,' he said. 'So what? Quiet, Renko!'

The dog looked up at its master, licked its chops but continued to make weird yowling, growling sounds.

'What kind of dog is that?' I asked.

'Caucasian Ovcharka,' he said.

'It must weigh two hundred pounds,' I said.

'Probably. They're a bugger to train, and I haven't managed it successfully, so be careful. He's an aggressive bastard, and he won't listen to me, especially if he's got your head in his jaws.'

'I'm not here for trouble.'

'I just want to be left alone,' he said.

'I know. I would too, if I'd gone through what you suffered.'

'I lost everything.'

'Yes. I lost my wife too. I don't want to lose my daughter.'

His gaze drifted beyond me, as if he was checking to see if I had company.

'Inside,' he said. He moved away from the open door, wrestling with the dog which was growling more loudly now that I was daring to cross the threshold.

We walked through a dingy hallway to a living room that really ought to have been renamed a dying room. There was nothing in it beyond a chair, a small table, a couple of books and a lamp. A rug that Renko rested upon. He went straight there now, and lay down to gnaw on a plastic toy.

'I'd offer you a seat, but...' he said, and sat down. 'I'd offer you a drink too, but...'

'That's kind of you, but I'll not trouble you for long,' I

said. 'I wondered if you could tell me anything about Graeme Tann. Did you get to know him while you were inside?'

'What makes you think I was on Red Row?'

'You *were* on Red Row. All…' My words faded out. 'You were on Red Row,' I said, again.

'All the nastiest bastards were on Red Row. Is what you were going to say. Or words to that effect.'

'Yes,' I said. 'What you were put away for was deserving of that wing. But you didn't do it. So it doesn't matter. Why get precious about it?'

'Because I thought about it,' he said. 'Because me and Carmen, we were going through a shitty phase of our marriage. I say "shitty phase" but I might as well just say "shitty marriage". We were at each other's throats constantly. I used to fantasise about murdering her. I was glad when she was killed.'

'Okay,' I said. He seemed euphoric, as if he'd let loose a demon that had been clamped to his mind for decades. Maybe it had. Maybe he'd never confided to anybody before. He looked guilty and thrilled, his blue, wet eyes wide and confrontational. 'I'm not here to judge you. I just want to know about Tann.'

'Graeme Tann paid me no heed,' he said. 'And I kept to myself. I was busy with appeals. How would you feel if you were innocent and you suddenly found yourself in the middle of a bunch of people who had killed for pleasure, who had laughed and danced in blood, taken trophies, added another notch to an already big tally?'

'I'd keep my head down,' I said.

'Exactly. And that's what I did. For six years.'

'But that doesn't mean you didn't see anything. I'm just looking for an "in", Frank. Graeme Tann murdered my

153

wife. It was a brutal, shocking murder. And now he's out. And I don't know where my daughter is.'

'I don't know how I can help,' Pastor said. 'I saw him. Of course I did. He had his cronies.'

'You see,' I said. 'That's interesting to me. "He had his cronies." So... what? He wasn't a crony? He didn't seem... subservient to anybody, in your eyes?'

'I wasn't making any kind of study while I was in there,' he said.

'Of course not,' I said. 'But he was... what? Some kind of kingpin? A leader?'

'Yes,' he said.

Renko stood up from his rug, the plastic toy – what looked like a giant raspberry – squashed between his jaws. You could feel the heat off this monster from six feet away. I wondered who would come off worst in a battle between him and Mengele. A tie, I reckoned. Or they'd probably get on like a house on fire. No pun intended.

'I saw his cell once,' he said. He was looking at me curiously, and it made me think of people who are gearing up to do something extreme and perhaps foolish, like BASE jumping, or free climbing. It seemed as though he was assessing me to see how I would take what he was gearing up to say. 'I was helping the wardens shift furniture. We had to change the chairs in some of the cells. They were wearing out. Tann got a new chair. I noticed your name was on one of the walls. He'd written it on a piece of paper and it was stuck to the wall. There were other names. I thought maybe it was some kind of list of grievances. A shit list.'

'That doesn't surprise me,' I said. 'I'm top of some shit lists compiled by some of the nicest people you're ever likely to meet. So it makes sense I should be on the shit list of a complete shit. Give me something else. Give me something I can use.'

'I need a drink after all,' he said, getting up. 'You might think it's easy to dredge this stuff up, but we're talking over ten years ago. This is a time I've been trying to forget, I'll have you know. You turning up puts me back in the middle of the shitstink corridors and nightsticks smacked across the back of the legs.'

I made to follow him to the kitchen but Renko growled at me. I allowed the dog to lead the way. The kitchen was a slightly more interesting place. Here was a tiny TV and a radio and a bench filled with green plants. A stack of newspapers tied together with gardener's twine. I leaned against a chair while Pastor fixed himself a whisky and water.

'Want one? Or is it too early for you?'

'What about those miniatures?'

He picked up a handful of vodka miniatures and he tossed them my way, along with a plastic cup. 'I've had those for months,' he said. 'I can't stand the stuff. It's like drinking surgical spirit.'

I wasn't going to waste time correcting him, or educating him on the superiority of 'burning wine'. I got the Smirnoff down me while he sipped his drink and watched Renko do that shameless begging routine that all animals fall into when they sit in the room with all the food.

'I'm stunned,' I said, 'that the authorities are no closer to catching him now than on the day of the riots. I mean, what is he? A shadow? How does someone like that just disappear off the face of the earth?'

He shrugged, his glass paused on the moist surface of his lower lip. The haunted look in his eyes had softened somewhat, but he still looked damaged as hell. 'It strikes me that he's the kind of person who would have something set up, all ready for him if the breakout was a success.'

'Any ideas?' I asked. 'Any clue as to where he might have gone? Maybe you overheard some plans.'

'Maybe I didn't. But what would you do? Boat in a harbour waiting to take him to Spain. Someone's cellar or attic. Maybe he's living rough out in the sticks. He's a survivor, isn't he?'

'Graeme Tann was a streak of piss before he was put away,' I said. 'He was a pathetic little shitehawk. What happened to him in prison? What turned him into Cool Hand Luke?'

Pastor swirled his drink and positioned his nose above the whisky, as if the answers to my questions could be discerned in its vapours. 'People in prison miss their home comforts. Graeme Tann was able to provide them.'

'You mean like blowjobs and buggery?'

'No,' Pastor said. 'He was like a gofer. He could get you what you wanted. That's power, in a place like that.'

'Like what? What could he get you?'

'Booze, pills, weed, wank mags. The usual stuff.'

'How did he manage it?' I asked.

'There was a tunnel. Small one. Out in the exercise yard, went all the way up to the fence. One of his contacts on the outside met it coming the other way. They put rails in. Remote-controlled cars...'

'I know. I saw it.'

'It's not uncommon. What was uncommon was how quickly Tann could get you your luxury items. It was as if he knew he had to make a success of this venture if he was to slide up the food chain. And he did. By the time a splinter group wanted to take over his operation he had serious muscle protecting him. Imagine that. Hard bastards at every turn, watching your back for you. Needless to say, he wasn't put off.'

'Inside and out,' I said.

'I'm sorry I can't give you any more than that,' he said. 'And you're welcome to search every room in this house if you think he's camping out here.'

'I don't think that,' I said. 'I don't know what I think. I'm grateful to you. It's been a change to meet someone who wasn't obstructive.'

'I've done nothing,' he said. 'I told you what I know.' And then he said a very strange thing. 'How obstructive are you?'

'You what? I don't...'

'Forgive me if I'm out of line,' he said. 'I spent a lot of time waiting, you know, in prison. I spent a lot of time watching people. Just watching. I saw how people got on and didn't get on.'

'What are you saying?'

'I just wonder if you might not be making things harder for yourself.'

'You're talking to me, aren't you?'

Pastor smiled and his wrinkles sprang out of sight, showing me how he might look without the sorrow in his life. Renko made a high, inquisitive noise, completely at odds with his size, as if to remind me he was there. I risked losing my fingers by putting my hand out to him but he allowed himself to be stroked and I felt a little better, my skin engulfed by all that fur and warmth.

Pastor watched, and he seemed impressed. 'Last person who tried that got a face full of growl.'

'This dog is soft as baby shit compared to what's waiting in the shadows for me when I get home.'

'You have dogs?'

'I have a dark angel of death. With tuna breath.'

'I don't really miss having a girlfriend.'

We laughed and I realised I'd liked him from the moment I saw him. It saddened me to think that I always went looking for the bad in people. Picking at the black threads, no matter how small they might be. Nature of the job, I supposed. But more likely nature of me.

'This tunnel,' I said. 'The rails—'

'Ah yes,' he said. 'I can't be sure, I'm no Sherlock Holmes, but I don't think you need to be. I put two and two together... One of the guards, guy called... what was his name... Collins. I forget his given name. He was always hanging around Tann. But not because he knew he was up to something. I always thought Collins was bent, on the take no matter what was being handed out. And he had a hobby. Model train enthusiast. You'd see him sometimes with his mug of tea, poring over these catalogues, picking out some new locomotive.'

'I see what you're getting at,' I said. 'And it doesn't surprise me. You'd need inside help, if you wanted to pull a scam like that.'

All the Smirnoff was gone. My mouth was sticky. Dehydrated. Once I realised that I thought I could feel crystals gathering in my blood, my brain shrinking back from the membrane at my skull, tongue turning to pumice.

'Graeme Tann is one of those people you find surrounded by muscle in the slammer,' he said. 'I guess you find that sort of thing whenever you have someone who can magic goods into your hand. He was the Baron. And it's always nice to know you've got protection, but he never, not in the time I saw him, made use of any of it. It was uncalled for. Unrequested. What I'm trying to say is, he didn't ask for it.

And he didn't need it. Compared to everyone else in that place, he was a live wire. Prison didn't seem to strip him of his life, it augmented him. He's one of the most driven people I've ever seen. And I think he's the most dangerous person I've ever seen too. But it wasn't any kind of Charlie Big Spuds thing. You only had to look at his eyes to see it. They were weird, those eyes. As if he was in the moment, fast on everything, but at the same time also far away, as if he was living in his head.'

'I visited him,' I said. 'In the summer. I tried to needle him. But he turned the tables. Got under my skin. Effortless. I lost it and went for him and he floored me. This with shackles on. I know what he's capable of.'

'I hope you do,' Pastor said. 'But my advice to you would be to do what I've done. Find yourself a hole well away from the bright lights and dig in until they catch him. He's no ghost. He can't hide for ever.'

I nodded. 'I'll just grab a glass of water and I'll be gone,' I said.

I drank long and hard until I thought I could hear waterfalls in my belly. I thanked Pastor and wished him good luck. It was hard to leave, to put myself back out there where *he* was, despite the spartan feel of the house. But one foot after the other, cinch the jacket around the aching muscles, because *she* was out there too.

'I was going to ask you,' I said at the door, 'when you think you'll be ready to… I don't know… reintegrate… get back to daily life. But I was thinking and, well, you seem fine. This is… nice.'

He nodded. 'You can't reintegrate into something that isn't there any more,' he said. 'This place is good for me. I can't cope with—' and here he flapped his hand at the sky,

'—any more. You find your nest and you dig in. And that's me done.'

I drove along empty lanes, hating the conspicuous car for once, and checking my mirror so much I was in danger of piling into a hedge, but I was not followed. That itch though, that certainty wouldn't get out of my muscles. Someone was looking for me. The four that were left. I eased off the mirror, tried to relax and fantasised about doing what Frank Pastor had done. Bolthole. Isolation. Maybe one day, afterwards. I couldn't sell up and move out knowing there was some kind of contract on me. And I couldn't get out of London while Sarah was at risk.

First though: A11, M11, M25, A2. Sometimes I feel like a travelling salesman. It's just me and the car and my foot on the pedal. And there's nothing to hawk but an idea. Hope. But nobody wants to trade in that these days.

15

I got to Rochester in three hours. I was on his street at a little after ten a.m. To pass the time I did a little digging online and found a newspaper article from a couple of years previously about Collins, Terence. He'd given decades of service to his profession and had bowed out while employed at Cold Quay. Cake and fizz and a gold watch. He was looking forward to his retirement, apparently. Who could blame him, going toe-to-toe with the mental cases in that place? He was going to devote his time to his grandkids and his hobby: model trains. That was quite a comedown from being threatened every day by some missing link with his teeth filed to points and a tattoo of a noose around his neck. I might be going OTT a bit on the description, but I'd met plenty of scary beasts who called prison home. People who'd sooner bathe in your blood than look at you, and have your head on a pike by the tub while they did it.

An hour later I saw him emerging from his house in a thick jumper and nicely pressed slacks. I parked the car and followed him into town. I'd never been to Rochester before but I'd heard it said that if Kent is the Garden of England,

Medway is its compost heap. It didn't seem too bad to me, but then it wasn't a weekend night on the high street when most places display their true colours, invariably in shades of red.

I watched him buy a newspaper and go into one of those coffee shops with lots of ironic crap paintings on the wall, big, well-worn armchairs and distressed tables. I was distressed too, when I went in after him and saw the prices for the breakfasts. I ordered one anyway, as did he. I had a pint of lager with mine, though, while he had coffee, and beggar the distaste on the waiter's face. I wolfed everything down and, good boy that I am, resisted the temptation to order another cold one. I was finished long before him, so I leafed through a magazine while the overloud MOR aural sick poured into one ear and out the other.

When he was full of sausages and good cheer, he set off back towards Curzon Road. I intercepted him as he crossed the railway bridge.

'Mr Collins?' I said. 'Terence Collins?'

'Terry,' he said. He didn't seem at all fazed by a stranger uttering his name. He was smiling. Maybe this kind of thing happened all the time. I decided to take advantage of it. I stuck out a hand and gave him a disarming smile of my own.

'I'm a journalist,' I said. 'From Milton Keynes.'

'Journalist,' he said. The smile remained. 'Which paper?'

'The *Messenger*,' I said, guessing wildly. 'I'm doing a piece on prisons. About how life in prison for inmates, as well as staff, can accelerate ageing.'

'Can it now?' he said.

'Yes. There was a study in the States some years ago that found a sentence of two decades will reduce life expectancy by around fifteen years. But the officers suffer too. Heart attacks, ulcers, depression, alcohol abuse. All down to stress. Long hours, unpleasant conditions, locking horns every day with dangerous criminals…'

'You're quite some distance from Milton Keynes.'

'I am, yes. But that's because of you.'

'Why do you want to talk to me?'

'Well I remember reading that story the paper did about you retiring. From Cold Quay. That's the link to MK, of course. I found your comments to be intelligent and thoughtful. A cut above the usual narrative.'

'That's very kind of you to say.'

'Not at all. It makes an impact, that kind of thing, in my profession. All too often you get people trotting out the same lines. The same clichés.'

He was maybe late fifties, early sixties. His hair was silver. I noticed that although he was neatly dressed, there was dirt under his fingernails. And he had shaved this morning: his skin was dry and red, a little shaving cream that he'd missed dried to thin curd on the underside of his jaw. I thought, *He was married; she's gone.*

'Come back to the house,' he said. 'We'll have a cup of tea.'

It was nice to meet someone for a change who wasn't suspicious or combative. I felt bad about duping him and thought about coming clean, but I supposed it didn't matter. My imposture wasn't hurting anybody.

He got us inside and I followed him straight to the kitchen. The faint smell of last night's dinner clung to the fabrics and carpets. Pictures on the wall. Flowers. Butterflies. Inoffensive: she picked them, he hung them, he never took them down.

'You live alone, Mr Collins?'

'Terry, please. Yes, yes, Mrs Collins went the way of all

flesh five years ago. But she's still with me, obviously.'

'Of course,' I said. She was with him in the way he ironed his shirts and got his hair cut every six weeks. She was in the meals he cooked for himself. I imagined him standing in front of the wardrobe, waiting for her to point out which clothes to choose.

'I didn't catch your name,' he said.

'Joel,' I said. 'Joel Sefton.'

He stuck out his hand and I almost told him we'd played that particular game, but I had to act nice. This was his home. He was all right. I accepted it.

He folded it back towards me so that my fingers were bending against themselves. 'This is a simple defence hold that we're taught during training,' he said. 'The police use it too. I've used it many times. It's most effective. You need minimum effort and the victim cannot counter at all.'

'What are you doing?' I asked. He kept tweaking his grip every time I made to readjust my stance or tried to grab at his arm with my free hand. The pain was causing me to buckle at the knees.

'Who are you, really?'

'Joel Sefton. I'm a journ—'

'You're no more a journalist than I am a lion tamer,' he said. 'The newspaper in Milton Keynes is the *Citizen*. There is no *Messenger*.'

'I'm freelance.'

'Who are you?'

'I'm Joel Sorrell,' I said. 'I'm a private investigator.'

'What are you doing here?'

'I wanted to talk to you.'

I told him the whole sorry mess about Rebecca and as soon as I mentioned her name he let me go. He made mugs of tea and put them on the table. He supplied a plate of chocolate digestives.

'You should have just told me the truth,' he said. 'I would have talked to you.'

'I know,' I said. 'Force of habit. You find yourself smacking your head against so many closed doors you don't notice when they're open.'

'Your name cropped up, from time to time, now I recall,' he said.

'In conjunction with Graeme Tann.'

'Graeme, yes.'

All the things I could have asked him, this man who had seen Tann up close on a daily basis.

'What was he like?'

'He was a model inmate. Respectful, helpful, we never had a peep out of him in all the time he was there.'

'And then he burns the place down and goes on the run.'

Collins smiled but it was bitter and ugly. 'There was nothing in his behaviour to suggest that he was going to start a prison riot.'

I sipped my tea and stared at the chocolate digestives. I could think of plenty in his behaviour, but Collins was obviously having none of it. He might not have come up with the stock platitudes in his newspaper interview, but I was playing responsibility bingo now and I knew he was going to say something along the lines of 'not on my watch' some time soon.

'Why did you retire?' I asked.

'I'd done my time,' he said, and gave me another look at that bitter little smile. I got the impression he'd regretted his decision, even despite what had just happened at Cold Quay; that he preferred to be there, among his mates and the maniacs, rather than the ghosts in this house. 'It's true. It's a stressful job. If you allow it to be. I was a good prison officer, I think. And enough governors and prisoners said so themselves over the years.'

I cut through this little masturbation session and asked him if he'd seen anything to suggest there might be a riot on the horizon, before he'd left.

'Not really,' he said. He took a sip from his mug. There was a picture of a woman wearing an apron and brandishing a rolling pin beneath the legend: I'M IN CHARGE. 'I mean, there are always little rebellions going on all the time. Inmates chancing their arm, pushing their luck. But it's all bluster in the main.'

'So why this catastrophic failure? The place was razed, Terry.'

'Overcrowding was a problem,' he said. 'And facilities, while not what you'd call "Victorian", were less than ideal.'

I wanted to get out. I was sick of his tea and his biscuits and the bottle of Fairy liquid by the sink, the carefully folded tea towel on the handle of the oven. A letter rack contained a Hornby model train catalogue. A polythene bag contained two miniature trees, around the size of my thumb.

'Things weren't so bad when I was there. I can't imagine what went wrong after I'd gone.'

Tick.

'Tell me about Graeme,' I said. 'I got the impression he was a sad little wanker who mooched about getting his kicks staring at women undressing through cracks in the wall. Quiet. Pathetic. One of those weak little piss stains in life. Boring and forgettable.'

'Pity,' he said. 'He thinks the world of you.'

Bitter smile. I matched it with one of my own.

'Sorry,' he said. 'I didn't mean to be flippant.'

'Never mind,' I said. 'Turns out, anyway, Tann has some clout. Who'd have thought it? Enters a tough prison as someone you'd think would be odds-on for a full-on anal assault in the showers, ends up cock of the walk. How does that happen?'

'I noticed Graeme Tann was not what you'd call intimidating. But there are other ways to curry favour.'

'Noshing off the guards?'

Bitter smile. 'I was thinking more about supplying inmates with, um, luxury items.'

'You mean drugs.'

'Drugs, tobacco, chocolate, men's magazines. Et cetera.'

'And how would they do that?'

'Good contacts on the outside. Some way of smuggling the gear in.'

'And how would they smuggle the gear in? High-security prison. Diligent prison officers on duty. I doubt anything got past you when you were doing your rounds.'

He picked up a biscuit and snapped it in half. The dried scurf of shaving cream was flaking away from his skin and catching in the fibres of his jumper. Through the kitchen window I could see his garden; he'd been at it with a spade, digging up turf. He saw my scrutiny and put down his halves of biscuit.

'Getting rid of my lawn,' he explained. 'Too much of a time suck. You need to be mowing it two, three times a week in summer. I'm no green fingers. Going to put in some decking and gravel. Get a Japanese maple.'

I wondered what the late Mrs Collins would have made of that. The garden was her passion, I'd have thought. I imagine he had wrestled with his conscience for many a day before that tang tucked into the soil.

'How do you fill your days then, now that you're a free man? Other than wrecking your back yard? Do you have grandchildren?'

'No. My wife and I couldn't have a family. But I have a couple of hobbies that keep me occupied. I go fishing. I've got a season ticket at Gillingham – supported them for fifty years man and boy. I like to cook…' His voice trailed off, as if he was going to add some other things, but had thought better of it.

'Where do you keep your train set?' I asked.

He started, as if I'd read his mind, but then he saw the catalogue and the miniature landscape scenery, and he snatched them up and put them in a drawer.

'What did you get out of it, Terry?' I asked.

'I don't have to talk to you. I'll call the police.'

'I'll save you the bother and call them myself. I'm sure they'd be interested to know that I found a tunnel down at Cold Quay. It's how all those tasty treats were getting in and out of the prison. Did Tann have something to do with it?'

He stood up. 'Well, since you've worked it out by yourself, you might as well come and have a look at my pride and joy.'

'Just get on with it, Collins,' I said. 'I haven't got time to fuck about.'

But he was going to have his way. I followed him through the hallway to the stairs. I didn't like the look of this. I imagined him taking me into a room where there were lots of cleavers, and the floor was covered in plastic sheeting. We went up and he led me into a large bedroom that had been converted into a Thomas the Tank Engine wankfest for grown-ups. He flicked a switch on a table and trains started slithering along tracks.

He'd gone the whole hog, adding stations and textured

landscapes and people standing on platforms. He must have spent thousands on it. Pounds and hours.

'Yeah, it's all fascinating,' I said. 'Now what happened at Cold Quay?'

'I set up the tracks,' he said. 'I got a cut of every transaction. Drugs coming in. Weapons.'

'Weapons?'

'Yes. Knives, mainly. Shivs. Never used. More for intimidation purposes. I wanted out. Two years of trundle back and forth and I could afford to retire.'

'I don't care about that. I want to know about Tann.'

'Tann was interesting. He was like... I don't know... a glass of tap water when he came in. He was there, but you wouldn't notice him unless you were looking for him. He sat and watched. He was a sponge, soaking up the prison politics, the cut and thrust. He was endlessly flexible, like I said. Yes sir, no sir. And then suddenly he was arranging things for people. He was the man you went to if you needed a dirty book, or a bottle of Jack, or an eighth of resin.'

'And that kind of ability means brownie points.'

'He wielded immense influence. Nothing much to look at, Graeme Tann – at least not back then, he's bulked up a bit in the last few years – but who needs physical intimidation when you've got everyone in your pocket?'

'Including you.'

'I've been up front with you. I didn't have to be. I'd appreciate it if you kept this between ourselves.'

'Why should I?'

'How about if I share a little extra information with you?'

'Like what? How you used to dress up as The Fat Controller and let Tann lick your whistle?'

'Tann used to get visits.'

'All prisoners get visits. Christ, even I visited him.'

'Ian Mawker,' he said.

'Mawker?'

'Ian Mawker visited Graeme Tann on a number of occasions. And I have it on good authority that he was there on the day of the riot. He was there when it was *happening*.'

'Whose authority?'

'Good authority.'

'So what?' I said. 'Maybe he was there because I asked him to try to get some information out of him.'

'Because that's how things work, isn't it? Civilian you instructs high-ranking officer to be his servant.'

'So why was he there? Why was he visiting Tann?'

'Ask him,' he said.

I felt anger rising. At him with his crooked little cryptic smile. At his games. 'Enjoy your choo-choos,' I said. 'I hope it was all worth it.' I left before I succumbed to the urge to take one of his locomotives and force-feed it to his anus.

16

I risked it. How hard could it be? I mean, I now looked like some fascist nut. I needed to get my laptop and make sure I'd turned off the iron. Maybe I just wanted to be a stubborn prick and to show anybody who was watching that I wasn't going to be cowed by them.

Just to be safe, though, I got in through the alleyway at the back, letting myself in through the communal door where all the bins are lined up. I hurried up the stairs, quiet as I could be, checking carefully at each turn because I was sure there'd be some nutcase who'd been put there to wait for me on the off-chance that I would show up like some stubborn prick.

Nobody here. I couldn't believe Tann wouldn't have this place staked out; surely he'd know this was my pad by now. If he held sway over a dodgy screw at the nick, then there was every chance that he had informants who knew how to hack into personal files and extract this kind of data.

The flat, without Mengele, was quiet and grey. He really brought the place to life, even if his raison d'être was to deliver death unto all. I retrieved my laptop from behind the sofa cushion and stuffed it in a rucksack. I looked around the flat longingly, wishing I could stay, but it was too risky. It was mid-afternoon, the sun leaving the sky, which was turning the colour of petrol. I'd suffered a long wait coming back, the motorway reduced to one lane because of an accident. I was hungry and tired, but I was always hungry and tired. I'd forgotten what it felt like to be rested and replete.

I went out the way I'd come, stealthy as a ninja wearing slippers. Back in the car. Back on the road. The whole operation had taken just over five minutes.

Except.

Well, there was a car behind me.

London, you say. *No shit*, you say.

And yes, it may well have been my paranoid guardian angel whispering away in my ear, but part of me was trying to persuade me that I'd seen the car earlier, as I had arrived. Not that it was particularly remarkable. Just a silver-coloured Skoda Octavia. Two people sitting in it. But I'd noticed it, even if only peripherally via the sleepy back brain. And I'd noticed it again now, as I drove through Marylebone in the direction of Marble Arch. I kept telling myself it was nothing, that I was reacting like a hair trigger, and that at every roundabout or traffic light they would turn a different way and I could laugh at myself for being the world's biggest tool. But they kept on after me, staying three or four car lengths clear, staying on me even when there were cars or buses between us. I turned left and turned left and turned left until I was back where I started and they were still there. It was as if they didn't care that I could see them. They were relentless.

And so now what? They were either Tann's lot or Mawker's lot. I could either try to lose them or I could confront them. There was something attractive about that: blocking them at a red light and swinging the door open. If it was Mawker's lot, they might just tell me to get back in the car and stop acting like John Wayne. If it was Tann's lot, I might just be turned into a fine red mist. But then if they were after me to kill me they could have done that already. Who'd have thought being followed could be such a brainteaser?

Lose them, then. And do it quick. I dropped into second and hurled the car into a side street, got up to third. Touch the brakes and hard right, really make those tyres sing. I opened the window and listened. An engine protesting – but it could just have been the echoes of my own as I toed it through built-up thoroughfares. I slalomed left and right down a series of streets. I was near Brompton now, around the back of the V&A museum, heading towards Sloane Square. I planned ahead: charge across Chelsea Bridge and get on to Nine Elms Lane, try to find somewhere to hide in the little jungle of warehouses, depots and distribution offices between the river and the railway line.

I was close to the south side of the bridge, Battersea Power Station like a table turned turtle to my left, when I heard and felt a pop just above my head. There was a sting of pain: blood started leaking into my left eye. I turned to see a bullet hole just to the left of the rear window. I hadn't been shot (but I wondered by how many centimetres... or millimetres... I'd escaped the bullet); it was a metal splinter that had grazed my forehead. Looked worse than it was. I was more put out that they'd damaged the Saab than the fact they'd got their shooters out in broad daylight after all.

I wellied it, and came screaming through Queen's Circus at the foot of Battersea Park at close on fifty miles per hour.

Another pop: one of the tyres shredded and control went walkabout. I managed to steady the car somewhat, but she was drifting and the steering wheel was becoming more and more unresponsive until it felt as if I was trying to wrestle it free of an invisible grizzly, intent on mashing us into the wall. I got over the railway bridge but by then I could hear ominous grinding from under the car so I brought her to a stop and got out smartish, tense against the sound of an engine throttling up, and a third shot, which I might or might not hear.

I sprinted along the main drag, looking for a place where I'd be able to shake off my pursuers, but they were stickier than a teenager's sock. I thought about crossing the road and trying my luck in New Covent Garden Market, but here they came. If I tried to get over the road now I'd be in full sight of them: they'd turn me into chunky Joel salsa. I heard the squeal of brakes and car doors charging open. No voices. No entreaties to stop. Death was all over their lack of vocabulary. Silent. Final.

I did hear the gunshot when it came, for the record, as it whanged off a length of metal fence about a foot from my left ear. I couldn't help thinking, uncharitably, that had Mawker shown the same kind of commitment and effort over the years then Tann might have been apprehended long before all of this had ever happened and Sarah would still be at home.

I jinked left down Kirtling Street, Battersea Power Station just up ahead. The site traffic entrance was heavily populated by guys in orange jackets who watched, bemusedly, as I came clattering by. They disappeared too, though, when they heard the gunfire. I don't know if it was because of the acoustics or whether I'd put some distance between us, but it sounded as if that shot had originated further away than before. I risked a glance back but couldn't see anything. I kept going along depressingly colourless access roads, past rusting gates topped with razor wire. The tarmac here was layered with pale dust. Cement, most probably. Another shot. Close to my foot; I saw sparks fly off the blacktop. Time slowed. I heard the breath in my lungs churning through each bronchiole. I felt the pulse of blood reach every capillary extreme. Ahead was a squat building with metal shutters and niggardly-looking windows. To the left was a ready mix plant dominated by a mound of sand twenty feet high. Warning signs were plastered all over the gates:

SAFETY STARTS HERE. LOOK AFTER YOURSELF, LOOK AFTER EACH OTHER. USE FLASHING BEACONS OR HAZARD WARNING LIGHTS BEYOND THIS POINT.

On, past a rank of front-end loading static bins. To the right, construction barriers and signs warning that demolition was in progress, but over the fence it was just flat concrete and a single lobster-red digger. Nowhere to hide. In front of me a host of vans and more hi-vis and helmets.

'Help me,' I gasped.

Another gunshot. One of the construction guys went down holding what remained of his knee between two suddenly crimson hands. His screams echoed off the acres of pristine glass on the new residential area behind him.

Fuck it, I thought, and charged through the lot of them before they knew what was happening. They were all either trying to help their colleague or fleeing the scene anyway. Nobody cared that I was bolting for the main doors and the

175

millions of square feet beyond. A LUXURY COLLECTION OF
SPACIOUS SUITES AND 1, 2 AND 3 BEDROOM APARTMENTS AND
PENTHOUSES, the banners gushed. LAST FEW REMAINING. It
could have been describing my nerves.

I got inside, relishing the darkness, and concentrated on
making myself vanish. I had to calm my breath down though.
Half a mile flat out had me whooping like something trapped
in a vacuum cleaner. I folded myself into shadow by something
shrink-wrapped in plastic, and forced myself to relax.

I thought of all the times Rebecca had cajoled me to attend
yoga classes with her and all the times I'd cried off because
I felt it was just so much hippy horseshit. I couldn't touch
my toes. I didn't want to touch my toes. I didn't want to
commune with nature or meditate on my chakras, wherever
they were and whatever they were doing. I didn't want to
have twelve-hour sex sessions. Well, I did, but I didn't want
to have to be in the lotus position, twitching my hips once
every twenty minutes while breathing in the steam from a
cup of green tea and listening to Sting play a lute with his
lingam... or whatever Tantric sex entails.

I wish I'd gone now. Not only because it would have
meant more time with the person I spend no time with any
more. But because it might have taught me something. I
might actually have learned how to control my temper, how
to calm my body when it was stressed beyond all reason.

Instead of this confused sack of grunts and twitches,
cracks and calamities.

But little by little, I came down. If there were two
following me then the chances were they'd split up. I guessed
the workers were too engrossed in their pal's knee, or in
getting away, to take much notice of what I was up to, but
there was every chance someone had seen me duck in here,

which meant that they might pass that information on to my pursuers, especially if there was a gun being pointed at them.

As yet, nothing. I gave it another five minutes and then I gave it five more. Where I was crouched cast no shadows. I'd left no footprints. There was one drop of moisture on the floor between me and the entrance. Perhaps sweat. Perhaps spittle. Nothing else to suggest anybody had been in this part of the building since the fitters brought in the rolls of carpet and the furniture, all packed and stacked and ready to be laid out.

My leg was screaming at me and so I allowed myself to unfold a little before cramp seized me up completely. And then I saw movement. The slightest change in the angles of light cast across the floor. Someone was coming in. Or rather, was already in and was moving deeper.

I slid backwards, away from the shrink-wrap, but remained within its shadow for as long as I could. By the time I'd reached the rear of the room, where a corner would lead me to a corridor where, presumably, the lifts were stationed, I heard the soft crackle of a hand as it shifted over the tight bindings of polythene.

I got up and hurried to the lifts, which gaped open but had no electricity to run them. I bypassed them and skipped up to the next floor. Here I eased open one of the windows, complete with criss-crosses of tape to protect the glass against random impacts of debris. I got out on to a gantry and scampered to where scaffolding still clung to one portion of the new building. I was down and over the fence and on Cringle Street heading east within sixty seconds, pushing hard but keeping one eye on that window and one on the road in case they worked out what I'd done and got back on my heels.

Lots of cars. No cabs anywhere. No police. Bus stops

without buses. I felt the aches and twinges from my injuries, and the training I'd undertaken with Danny Sweet, and the game of footsie I'd played with Karen Leonard's gammy clutch. Yoga might have helped with all of that too. I determined to get into it if I managed to see this day out without anyone putting any holes in me.

I got off Nine Elms Lane, anxious by how busy it was and how exposed I was, and ran down to the riverside. I don't know what it was, but I didn't feel I'd done enough to lose them. The anxiety wouldn't go away. Usually, if I know I've got a tail on me I can work out who it is and get rid within a matter of minutes. But there was something about this tail that spoke of a deeper professionalism, a more serious commitment.

The figures in the car. The guy who didn't have the gun.

I'd seen him for what, maybe less than a split second? Hunched over the wheel, in profile. A hint of hair. A glimpse of jacket. Dark eyes. Angular jaw. Not a shred of fat on it.

Stop with the guess who. You know who.

I didn't want to accept that, though. Because if it was him, I wasn't clear. And I wouldn't be clear. What I had ahead of me would make Butch and Sundance's pursuit by the superposse look like a game of kiss chase.

I was saying his name as I ran, chanting it in time with my footsteps. I didn't want to entertain the thought but I didn't need to. My chattering teeth gave my fear a voice.

Henry Herschell. Henry Herschell.

I'd known Henry Herschell for many years. We'd developed, if not a friendship, then a grudging admiration for each other. We'd never crossed swords in the criminal world. Mainly because I wouldn't dare. He was one of maybe four or five people that put the shivers through me.

But I'd helped him out once, saved him some money on a business deal that was headed south because of a bent partner. And I liked him, despite myself. I liked how he was polite and always well dressed. I liked, too, how wiry and supple he was. I envied him the way he moved, relaxed like a panther but with ready muscles. He was potential kinetic energy, even when he slept. His wife was Japanese – Oka Ino her name was, from Nagasaki – and apparently her nickname for him was *Shinnichi* because he was a sucker for anything from Nippon.

He worked wherever he could find a pay packet (an admirable trait, but one that appalled me right at this moment) and I remember one night at Tuzie's, a strip club on Brewer Street where he sometimes worked the door. I stopped by to have a drink with him because I'd seen a beautiful leather jacket he might have liked in a vintage clothes shop in Kensal Town (he was always complimenting me on my own). We sat at the bar and all the girls waved at him and blew him kisses on their way in or out. Because he wasn't just a bouncer. He was a bodyguard and sometime confidant to these women – Jazz Maggs, Abi Valley, Dotty Pillows – and that was something that maybe I could work to my advantage.

So I thought we were kind-of friends – as much as it was possible to be kind-of friends with someone who flirted with the lower echelons of crime – but friends didn't take pot-shots at you in SW8 with what sounded to my educated ears like an 8mm Baikal self-defence pistol adapted to take 9mm rounds. Although that said, I could probably think of a few who wouldn't say no if given the opportunity. Tokuzo would say no. But only because she'd rather come at me with a flamethrower.

He'd allowed himself to be persuaded to have a drink

– a small measure from a bottle of Gekkeikan sake the management kept behind the bar especially for him. He offered me some, so we sat there sipping rice wine while everyone else drank £20 pints of shit lager.

A paper fan stuck out of his top pocket. Henry Herschell is a master of Tessenjutsu, a martial art involving use of an iron fan, and his facsimile was a symbol of his prowess. He was something of a clothes horse; he liked to wear silk shirts and expensive moisturisers. He carried a steel comb with him – not a weapon, this, but I imagined he could do some damage with it anyway – and he would whip it out theatrically from time to time to keep his immaculate hair (gleaming with Sweet Georgia Brown) in check. I knew a number of people who expressed surprise at being told of his heterosexuality.

I liked to ask him about Tessenjutsu, how he got into it (it wasn't exactly a front-page martial art like karate or judo) and what he was up to (which always guaranteed me an arched eyebrow and a finger pressed to the side of his nose. '*Himitsu*,' he would say). Every year he and Oka holidayed in Japan where she caught up with her family and he brushed up on his Tessenjutsu skills. He once brought me back a bottle of red ink called *momiji*. I was grateful to him but I could never shake the murmur from my head that this was some kind of friendly warning. *Momiji* translates to maple. And it was the colour of autumn leaves. The colour of death. Maybe not. Maybe.

There is only so much hiding you can do. There is only so much waiting you can tolerate.

But I knew about him. His endless patience. The discipline he displayed. He'd sent me a card when I was in hospital for a spell after the fight I'd had with the Four-Year-Old. It contained a picture of Mount Fuji at sunset; I remembered the wording too, a death poem by Basho:

> On a journey, ill;
> my dream goes wandering
> over withered fields.

How did someone harden their heart to be able to act against a kind-of ally? How did you anaesthetise yourself against the pain your wife would feel were you to die? And the word on the street was that Oka was pregnant. So what the hell was Henry doing playing silly buggers?

I heard the soft collapse of dirt and stones. Grit under stealthy tread. Here we go.

I heard the engine of a barge on the Thames behind me. He wouldn't expect it. I wasn't expecting it. I went for it. You stupid twat. Twat. Twat. Twatwatwatwatwatwatwatwatwatwat...

I leapt over the wall separating Riverside Walk from ten feet of nothing and then up to my knees in silt and shit. I saw the barge pilot jerk his head towards me and then spread his arms as if to say, 'What the fuck are you?'

I couldn't agree more. But I was still alive. I beckoned him over but he wasn't having any of it, and why should he? From his viewpoint I was a cretin who couldn't commit suicide properly. I struggled on towards the water and by dint of clumsiness and determination found myself suddenly swimming. In the Thames. I got out of this okay and the first thing I'd need to do was visit the doctor's for a tetanus injection as well as a common-sense booster.

I couldn't tell if there were any more shots at me; the water was choppy, the sound of it slopping against the hull of the barge was louder than I'd expected. I reached it as the pilot was trying to turn away. Luckily the current was in my favour. It was comical, but if I didn't get a hold of the damn boat, I'd be dead. Drowned or shot. Neither held any particular attraction to me.

'Get the fuck off,' the pilot yelled, as he saw me trying to clamber over the side. The water in my clothes must have doubled my weight. It was hard enough just to cling on.

'Please,' I gasped. 'I'm in danger.'

'You'll be in danger if I have to leave this wheel and come and beat your fucking head in,' he said.

A shot splintered about a foot of wood from his starboard side. I felt some of them sting my face.

'Jesus fucking Christ!' he yelled, and instinctively threw the wheel away from the death being spat at us from the southern shore. I looked over my shoulder and saw a flash of exotic green: the lining in one of Herschell's jackets no doubt.

I scrambled on board and shambled up to the pilot who was casting glances around him as if he was being assaulted from all sides.

'It's only me you need to worry about now,' I said, and turfed him overboard. 'You can swim, yes?' But I wasn't paying much attention. I tossed a life ring over the edge and concentrated on getting across the water to Pimlico.

No more shots. Which meant they'd either given up, found a boat of their own, or they were getting back to the car, knowing what I was up to. I reckoned they were intelligent enough for that latter option, so I kept my eye on the closest of the bridges – Vauxhall – for any insanely fast cars driven by a man who liked wearing Armani suits and patent-leather shoes.

I ditched the barge at Westminster Boating Base, just south of Grosvenor Road. I was in a taxi within minutes and I got the driver heading east, as close to the river as possible at all times. I needed to keep an eye on it, and the road behind us. My clothes were sodden. I checked my phone and found it was still working – thank Christ I'd invested in a waterproof case.

Fuck you, Henry Herschell. Fuck you and your so-called ninja skills. Iron fan? Iron fanny more like. I beat you. I got away. Comb your hair and fuck off.

Nothing on the river. Plenty on the roads. But nothing I… Recognised.

Hang on. Yeah. Here he came. Silver Skoda. He was like a cat with a moth. I told the taxi driver I'd give him a tip to remember if he could lose the cunt, but he drove like a grandma with glaucoma who's had a few sherries. We crawled along Victoria Embankment while he hemmed and hawed about licences and speed limits. The Skoda was almost literally up my arse.

I got out at a red just as it was changing for green and skipped up Farringdon Street. I heard car horns sounding. I heard car doors slamming. I heard leather slapping on pavement.

I shot through a sandwich shop, vaulting the counter and body-charging any number of white-aproned salami jugglers out of my way. Through kitchens, through stock rooms, out into car parks, across quiet roads and into noisy loading bays and warehouses. Now a hotel laundry. Now a taxi rank. Pushing and pulling. Trying to reach top speed and failing due to traffic – human and car varieties – failing due to slow muscles, injuries, tired blood, tired minds. But that meant he was too.

Someone tried to rugby tackle me coming out of a pub on Pancras Lane; not the people hunting me, some have-a-go hero attempting to show me the errors of my frantic ways by delivering some of his own. I kicked him in the shoulder and told him to piss off. I could hear footsteps charging across concrete. People shouting. Maybe Henry didn't care about stealth now. He just wanted me in the ground and he didn't care how artful it looked any more. I got onto another main road and sprinted for height. All the skyscrapers here for me. Hungry for company. Staring down on this pathetic, sweaty, Thames-stained curiosity.

I U-turned and switchbacked and feinted and swerved. By the time I reached the Splinter it was getting dark and I was half-crippled with a stitch. I slowed down, though, and tried to remain mindful while my lungs bellowed like a bagpiper's arm.

Up.

I tried to be quiet, but I was knackered. Every step felt like a challenge, every breath a chore. Gravity was pulling my feet down as heavy slaps on the poured concrete. I heard the chitter of radios, but my luck was in: they were always from a distance. Footfalls passed where I had been moments ago, or where I was due to tread.

I couldn't hear any sounds of pursuit. Not that I would. I had to presume, despite the hours of dodging, that I was still in jeopardy. I could not underestimate Henry Herschell.

This time I did not go as high as possible. I didn't want to leave myself with only one direction of escape. But I also didn't want to put my architect friend in any kind of danger.

I found a room that was full of the clean, slightly scorched smell of freshly sawn wood. There was a table in here covered in blueprints and coffee cups. I wedged it into a corner and positioned heaps of waste – swathes of heavy-duty polythene wrap, lengths of stripped electric cables, spent containers of silicone grease, bulk containers – and equipment such as ratchet straps and pallets against it so it looked like a conscientious worker had gone to great lengths to make the room tidy and accessible.

I got underneath the table and rested my head against a wall of chipboard. It felt as if my pulse was trying to dent it. My heart was playing merry hell, but I didn't worry too much about that. It meant I was alive, violently nerve-shreddingly alive.

I didn't think I'd sleep. I was shattered – I must have run five miles in world-record time – but my nerves were jangling like a piano in an earthquake. Sleep I did, though, despite everything, and it was deep and untroubled, which is why I was instantly on my mettle when I came to, because I was still tired, and it was still dark. My wet clothes were drying. Something had roused me. What was it? Wind fluting down through the gaps and ginnels? A mouse scampering through its opulent penthouse? I felt sweat break out at my hairline. The merest scuff of a foot?

He was just outside the room. I'd been tired when I put together my little den. Now I saw it for what it was. Not a conscientious worker's pile at all. A hiding place. A dumb, obvious hiding place. If you were looking for someone and walked into a room and saw a man-sized pile of junk, you'd check it out. I'd been lazy and careless. I heard the light touch of a shoe again, and knew it was Henry. He seemed to be stalking around just outside the room, as if reluctant to come in here and finish it. Perhaps he was a vampire, and needed an invitation to cross the threshold.

There was no point in trying to jump him. No point in trying to run away. I'd be wearing that fan like a coxcomb before I got to the doorway. I was at the end of everything. Suddenly I didn't care. I just wanted some kind of answer before the long, dark underscore.

I stood up.

I saw a figure move just past the black oblong of the doorway, moving in a crouch, and he was elegant and lethal.

I moved too. Nowhere near as elegant, nothing like as lethal, and watched him disappear into the grainy dark. A chance. I started in the opposite direction. I don't know why I didn't head down the stairs. I guess because it meant more running away, more hiding, and that kind of life is too demanding, physically and mentally. So I kept climbing, desperately hoping that whoever was after me – Henry, you know it's Henry – might give up, feeling as tired and cold as I was (although perhaps not quite as damp), or as jittery where heights were concerned.

I tripped over the body of the security guard on the penultimate floor. There was a lot of blood but it wasn't immediately obvious as to what had drawn it.

What it might mean was that Henry had done a check of the uppermost storeys and was now making his way down, in which case I'd given him the slip. What it also meant, though, was that he'd been to the summit, where the architect was probably holed up.

I climbed the final flight, certain I was going to find him dead. Henry was no mass murderer, I was sure. But he would leave a clean canvas; he couldn't risk anyone identifying him. That he'd killed one innocent told me that he'd get rid of whoever crossed his path, contract or not.

I couldn't stand the thought of being pursued again, but I guess I had to force the issue. Otherwise it might recur at some unknown future date once Henry had refuelled and repaired. Not knowing what was coming was unbearable.

But then, his tread again. Searching, indefatigable, cat-soft. I had underestimated him. I had thought he might go. But no. He was here.

All of London stretched out before me.

'Joel.'

I turned and he was there, six feet away. The fan in his hand opening and closing like the deliberate certainty of a crocodile's jaws.

'Henry,' I said. 'What do you think of my new place?'

'You led us a merry dance today, Joel.'

'What is this? Why?'

'Money,' he said. 'It's always money.'

'I'll give you money,' I said. 'Tell me who's paying you.'

'You can't pay what he's paying.'

'Tann.'

'Does it matter?'

'Have you thought about where Tann's money is coming from? He was a handyman in a leisure centre, for fuck's sake.'

'I don't care where the money comes from. The down payment seems real enough,' he said. 'I can hold it in my hands. And I can spend it in the shops.'

'I thought we were friends,' I said. 'Kind of. You're better than this. A contract killer? Really?'

'There's nobility in any form of work.'

'Fuck off, Henry,' I said. I was getting angry now, and that was good, because it was putting some iron in my voice, and taking the shake out of my muscles. 'Don't try to justify what you're doing. You make it sound like something worthy.'

'*Kishi kaisei*,' he said. 'Wake from death. Return to life.'

I was so tired. And I was bored of this man's Wapanese schtick. 'Fuck's sake, Henry,' I said. 'Put your miso paste away. You're from fucking Tulse Hill.'

His fan was catching the city lights. Bamboo and steel.

187

It was beautiful and lethal. I guessed that his killing stroke would not come from that. He was married; she was pregnant. He didn't want any kind of evidence of a fan wound to the head on my body; he'd go away for years. He wanted this to look like an accident.

'I studied for years,' he said. 'I wasn't interested in karate or jujutsu or kendo. I wanted to do something unconventional. And I liked the idea of the war fan. The idea of carrying something seemingly innocent into an arena of death where swords were not allowed.'

'But you're attacking me,' I said. 'How noble is that? Doesn't your art have something to say about aggression? Isn't it all to do with self-defence? I'm sure your sensei would be disgusted with you.'

That stung him, and I was glad. It meant maybe a notch up on the rage monitor, which meant possible clumsiness, which meant that I might have some window of opportunity to counter.

'What do you know?' he spat.

'I've dabbled,' I said. 'I know a little karate. Silat. Krav Maga.'

'Diluted,' he said. 'Lesser forms. Jack of all trades.'

'We'll see,' I said, but my voice was claggy with fear. I felt a sinking inside me. My hands shook like a wet dog. I was back in Silex Street in the dark, footsteps echoing all around. A dark figure coming for me, arm raised, a machete gleaming at its summit, the polished blade sucking in all the light available and reflecting it right into the meat of my heart.

Henry darted in then and I found it hard to counter because of the doubt backing up inside me. I blocked and retreated as best I could. But I was weak. He was liquid fast, strong, sure. I bet the fucker did yoga. Henry had taken sides, and it seemed the weight of the green in his bank account mattered more than anything. I was utterly spent, but I had to hope that he was too, to a greater or lesser extent, despite these pyrotechnics now. He'd been on the go, maybe when I was kipping, and so I might have some kind of sleep oneupmanship. But there was always his fan, flicking between us like a cast-iron cobra.

'You're married, Henry,' I said. 'What if you don't come home today?'

'Don't underestimate me,' he said.

'I don't,' I said, trying to remember the moves. When you only go at it half-arsed like me, you can't ever expect for it to become instinctual. He thrust the fan at my face and I countered with *jodan age uke*. But I was slow and uncommitted. I was a poor-quality YouTube demonstration. He moved into the space below my upraised arm and slammed an elbow into my floating ribs. Searing pain. I wondered if he'd broken one.

'What's her name again?' I grunted. 'Oka? I heard she was up the duff.'

'Shut up,' he said.

'What would she say if she saw you tonight?' I asked. If this rib was broken and had punctured my lung I'd not get much joy out of him. It would be a one-way fight. 'You have regular work, as far as I see it. A way forward. You don't need the easy way out. Not at the expense of a friend.'

'I don't have any friends,' he said. 'I have opportunities.'

I tried a snap kick to his groin but I only ended up looking as if I was trying to flick something unsavoury from the sole of my shoe. He was greased elegance. He countered with a kick of his own and it caught my thigh and I felt the whole side of my leg turn numb. He followed up with a chop to my neck with the fan and I ducked, but not so fast that I could avoid what felt like a scalping. Fire raged across the top of my skull, and I felt blood leaking immediately down the back of my neck. Maybe I was wrong about his intentions with that fan. Maybe Phil Clarke would lay me out on his post-mortem slab and see the fatal wound and nobody would have any idea where it had come from. I wondered if I'd have enough time before I died to write the word 'fan' and draw an arrow to the hole it had made in me.

I just wanted to talk to Henry, to hammer out some kind of agreement, but I was too exhausted to speak and these exertions, the pain flaring in my side every time I moved or breathed, were reducing me further. That and the black dog, the lack of confidence or belief. The conviction that Death was watching this fight from the shadows, egging Henry on while it widened the mouth of the shroud in which it would tote my soul to Hell.

Happy thoughts. That's right. Stay positive.

I concentrated on staying upright and hoping that he'd make some kind of positional error that would allow me to strike and send him over the edge of the skyscraper into eternal night.

He came again, feinting to kick and then flicking out the fan in the direction of my eyes. I'd estimated the feint and sunk low to combat it, but I hadn't expected the finesse. I felt the iron blades connect again, skimming across my forehead but although there was blood, I hadn't been skinned to the bone.

I hit back with some unsophisticated moves of my own that had found traction in confrontations in the past: an inside chop to the calf; a palm heel strike to the groin; *mawashi geri*... It gained me some space, a little time; it in no way incapacitated him. There was no backbone to it.

'I train three hours a day, seven days a week,' he said. 'I eat a lot of protein and fresh vegetables. I'll have one drink a week, if that. I've seen you put away a bottle of vodka in one evening. How do you think we compare on the scale of fitness, of physical possibilities?'

I tried to not listen to any of his shit. Instead I threw a bracket of metal at him, not knowing where it was from or what it was for. All I knew was that it would give him pause if it hit his bollocks or his brainbox. I didn't think of the ramifications of allowing the metal to fly out of the skyscraper and into clear air above the houses and flats and offices below. Luckily for me it hit him, but nowhere vital. He let out a yelp of pain anyway. And I thought, *I got him in the forearm or the wrist: target those, and make it matter*.

The next time he sashayed in with his fancy fan akimbo, I jinked out of his reach and performed a *yoko geri keage* – a side snap kick that of course he was expecting – but I reinforced it with a reverse hook kick. I managed to connect with the side of his head, pushing him off balance. Knowing I had a split second I followed up with a kick to the left hand, which he was now favouring, putting it out of commission even as he folded into my attack, whipping his fan around to strike at my kidneys.

No joy there, I thought, knowing that my piss filters were protected by a good lining of thick leather. But it was just part of a series of assaults, a pattern offensive designed to reduce me physically and psychologically. If you're up against someone who knows what they're doing and has done it every day for years then you're more likely to feel inadequate, no matter how experienced you feel you are. The compulsion was strong inside me now to just shrivel up on the floor and wait for the killing strike. Give up. Let it happen. It would be over in seconds.

And then I was stunned to find myself in a position where I could cram my boot into that precious space between a man's legs known technically as the knackers. I didn't need asking twice. He went down grunting like a boar. I followed it up with a jab to his nose and a near simultaneous strike to the hand holding the fan; the weapon went skittering away across the dusty floorboards. I was on top of Henry, besting him by a good seventy-five pounds, and his fight was done.

'What now?' I asked. 'You going to sweet talk my chi to death?'

He smiled. I smiled. And then he launched me.

I wasn't expecting that. I thought I had him pinned down fast, but he shifted like a fart in a wind tunnel. The smile disarmed me. I must have relaxed my grip, no matter how minutely. I'd been thrown to one side as swiftly as a right-wing newspaper in a left-wing reading room. But then someone else was next to him, blocking his efforts to retain his *tessen*, striking out on his own with a length of iron pipe and launching Henry backwards towards the edge of the building space.

I went to him, reaching down to pick him up, to demand some answers, when he kicked out at me and found the edge of my jaw. I saw stars and toppled over. The next thing I knew I was rubbing my face and Henry was standing right on the edge of forever. A lump the size of a child's fist had risen from Henry's forehead. The architect was standing close by, holding the pipe, breathing fast, his face hard and determined.

Henry said: 'There's a legend in Japan that if you jump from Kiyomizu-dera, the Buddhist temple in Kyoto, and manage to get away with not being injured, that all your wishes will come true.' Blood fizzed from his nose. There was fear in his eyes, but also determination. I was finding it hard to breathe. Two people miles up in the sky who kind-of liked each other. Blood and fear. This fucking life. This job that we did.

'Don't do this,' I said. 'We can all walk away. No tragedies. Think of your wife, Henry. Think of Oka. Think of your unborn child.'

But he wasn't listening. To listen was to lose face, I guessed, and Henry wasn't the kind of person to do that. He was all about honour, despite his background. I wondered if that was a good thing, to change your viewpoint no matter the kind of life you'd lived, the upbringing you'd enjoyed or endured. I imagined it didn't make any difference at all to him. I guessed he thought he was free, no matter what choice was made.

He stood on the brink and his face was serene. He was in Japan. He was at the temple in Kyoto. Survive this and there was milk and honey for eternity. Only this wasn't a survivable hop. This was eighty metres plus. And you didn't come back from this kind of dive, even if you believed you were blessed.

'Tell me where he is, Henry,' I said.

He said: '*Tōdai moto kurashi*,' and stepped off the edge.

17

Minutes later the architect was telling me to go, *just go*, that this place would be flooded with police before long and then I wouldn't have a chance to get clear for hours.

'What about you?' I asked.

'I know all the best hiding places,' he said.

I got moving.

I studiously avoided going anywhere near the spot where Henry had landed, though I knew if I'd buried him with some of the sand available on site it might give me some valuable time. Instead, I was violently sick and had to crouch down for a few minutes until my limbs stopped trembling.

The pain in my ribs was sharp but manageable, at least for the time being. Nothing a fistful of Nurofen wouldn't budge. Tender examination suggested there were no complete breaks. Fractures I could live with. Breathing would hurt like bastards for a week or so, but I've been with some form of pain or other for so long it would feel wrong if it wasn't there at all.

Now get up and get out. On to the next bit of business. Attaboy.

But I couldn't move. It felt good, hunkered down, my boots dusty with cement, close to that puddle of my own hot waste, a symbol of all I'd become. Getting up meant opening myself to attackers, presenting a bigger target. They'd barely see me if I was scrunched up like a mouse. I could stay here all day. Even better if I shut my eyes.

Sarah used to do that.

She did, didn't she?

She'd play hide and seek and choose a crap place to hide, but then she'd shut her eyes because she thought she wouldn't be seen.

It didn't help that she called out 'I'm here' when the seeker came looking.

Come on, Joel. We're all waiting for you.

What Becs would call out when she and Sarah were at the table for the evening meal. It was the one sacrosanct in our lives. We always ate dinner together. None of this trays-in-front-of-the-TV malarkey. No newspapers, no gadgets. Three people eating, engaging. But now that line carried a weight to it, an ambiguity I wasn't sure I liked.

I heard the groan of a lorry. I got up and walked to the fence. Here it came, crawling along Cheapside, bed loaded with aggregate and rebars. I saw three guys in the cab. More would be on the way.

I slipped over the fence just as they turned into the construction site. I almost didn't make it. Dizziness gripped me and I nearly fell backwards; they'd have me in their sights then. Lots of explaining on the cards, especially when their digger picked up a pile of Henry porridge.

I got on the phone and asked Jimmy Two to help me out. I needed an emergency fix on the Saab, or a replacement if that was unlikely. Soon as.

Back on the street I had to stop every hundred yards or so to catch my breath. The fear was all over me. It was like suddenly coming to in a strange part of town after a weekend bender to find your wallet empty and somebody's tooth embedded in your bloody knuckle (although, to be fair, that only happened to me once).

I didn't want to stand there for ages frightening off taxi drivers, but I didn't want to get into any conversations either. So I hopped on the first bus going north – a 214 – and promptly fell asleep.

I rapped my head against the window and snapped awake. The bus had taken a sharp corner in... where were we? Gospel Oak? I got off and thought about breakfast. I needed something in me, if I could stomach it, but maybe not pancakes.

I walked up to Hampstead and bought a bag of doughnuts and coffee from a sandwich shop. I ignored the funny looks. At the water fountain I rinsed away all the blood that was congealing on my face and knuckles and ate the doughnuts, one after the other, in quick bites, relishing the hit of sugar. I drank the coffee while it was still too hot. I became aware of people hurrying by, the usual gyre of cars and buses and black cabs. The farting, sooty exhaust on a vintage delivery van. A noisy parakeet in a plane tree.

I stood up and this time there was no accompanying disequilibrium. I don't like that spatial special effect, and it's acutely unfair when I don't even have a head full of vodka to cause it.

Every time I blinked, though, I caught a frame of Henry in attack mode. The only way I could escape it was to staple

197

my eyelids to my forehead, or maybe even go on that short walk to infinity that he'd taken.

But maybe there was another way.

I snagged a taxi on Pond Street and in the few minutes it took to skip up Rosslyn Hill the Polish driver was foaming at the mouth about the Syrian immigrants pouring through the border threatening to take his family's jobs.

I headed along Flask Walk to Stodge, admiring the sleek, gutsy coupés and convertibles, and thought about the car I might choose to drive now if it transpired the Saab had gone skid-plate up. I'd had no call from Jimmy Two as to the seriousness of the repairs. My mind filled with Aston Martins and Bentleys, but I could probably find just enough spare change to buy something built in the Eastern Bloc in the 1960s, held together by spit and willpower.

Danny Sweet's staff were arranging tables. The front-of-house penguin was being talked through the lunchtime menu when I reached him and asked where Danny was to be found. He gestured with his head towards the kitchen, wearing a look that said *of course*. I left them to their talk of quenelles and mushroom foam and pushed through to the engine room. A chef was washing salad. Or maybe he wasn't a chef. Maybe he was a sous chef, or a prep boy or an underling, someone further up the food chain than a dish zombie but a couple of links down from soup ponce. I have no idea. Danny was haranguing some poor… saucier? sauce whipper-upper? gravy monkey? for filling squeezy bottles with beef jus before it had properly cooled. He used the word 'cunt' liberally, as if he was adding salt to a tureen of steamed cabbage. And if 'cunt' was salt, then 'twat' was pepper. The poor saucejack cringed before Danny like a leaf of spinach before a blowtorch.

'Do you think,' I said, to try to distract him from the roasting of his staff, 'that it helped to become a celebrity chef because you had the surname Sweet?'

He didn't seem surprised to see me, but he was surprised by my demeanour. He hurled a copper pan at me and I ducked just in time to see it carom off the corner of a fridge and into a pile of potato peelings.

'I'm no fucking celebrity chef,' he roared. 'Do you see me getting my big hairy pepper grinder out on *Can't Cook, Won't Wank*? Am I in the TV studios at the weekend showing people how to spunk the perfect Hollandaise on their ham and eggs? No. I'm in here showing thick twats like this cunt how to fucking cook. Do you want a fucking coffee?'

'I'd love one,' I said. 'You should have a sit down and some camomile tea. You've got veins thicker than my fingers sticking out of your forehead. You're herniating.'

He got some beverage slave to sort out *due espressi* and we sat in his empurpled restaurant. The silver teaspoons were tiny in his hands.

'You know what you should do?' I said. 'Origami serviettes. Take your dining experience to a whole new level.'

'Fuck off, you plebian tosser,' he said. 'And it's napkin. "Serviette" might work if you were eating shit chip butties in a Warrington mankhole. Not here.'

'Says indigenous Hampstead man. You're from Kirkcaldy, aren't you?'

'And proud of it. I used to catch flounder from Tiel Burn that were bigger than me when I was two years old. Mum helped me gut 'em and cook 'em.'

'So go and open a Michelin-starred restaurant there,' I said. 'Deep-fried Mars bars with rosemary ganache… whatever the fuck a ganache is.'

'You've perked up,' he said. 'Look at the state of you. You look as if you've been headbanging in a rose bush. Do you need a plaster?'

'I'm all right,' I said. I touched one of the fan wounds and it stung like fury, but the bleeding had stopped.

'What are you doing round here, anyway? I'm not going for another old man's jog around the Heath with you again.'

Now we were at the crux of it, I didn't want to say. Danny Sweet is a man's man. Moreover, he's a bastard's bastard. He doesn't like to see weakness of any kind. Though he might have steak tartare on his menu, he certainly doesn't like the mincing of words.

In the end it just fell out of me: 'I was hesitant, and I almost died. There was a weapon involved. I don't think I can do this any more.'

He didn't say anything. He took the coffee cup from my hands and placed it gently on the table. He held up a finger to *Aptenodytes patagonicus* and took me to the magic doors. He unlocked them and we went through.

I'd been here before, of course. And it was why I was here now. I needed to find a way to shift the burden that was weighing heavy around me and Danny Sweet was the only person I knew who might be able to help with that. Fear was turning me sluggish. Was there a better way to prise its fingers from my throat than spend half an hour in this illegal bear pit?

It hadn't changed much since my last visit. The fug of male sweat was thicker, maybe. The puddles of dried blood on the floor, the crazy splashes of it on the walls were more numerous.

Danny snapped his phone shut. 'Mungo the Child Crusher is on his way,' he said.

'Who?'

'I'm kidding. His name's Eric.'

'So you're still doing this?' I said.

'Yes,' he said. 'And you know it. That's why you came to me.'

'I don't know why I thought it was a good idea, really. Fight fire with fire?'

'It costs considerably less than lying on a brain masseur's couch doing Rorschach tests. And, I'd argue, it's safer and more fun.'

'Fun? Christ.'

'Come on,' he said. 'When you go toe-to-toe with a naughty man, when you land the critical blow, you can't tell me that doesn't feel good.'

'I honestly do not feel any pleasure from hurting another human being,' I said.

'Bollocks,' he said.

There was the squeal of hinges as the door was opened.

'That was quick,' I said. Cartoon heavy echoes on the concrete steps. 'Who's this? The Hoxton Creeper?'

'Eric's one of my chippies,' he said. 'He's putting new window frames in the conservatory out back.'

Eric arrived smelling of hot sawn timber. His boots were tanned with sawdust. He wore a utility belt loaded with tools: hammer, Stanley knife, measuring tape, screwdrivers. Nails jingled in a pouch when he walked, like spurs on a cowboy.

'Do you ever wear that and pretend to be Batman?' I asked.

'Fuckeryou?' he said. He spoke in a hurry, as if the spaces between words were a luxury he couldn't lay claim to.

'I love it,' Danny said. 'You just have this face, this way with words that instantly gets people spitting blood and piss.'

'I was being friendly,' I said.

'You insulted him,' Danny said. 'You implied that his work equipment was a toy.'

'I'd pretend to be Batman if I was him,' I reasoned.

'Iknowyou,' Eric said. He was peering at me as if through fog. 'User copperwonce. Youput my babybrotherTony behindbars.'

'It was kind of my job,' I said.

'Oh,' said Danny. 'Well this adds a little spice, doesn't it? Eric, if you're in the mood, Joel here has come down to the mosh pit to try to battle some demons. I wondered if you might fancy a break from all those pieces of oak upstairs.'

He didn't need asking twice. He made a great play of removing his tool belt and draping it delicately over the back of a chair. Then he rolled his sleeves up. There was the obligatory tattoo, a Chelsea Football Club crest. Another reason to not care too much about stoving his great haggis of a face in. 'I bet that's recent, isn't it?' I said, nodding at the blue lion carrying its Polo mint on a stick. 'Post success. I bet you didn't have that when Chelsea were kicking lumps out of teams in Division Two in the late eighties.'

'Hoojoo sport?' he said.

'It doesn't really matter, does it?' I said. 'But we've won four European Cups more than you have.'

'Shouldaknown,' he said. And came wading towards me.

'Hang on,' Danny said. 'Let's make this interesting. We don't want Joel to have too easy a ride of it.'

'Easy?' Eric said. His face twisted with offence, confusion and hurt.

'Pick a weapon,' Danny said. 'How about that box cutter?'

'Fuck off, Danny,' I said.

'You're not going to ever get better unless you stare it down, Joel,' he said. 'A punch-up won't wash. You've got to be James Stewart climbing the bell tower. Roy Scheider getting on board the *Orca*—'

'Wotsy onabout?' Eric asked. I shook my head.

'—Sigourney Weaver stripping to her smalls. You've got to face your fear and wrestle it into submission.'

'It's not about the knife,' I said.

'Yes it is. It's all about the knife. Eric.'

Eric dutifully picked out the Stanley and ratcheted a couple of inches of razor from its mouth. 'Whatify cuttim?'

'He'll thank you for it,' Danny said.

'Idunno.'

'He'll pay you as well,' Danny said. 'Won't you, Joel?'

'I'll give you a hundred quid,' I said. 'But I'd rather we forgot about the knife.'

'The knife stays or you go and find yourself a couch and someone who wants you to talk about your mother.'

Why should I have been surprised? You go courting madness, you end up in a room filled with it.

Eric seemed happy, absolved of any blame should he slash my face to ribbons, plus money, plus vengeance for Tony. I couldn't even remember who he was or what he'd been put away for, beyond having a criminally stupid brother.

And so here he came, and I couldn't separate the blade from the person who wielded it. Eric was overweight, dimmer than a ten-watt bulb; his monobrow was probably more intelligent than he was. But the blade elevated him. And the closer he got, the more it pressed him into the background, until only that triangle of silver mattered, and I could feel its heat and penetration before it had gone anywhere near my flesh.

I felt myself dwindling.

A voice came through the black clouds. Danny: 'Fear is man-made,' he said. 'More specifically, it's *you*-made. It's personal and intimate. It's not the knife, it's the fucking knifer. Being scared is overrated. It's so yesterday. It's for fucking kids. Anyway, Joel, what's the worst that could happen? He slashes you up and you die. Big wank. It's better than pissing into your cushions while a nurse who despises you feeds you custard in a care home. And who'd miss a cunt like you? The mixologist at One Aldwych?'

The voice helped. His sweary, know-all voice. The voice he'd worked hard on in order to remove any of the Scottishness in it, to mould it into something posh-casual. You might hear it in Notting Hill or Hoxton.

It helped to dull the anxiety, but even though Eric was easy enough to best, and I was a good boy, refraining from stamping his head into a disappointing brawn, I knew I'd have to find a different way of coping, because I didn't want to have to think of Danny Sweet's voice in my ear every time someone pulled an edged weapon on me. At least now I knew I could do it. *And maybe*, I thought, as I peeled off some notes and gave them to Eric, thanked Danny and bid him goodbye, hoping never to see him again, *he was right in one respect*.

I'd developed a Pavlovian response to the unsheathing of a blade. That was all. It was a related absence of control that bothered me. Death held no fear for me. I knew that. How could I fear death, any kind of death, when even my violent murder would most probably come nowhere near the brutal death that Rebecca suffered? It was more that I feared checking out before I'd made everything right. I didn't want to go without seeing Sarah again. I wanted my life to be put in order before it was snuffed.

My hands felt dirty where they had touched the bills. And my guts were trying to repel the taste of Danny Sweet's coffee. It had been an ugly, desperate act. But necessary, I felt. I'd found some way of overcoming a difficulty. That was life, I supposed, in a nutshell.

I ascended the stone steps while Danny cajoled Eric back to work. Just as I got to the door, I got a text from Jimmy Two, my miracle man, saying the car, though bruised and battered, had been coaxed back to action and – given my current travails – was waiting for me not outside my flat on Homer Street, but in a car park near Willesden Junction. I was tucking the phone away, a skip working its way into my stride, when it rang.

18

It was Lorraine Tokuzo. Her voice slapped me into alert mode; after the fights – Henry, and the less demanding, but equally necessary Eric – my body just wanted to shut down and dissolve in its juices of shock and exhaustion.

'Where are you?' I asked.

'We're both safe,' she said. Typical Tokuzo. Ask a sensible question, get the answer to a question she wanted to hear.

'I told you to get out of London.'

'You might have *advised* us to get out of London.'

'Lorraine, let's not play around. It's dangerous. These guys… they don't care about anything. They'll come for my weak spots.'

'I'm not weak.'

'I don't mean it like that,' I said. 'And you know it.'

'Never mind,' she said. 'Romy said she thinks she was followed yesterday.'

'What about you?'

'I don't know. We're jumping at shadows,' she said. 'I'm pretty scared. For me, for you. Romy.'

'This is what I wanted to avoid,' I said.

I heard a rumble in the background.

'Where are you?' I asked again.

'We're in a fauxtel near Heathrow,' she said. Fauxtel. That was what she called any place that didn't come with a chocolate on your pillow or complimentary bathrobes.

'What are you doing at Heathrow?'

'I don't know,' she said. 'Seemed like a good idea at the time. Anonymous. Grey. Getting lost among the masses. But there's only so much coffee you can drink, and after a while, it gets depressing seeing people piss off to the sunshine. Security were getting a bit fidgety too. You stick out if you've got no suitcases and you're just hanging around.'

'I'll call you when I get there,' I said. 'Sit tight.' I thought of getting Mawker to help out but he'd either point blank refuse – there was no evidence as yet to suggest Tann was going after anybody but me – or he'd ride in there with half a dozen screaming squad cars and cause a stampede. Half the people at airports are already touching cloth without a bunch of sirens and rifles making things worse. I was back at my car and heading off within the hour.

But I knew I couldn't go straight out to the airport. I was reluctant to do it for any number of reasons – including a building desire to get right in Mawker's face about his visits to Cold Quay – but en route to Heathrow I took a slight detour. I sat in the car for ten minutes on a road just north of the cemetery at Roundwood Park, summoning the nerve to get out and get on with it. And that walk to the door was one of the hardest I've ever taken. I'd passed on death news before, but I'd never broken it to a pregnant woman, nor told her that I had played an instrumental part in his demise.

I'd never met Oka before – Henry had quite rightly kept

her away from his work, especially at Tuzie's, which was the only place I'd ever encountered him.

The doorbell produced a subtle chime – I should have guessed; no strident cliché tones for Henry – and she answered within seconds, as if she had been waiting at the door for a visitor. Perhaps she had; her husband had been dead for hours, and for hours prior to that he'd been galloping around London after me. He didn't strike me as the kind of person who would keep someone waiting, let alone his wife. Henry was renowned for his punctuality and reliability. She would know something was amiss. One look at her face told me she already knew, and I paused, considering the wisdom of coming here.

'It is all right,' she said. Her English was perfect, but the sing-song intonation from her native language remained. There was a flash of grey in her short black hair. 'They have been and gone.'

'Who's "they"?' I asked.

'Henry's comrades. They told me what happened. One of them said you might come here but the other said you could not be so stupid. And yet here you are.'

'Here I am,' I said. 'And I'm not going to deny any accusations of stupidity. I thought it was the right thing to do.'

'Will you come in?'

I flashed a look at the darkness behind her. She placed a hand on the bulge of her stomach as if to reassure me. 'For a short while,' I said. 'Thank you.'

'Please remove your shoes.'

I followed her along the hallway and into a room that contained a low table with a vase holding a single white flower. There was a framed Japanese ideogram on the wall. A stone bowl on the window ledge. That was it.

'Please,' she said, and indicated that I should sit on the floor by the table. I did so and she left the room. I closed my eyes at the ludicrous situation. Earlier her husband and I had been trying to gouge the life out of each other. And here I was, spoiling the feng shui.

She returned with a tray bearing a stone teapot and what looked like two eggcups. She placed the tray on the table and, with some difficulty, lowered herself down opposite me.

'When is the baby due?'

'In two weeks,' she said.

Sunshine kitchen. Toast-crumb mouth. Fingers laced through mine. Wide eyes. Joel. Pinch me. Slap me upside the noggin. Tickle my tits till Tuesday. We. Are. Going. To. Be. Parents. In. Two. Weeks.

'Joel?'

I had reached out and taken her hand in mine. I didn't know what to do. The child would grow up without a father. She would be more than enough – I could see that – but Henry was suddenly a memory, a myth.

'I liked him,' I said.

'He liked you.' Her voice remained smooth and steady but the catchlights in her eyes sparkled. 'You men,' she said. 'Violence never strays far.'

'What will you do?'

Her face was stone. Maybe she hadn't thought about that yet. Maybe there was nothing else on her mind. But then: 'Sell the house. Go back to Japan.' She didn't sound convinced. Neither was I.

She poured some green tea and stared into the steam. She had the kind of face that you could believe had never known a smile. It seemed born to misery, comfortable with it. But that couldn't be true. I wondered how a smile might transform her. I wouldn't be finding out soon.

'I knew Henry's work was… unconventional. But I did not realise he was involved in killing practice.'

She nodded at my bald display of scepticism. 'It's true,' she said. 'I know he was passionate about Tessenjutsu, but I didn't believe he carried it beyond the dojo walls. Or that he used it offensively. His sensei would turn his back on him, if he knew.' She hesitated. When she spoke again her voice was very low, barely audible. 'And so would I.'

'What did they tell you, these comrades?'

'A body was found in the City a short while ago. They said he fell from a great height. I was told I would not be able to identify him. Only from the clothes he wore.'

I thought of him standing on the edge, the wind flapping at his jacket, flashing its iridescent lining at me.

'He fell,' I said. 'He was not pushed. We fought. It didn't go well for him. But I suppose you could say he retained his dignity, at the end.'

'I understand,' she said. 'I am not blaming you.'

'Did Henry talk about the person he was working for?'

'He never spoke about any aspect of his work. And I never asked.'

'Is there anything you can tell me? Anything at all that you heard or saw? Anybody who came to the house you didn't recognise?'

A shake of the head. 'Henry was protective of his privacy. And protective of me. Our paths rarely crossed during the mornings and nights. He was always out, working. I saw him in the afternoons he wasn't catching up on his sleep. Sometimes we would go out for brunch.'

'And where did he go, other than Tuzie's?'

Her eyes flicked to the stone bowl on the window ledge.

'Nowhere, really,' she said. 'I didn't know his paymasters.'

I was restless. It was time to go. I finished my tea and stood up. I went over to the stone bowl. There was a key on a leather fob. A laminated piece of paper with the number 7 on it.

'What's this?'

'You have no right.'

'My wife was murdered by your husband's paymaster,' I said. 'Henry visited me once, when I was in hospital. His betrayal gives me every right.'

The hand on the belly again. To calm her, to calm the baby. Who knew? Who cared? 'It's a key to a garage,' she said.

'Where is it? What's in it? Your car?'

She shook her head. 'It doesn't belong to us. Henry was looking after it while the owner was... away.'

'Away? This is Tann's garage.'

She nodded. Stroked her child.

'Where is it?' I asked.

'Wallingford.' She gave me the address and accompanied me to the door.

'In Japan,' she said, 'ritual suicide was performed by the wives of those samurai who had brought dishonour on their homes. It was called *jigai*. You take a sharp knife and draw it across the throat, cutting the arteries clean through. A fast death. It was taught to very young girls so that they might be prepared in later life.'

'But times have changed,' I said, carefully.

'In some ways,' she said. 'For some people.'

'Your child will be happy and strong,' I said. 'You don't need to pass on the sorrow. You mustn't act rashly. There are positives to be gained from all of this.'

'I am struggling to see what they might be,' she said. A

hand on the belly. Her other hand swept her hair away from her throat and in that moment I saw how her suicide might go. I felt the skin on my arms pucker.

'I can put you in touch with people who can help you,' I said. 'They will give you good advice.'

'It's time to say goodbye,' she said.

I pulled my boots on and Henry's voice leapt up in my head.

'Can you tell me what... *To*... something... um... *day*? *die*?... *moto crashy* means?'

'*Tōdai moto kurashi*? It means, more or less, that "The base of the lighthouse is dark".'

'That's it?'

'Yes.'

In the street a rag-and-bone man went by. We stared at him. I felt lost in time, unfastened, as if I wasn't moving along at the same speed it was. Everything was playing itself out a few frames ahead of me.

'There is another Japanese proverb,' she said. Her voice had turned dry and bitter. The hand had not left her distended belly. '*Katte kabuto no o wo shimeyo.*'

I waited. I wondered about Oka, and what she had told me. I felt she was reining in much of what she had wanted to say, or do. I wondered whether it was true, her assurance that she did not blame me. And what might have happened to me were she not carrying the child.

'Having conquered,' she said, 'tighten the thongs of your helmet.'

19

The key was burning a hole in my pocket. I wondered what I might find there. I wondered if this garage, in the south-east of Oxfordshire, might not be where Graeme Tann was hiding out. But I had to help Lorraine and Romy first.

Heathrow, then. I still get excited whenever I get near an airfield. One of my favourite memories of Dad was when he took me to the viewing park at Manchester airport and we spent a couple of hours watching jets take off and land. As I approached Bath Road from the M4, a 747 sank before me, flaps extended as it came in to land. Now all I could think of was suicide bombers and hijackings and engine failures, and two women I cared about sitting in a grey room while someone mooched about outside, looking for them.

Their hotel was a cheap, nondescript little place with a farty little token gesture car park and neglected hedges. A woman at the desk with a face like a gravestone looked at me as if I had just offered to eat her children in a granary bap. There was nobody else in the so-called lobby. A birdcage luggage cart bore a misery-grey suitcase with a broken handle wrapped in parcel tape. There was the faint smell of fear sweat. People holed up waiting to get on pressurised metal tubes travelling eight miles high at 500 miles per hour with 150 tons of highly flammable fuel under their arses.

I texted Tokuzo to say I'd arrived. I got one back: 37.

I walked along a gloomy corridor punctuated with muffled sounds of TV and argument. I tapped softly at the door and she opened it. A sharp smell of vinegar. Romy was sitting on the bed behind her, knees drawn up to her chin. They both looked tired and edgy. Tension was thick in the room. I wondered if they'd been squabbling.

'So what's going on?' I asked.

'Can we just get out of here?' Tokuzo said.

'Let's just relax, okay? Let's not get up a head of steam over something that might be nothing. I'm in the car, we can all head back together. But not while we're in headless chicken mode.'

'I went out earlier,' Romy said. 'To get something to eat. We were both starving.'

'Why not order room service?'

'I'm not eating anything from this skank hole,' said Tokuzo.

'There's a fish and chip shop just five minutes away,' Romy said. 'I saw someone on the other side of the road. He had a phone with him. And he was talking into it. He watched me walk by.'

'As would any red-blooded male,' I said.

'He wasn't there when I was coming back. But there was a car, and it was just idling. I think there were two people in the car.'

'What kind of car?' I asked.

'I'm not good with models,' she said. 'It was black, I think. Black wheels too.'

'And what? It followed you?'

'Well no, it wasn't kerb-crawling me. But when I got to the hotel entrance I heard a car very fast in the street. I turned to look and it was the black car.'

I sat down on the bed. I felt Romy's foot move away, and then move back. Her toe dimpled my thigh. I gave her calf a squeeze.

'What do you think?' asked Tokuzo. She was biting the nail of her thumb. Those cat-sly hazel eyes looked muddy in the sickly gleam from the hotel room lights.

'I'm wondering if I saw a black car on the way here. And you know, I think I did. One of those thousands of cars might well be what we're looking for.' *But black wheels*, I thought. *A bit of a stand out. Something to keep an eye out for.*

'What about just now?' she said, her voice getting firmer. I knew that voice. It meant: *no more dicking about.* 'Anybody in the car park? Anyone shifty at Reception?'

'Other than the receptionist, no. There was a service vehicle in the car park, and a taxi. I saw a man walking a dog along Bath Road. Nobody sitting on a bench with slits cut into his newspaper.'

What to make of it? Maybe nothing. Maybe something. I had to consider it a threat.

'I think we've all spooked each other enough,' I said. 'Come on, let me take you somewhere safe.'

'Nowhere's safe, with you knocking about,' Tokuzo said.

'Seriously,' I said. 'There's this safe house I know about.'

'Stick your safe house,' she said. 'If it's so safe, why aren't you in it?'

'Good question,' I said.

'I want to go home,' she said.

'And how about you?' I asked Romy.

'I'll go with her,' she said. 'I can't stay with Dad. I won't stay with you.'

Get that 'won't'.

'King's Cross might be all right,' I said, because I felt I had to offer some crumb. There was no reason it would be all right. There was every reason it was being staked out like every other place in London that Tann knew I had a connection to. 'But first we have to drive out Oxford way.'

'Oxford?'

'Wallingford, to be precise.'

'Wallingford? What's in Wallingford?'

'Tut-tut,' I said. 'There's a glass-half-empty attitude if ever I heard one. What *isn't* in Wallingford? That's the question you should be asking yourself.'

'Why are we going there?' Romy asked, and I decided to drop the smart-alecness. I had been thinking about her soft mouth and the way she said my name. I hadn't been concentrating enough on the fact that she was scared and confused.

'There might be some information, or a clue as to how I can stop all of this,' I said.

'We're going to see someone?' Tokuzo asked.

'We're going to check something out. An address. A garage.'

'A garage? A lock-up?'

'Yes, a lock-up.'

'Great,' she said, and pushed past me. 'Don't expect me to be by your side when you open the door and find all the torture equipment.'

I coaxed Romy from the bed and followed them both down the corridor to the lobby where I paid their bill. The receptionist looked at me with those dead, dismissive eyes. Her crimped mouth, like a badly arranged pie crust, registered its disgust at this pimp and his bedraggled whores in a series of contemptuous moues.

'Get in the car, quick,' I said, scanning the road. The service vehicle had gone. The taxi driver was asleep in the front seat, his mouth sagging open.

I got in and started her up and within five minutes we were on the M4. Nothing in the rear-view mirror. Well, nothing black. Nothing nosing at the rear of the Saab at least.

I felt myself relaxing, bit by bit. I switched on the CD player and fired up Penderecki's 'Threnody for the Victims of Hiroshima'.

'Jesus Christ,' Tokuzo said. 'There are any number of reasons why I'm grateful me and you don't have a thing any more. And your music is top of the fucking list.'

'It's possibly not the easiest of listens,' I said. 'But why should it be?'

'I'd rather listen to cats screwing. In fact… isn't this an album of cats screwing?'

'Very funny,' I said. 'I'm so sorry that I don't have any dinner jazz, or whatever it was you liked to listen to. Fucking lift music.'

'Please turn it off,' Romy said. 'I've got a headache.'

I switched off the music and we rolled in silence. I wondered if Romy knew Tokuzo and I had been involved some years ago. Of course she would. Lorraine would have been counting out my bad points in excruciating detail. She wouldn't have enough fingers for it.

I got off the M4 at Maidenhead and drove north through green acres and golf courses, crossing the Thames at Henley and passing through places that sounded as if they must only be uttered by people with very clipped upper-class English accents: Bix, Nettlebed, Crowmarsh Gifford. That last was just around the corner from Wallingford, and we pulled up on the high street, a couple of roads away from the lock-up's location.

'You should wait here,' I said.

'Fuck that,' said Tokuzo. 'I want some sugar. I want an ice cream and a pint. You coming, Romy?'

'Some coffee would be good,' she said.

'Please, just don't fuck about. Keep your heads down. Back here in an hour, right? It's getting late.'

'Right, Dad,' she said, and blew me a kiss and flipped me the finger.

I watched them heading off in the direction of the off-licence and kept an eye on the human traffic for a while. But there were no interruptions in its stream.

I walked up to the right road. Halfway along it was a turn-off into an alley boiling with chickweed, colt's foot and nettle. The alley was flanked with garages and came to a dead end: crumbling concrete bollards, a wall of weeds, a single office chair bloated with rainwater. A streetlamp bathed the place in a sickly ochre glow.

The yellow double lines that edged the road looked to have been painted at some point just before the Iron Age. Some of the garages – the ones on the north side – were well tended, the paint was fresh, the weather-stripping intact. You knew the hinges and pulleys and sheaves were all adequately greased. The ones on the south side, though. Christ. They looked as if they'd been used as target practice for a Challenger 2 battle tank. They were scarred with rust and graffiti spray paint. Tags held sway: KNOWN, FUME, MAKO. Here was the lock-up that corresponded with Henry's key; the only one that was shut. I wasn't even sure it would open; the roller looked as if it was badly buckled and, sure enough, when I unlocked it and hauled it north, it seized up after about a foot.

'Fuckers,' I spat, and my voice shot around the close metal surroundings like a ricocheting bullet.

A final look around and I got myself dirty, crawling under the gap into a darkness that smelled like a retirement home laundry basket. Ancient fuel ghosts. Dog urine. Rat spoors. I felt my eyes water.

I got my pencil torch out and punched light into shadows that seemed reluctant to shift after years of bedding in. There was a switch on the wall but of course it didn't work. An old MG Midget stood on flat, perished tyres. I couldn't tell what colour the car was because the paint was scabbed and peeling and riddled with moss. Pigeon shit had hardened to meringue on the windscreen and roof. Its headlights were misted like cataracts. The car was surrounded by boxes, chests and lockers.

I sneezed hard, twice, and the sound was ushered away as if it had never happened. The ground underfoot was a thin soup of grit and oil. No shackles bolted to the wall, although Tokuzo's warning had me half-expecting it. No fridge filled with choice cuts. No lampshades made from human skin.

I started opening drawers and doors. I got through some of the big ones near the entrance first: kitchen carcasses filled with old tools, an engine incrementally rotting away, presumably from the car behind me, work clothes bundled in polythene. A stack of what looked like uncooked waffles, but on closer inspection were the asbestos grids from inside gas fires. I kept clear of those, keen to not fill my lungs with any nasty fibres. An ironing board. A small hill of paint tins. Empty oxyacetylene bottles. By those, a nest of stiff, desiccated rat pups.

The boxes contained magazines bundled with twine: *Radio Times*, mainly, but there were also copies of *Private Eye* and *Angler's Mail*. Another box contained a bunch of vintage damaged toys: Action Man without hands, Action Man without feet. A velvet bag filled with chipped marbles. Headless Subbuteo players.

So far, so *Steptoe and Son*. I checked my watch. I'd been in here twenty minutes, poking among Tann's worthless hoard. Why had he given Henry the key? What was he trying to conceal from the authorities?

I went back to the shutters and prepared to drag myself through the gap again. I'd missed something. The car. Obvious. Right under my nose. I peered through the dusty windows but could see nothing inside. I tried the door but time and rust had sealed it firmly shut.

I picked up a floor lamp and sent the heavy base of it through the driver's side window. I shone the torch inside, expecting to see a head in a jar, but there was just a bunch of Reader's Digest home improvement handbooks and a football coaching manual from the late 1970s. Tissues and travel mints in the glove compartment. I wondered if Tann had ever driven this thing, and whether the odometer – stilled at 96,013 miles – marked the end of his travels, the end of Rebecca's life.

I tried the handle of the boot and the whole thing came off in my hand with a shower of rust. Nothing in there.

Fuck it. Maybe Henry had the key because the *Radio Times* collection was worth something. I resisted the urge to set fire to the place and destroy everything. His gas fire waffles would survive, at least.

I thought about that for a minute, and went back to them. I covered my mouth and nose with the neck of my T-shirt and kicked the pile over. Deadly dust rose up in a plume. A metal box was buried beneath them. I plucked it out and took it over to the door. I tucked my T-shirt back into place and opened the box. DIY darkroom prints. Rebecca in the female changing rooms at the leisure centre, in various forms of undress. Wet and gleaming from exertion. My beautiful, young wife. Rebecca at home, in postures of death. I shouldn't have been surprised. The police found acres of this stuff pinned to his bedroom walls. But now: photographs of Sarah in her school uniform joking with classmates. Photographs of Sarah in the changing rooms, her pre-pubescent body pink and steaming from the shower.

I dropped the box and the photographs tipped out on to the filthy, fuel-stained floor. Then everything went blurred, and I didn't realise how much in danger I was until I vomited from the thick, black fumes. I'd set the damned garage on fire after all, in the midst of a rage that sent me spinning around the interior kicking holes in the carcasses, kicking out the headlights of the Midget, dragging all the cabinets and shelves down from the cracked, mushroom-mottled walls.

I dragged myself out and sucked in clean air. The heat was building. I could hear the pop and crack of glass and metal. Flames tongued the space around the shutters. I moved off before the whole row went up, and wondered what might be lurking inside each one. Nothing as grim as the thing I'd found. I thought about the visit I'd made to Cold Quay. The pathetic attempt I'd made to get under his skin. The way he'd flipped things around and tied me in knots. How he'd floored me without even trying. I should have gone for his eyes. I should have filed my fingernails to points and tried to rip his windpipe out before the screws could put themselves between us.

Romy and Tokuzo were leaning against the bonnet of the Saab when I got back, tongues chasing drips of chocolate and ice cream around the sticks in their hands. At any other time I might have made some kind of lascivious remark but now I just wanted to sit down with a hard drink and regain control of my heart.

'You look as if you've been wrestling with grease monkeys,' said Tokuzo.

'Did you find anything?' Romy asked.

'Some old friends,' I muttered. I didn't want to talk. 'Let's get you home,' I said.

I got the car started and ignored the rest of their questions. Soon they dried up and they concentrated on finishing their ice creams. The smell of it was making me sick. I put my foot down and we made it back to London in decent time.

I don't remember parking the car in the bays beneath Tokuzo's block. I don't remember going up to the flat, or putting my head down on the pillow. I should have eaten. I should have checked for danger. But after a day like that, I think I deserved just a little bit of oblivion.

PART THREE
GUET-APENS

20

I dreamed I was the guardian of a lighthouse in the midst of a terrifying storm. The rain was not rain but endless torrents of blood. Lightning was the finery in a network of veins, arteries and capillaries. Thunder, the combined screams of everyone on the planet who had ever succumbed to a killing blow. The beam of the lighthouse swept before a sea of tumbling bodies, and someone moved beneath it, in the cone of shadow, scuffling around the foot of the tower like a rat at a kitchen door.

The architect swung down from the ceiling like a giant bat, his face inches away from my own, inverted. He opened his mouth in a shocking smile; it looked like the horrible down-turned grimace of a great white shark. He said: *I know all the best hiding places.*

I jerked upright in bed and Mengele sprang away from me as if he'd been hit with a thousand volts. Breathe. Relax. Realise. Not bed. Tokuzo's sofa. Not Mengele, a cushion. I heard the reassuring ticks of the refrigerator and the chuckle of the broadband hub. I heard the ebb and flow of measured breath in the bedroom. I checked my watch. Six in the morning. Not as much sleep as I'd have liked, but sleep was getting in the way. I could sleep all I wanted when Tann was back in the slammer.

I lay there for a while trying to imagine what Sarah might do or what Tann might do if they were to meet. I wondered if Sarah would be able to deal with it, with him. *It won't come to that*, I thought. And she was smart. Street smart especially, but any other kind there was too. I thought of how she had made that den for herself on Silex Street. The nerve of her. I couldn't have done that when I was her age. I don't think I could cook at her age.

Thinking of Silex Street reminded me of what I'd found there. I fished in my pocket for my wallet and retrieved the train ticket. Bedford. What was in Bedford?

Lorraine had a bookcase given over to various Ordnance Survey maps she'd collected over the years. I picked one of them out and peered at the UK map on the back. Bedford. Bedford.

I felt myself go cold. Of course, whenever I'd visited, I'd gone by car. Sarah couldn't drive, or didn't have access to a car. So she went by train. From Bedford to Cold Quay was a twenty-minute taxi drive. Why else would she be in Bedford? There had to be some other reason. She wouldn't go to see that fucker. Not in a million years.

Why not? You did.

I had good reason.

Did you? Maybe she does too.

What possible reason would she have to go and visit the person who put her mum in the ground?

To see his face. To make him see her face.

228

I showered and got dressed and raided Tokuzo's fridge for breakfast. I had barely eaten a crumb the previous day. I was so hungry I could have eaten the arse out of a low-flying pigeon. I stuffed crackers and bananas in my pockets and gave head to a third of apple pie straight from its tray. Coffee I could grab on the lam.

I wrote a quick note and left it on the table.

Stay here. Stay safe. Call if aggro. I'll come back soon. J.

At the bedroom door I listened to them breathing some more, and felt an ache at the thought that once upon a time I had lain with both of these women and my own sleeping breath had mingled with theirs. And because of me, they were together now. I'd caused an awful lot of the fear in their veins.

I needed therapy. How do people get on with their lives, when their colours are nailed to the danger mast? Maybe they didn't. Maybe the domesticity was a sham. Because you can't switch off. Switching off is inviting trouble.

I got down to the ground floor and stood at the lift door for a while, checking the area. I don't know what I was expecting to find, but after last night's lax showing, I felt I needed to demonstrate a touch more diligence. Nobody around.

I texted Mawker:

on my way 2 see u – at nsy?

He texted back:

like fuk u r fuk off busy.

I texted back:

tuff shitz

I added a grinning dog turd emoji and walked the two

229

minutes to King's Cross Tube. I was at New Scotland Yard within half an hour. At Reception I asked for my favourite detective chief superintendent and waited outside by the revolving cheese.

'I told you I was busy,' he squawked. He was holding a case file and a coffee. He was wearing a grey shirt with hoops of sweat under the armpits that you could have fit a basketball through.

'You and me need a talk,' I said. Maybe the way I said it, without any added snark for a change, caught him off balance. He gave me an odd look, as if I'd complimented him, and then he tucked the file under his arm and told me to follow him.

We went up to his office and he poured me a cup without asking. I'd seen that before. It was a gathering technique. He was creating a buffer of time in which to consider all possible angles and possibilities regarding this visit. But he knew why I was here.

'I imagine you want to know how the manhunt is getting along,' he said, offering me the steaming cup of ground winnets.

'Yes and no,' I said. 'And I'm not drinking that. Put some down for the rats.'

'What do you want?'

Muscles were jumping all over me. What I really wanted was to pick up one of his office chairs and launch it through the window.

'Those words on the case file you gave me. Whether you wrote them or not. "GT visits".'

'If "visits" is what it meant.'

'Fuck off, Ian. "GT visits". And you know it. Because you made them.'

'What?'

'You were visiting Graeme Tann in Cold Quay. Admit it. Why?'

'Who told you that?'

'It doesn't matter who told me that. I'm a private investigator. I investigated. I found something out.'

'I might have gone to Cold Quay a couple of times. But not necessarily to see Tann.'

'Not necessarily? Why then? It's miles away from this little misery pit. What business did you have at a high-security prison? What possible reason could you have?'

He sipped his coffee, saw the light, grimaced and put it down. He put his hands on his hips. He looked like a shit supply teacher who's had a bad day and is about to tear into the disrespectful kids he's been trying to marshal for the past hour.

'You don't want to know.'

I shut my eyes and sighed. She wouldn't. She wouldn't. Please, God, don't let it be her. I opened them again and there was the red mist. I walked over to him, close enough to smell his coffee breath and the drenched polyester, ingrained with perspiration notes from years ago when he bought his shirt, quite possibly third-hand, from Corpse Reclamation Threads Ltd. My nerves were tighter than a porn star's G-string.

'I do want to know, Ian,' I said. 'And I want to know now.'

'You don't want to know now. Or ever.'

I got hold of him and he got hold of me. We wrestled like that for a while, trying to gain traction but we were both wearing shit shoes on a shit surface and we slid and grunted around like seals on ice in mating season.

'Why were you at Cold Quay?' I said. 'On the day it burned.'

231

'Leave it, Joel.'

I'd never hit him before. We'd always had those moments of close proximity pull me-push you. He'd headbutted me once. There was always a spice there, the potential for a ruckus. So I thought, *Fuck it. Risk arrest. It will be worth it to see him walking around with gaps in his teeth and a black eye.* Credit to him, as he sat there spitting blood between his lips, he didn't threaten me with a cell. He got up and came for me. He's sprightlier than you'd think, Mawker. He thudded a couple into my ribs, including the one that Henry had been playing notes on earlier, but it was fuelled with breakfast baps and p.m. pints. He was already out of breath and I'd suddenly lost the appetite for it. I just wanted his version of events and I wasn't going to get it if he was having a coronary, or trying to speak through a mouthful of gore.

I slapped his fists away and slammed my forearm into his throat, pinned him to the wall. I planted my thigh between his legs so he couldn't swing a limb at me.

'Talk to me,' I said.

He struggled against it for a while, his little eyes bulging like dumplings that had failed to rise in a pale stew, but he wasn't going anywhere. I felt his straining muscles suddenly crumple.

'Get off,' he said.

I stepped away and he pulled back a chair and sat down. He dabbed at his face with a handkerchief. Then he opened a drawer and pulled out a plastic bag. Inside was a large book, or what remained of it. It was partially charred.

'What's that?' I asked.

'Visitors book,' he said. 'Cold Quay.'

I didn't recognise it, but then the flames had been at it. My signature would be in there somewhere.

'Quaint,' I said. 'What's the story?'

He didn't say anything. He took the book out and pushed it across the desk. The sour smell of carbon. The cover flaked a little under my fingers.

'Never mind,' he said. 'It's not evidence. Not really.'

I opened it up. 'What am I looking for?' but I knew full well.

He stood up and poured more coffee. He went to the window and looked down at Broadway. Sip and stare. He wasn't saying anything else to me.

I flipped through the book. It was a hefty tome and had been initiated three years previously. First-page visitors included deliveries from Parcelforce, a visit from a local politician and a dentist. I flicked through the rest of the book. I found my name from the visit I'd made earlier in the year.

I turned pages. And here... of course. That date. That black anniversary. Sarah had come to Cold Quay prison.

I stared at her name and her signature. Sarah Sorrell. I felt a hit of happiness, despite the horror and confusion and hurt, that she'd kept my name.

'Sarah came to see him,' I said.

'Yes, she did. It wasn't the only time.'

Her name cropped up on the following pages. Weekly visits. 'When did you find out about this?'

'Not that long ago. You were still in hospital. When I came in to see you I overheard the duty sergeant talking to his shift replacement about a rumour that was knocking about. That Beauty was going to see the Beast.'

'And you didn't think to tell me?'

'It's none of my business. She's an adult. She can do what she likes.'

'It's *my* business though, isn't it? I've been searching for her for years, Ian. My life has been put on hold.'

'I thought I was doing the right thing in protecting you from this.'

'You couldn't stop her?'

'I told you, she can do what she likes.'

'Ian… Jesus Christ.' I threw the book on the floor. All the strength had collapsed out of me. I felt hollow, carved open like a Halloween pumpkin. 'I don't know what to do. I don't… What am I supposed to do?'

'Is this you asking me for advice?'

'No. It was a rhetorical question.'

He put his shit coffee down and sat in his chair.

'What a mess,' he said.

'What if he's out there, looking for her? What if he's found her? These visits… she could have inadvertently clued him up as to where she was living. And then the riot. He's out and he's got reciprocity on his mind.'

'There's nothing we can do,' he said. 'We don't know where he is. We don't know where she is. Everything is ifs and maybes.'

'What about his other visitors?'

'He had one or two, over the years. Nutters and freakshows in the main. A couple who were after mementos. One girl hitched down from Hull, fresh from college, wanted to marry him. We checked them all out. No joy.'

I sighed and the sound was the rattle of air through an old man. 'What did she want from him? What could she possibly get out of visiting him?'

I stood up. I had to get moving. That I didn't know where only made me more restless. I felt as though I'd been chasing ghosts, stains in the air, bruises in the memory. People who'd experienced some tangential involvement with Tann, like the way a moth will leave a tracing of its golden dust on the skin if it brushes you. This dust was coal black though, and it settled in the soul, a mark of Cain.

'I should get back to them,' I said.

'Who?'

'Romy and Lorraine. I picked them up from Heathrow last night. They worry they're being followed.'

'Let me take you,' Mawker said. 'I'll arrange for a plainclothes to hang about.'

The thought of going back on public transport was pretty grim, grimmer than sitting next to Mawker and his collection of cheap food stains. But I thanked him, and I meant it, and we headed for the car pool. I was feeling pretty bad about strong-arming the guy, though I was sure I'd get over it pretty qui—

The plainclothes was a woman wearing Gucci, Kevlar and a Glock 26. She introduced herself as Officer Stephanie Bradley. She was twenty years in the force and looked tougher than a dog toy. East London, mainly, with the Territorial Support Group and, later, with various crime and intelligence squads before her current position in SCO19. We all said hello as we piled into an unmarked Volvo S60 in the basement car pool. The car was being driven by a guy called Creamer, po-faced and fifty-something in a black leather jacket.

When Creamer swung into York Way I told him to lay off the pedal.

'Wait here,' I said.

'I'll come with you,' said Bradley.

I led her towards the junction of Caledonia Street. There was a black Mercedes, a C-class coupé, positioned at the eastern end of it. Two figures inside.

'I didn't see them earlier,' I said.

'Black Merc,' said Bradley. 'Are you sure? There's not a lot of them about.'

'You're right,' I said, admiring her sarcasm. 'Could be nothing. Black alloys though, see. Romy said the car had black wheels.'

'Might be something, then. No harm in being ultra cautious.'

'If they've been following me since Heathrow, why didn't they follow me to Scotland Yard?'

'Maybe they did.'

'I took the Tube to St James's,' I said.

'Maybe someone on foot.'

'In which case we lost him coming back,' I said. 'Unless he followed us in a cab and that would mean he'd know which car we were in coming out of Plod Central... sorry.'

'I've been called worse.'

I just wanted to go up to the Merc and tap on the window and ask them to stop playing silly buggers, let's all be friends and chat about what was up. If only life was so simple. If only I was so reasonable.

'How do you want to play it?' she asked.

'We can't let on that we've spotted them,' I said. 'They'll lose us or we'll catch them. Either way, they're not leading us to Tann. So how about I go in, tell Lorraine and Romy what's what, then you can watch them and the entrance while I drive the twit twins around town for a few hours till they get bored. Mawker and his chauffeur can keep tabs on them from behind. At some point one or both of them is going to have to knock off. Maybe they'll go back to the place where Tann is hiding out.'

'I guess so,' she said. 'But if they're here for you, what's to stop them gunning you down in the street?'

'Broad daylight. Busy. I reckon they're waiting for their moment. They've seen what happens when they come at me blazing. Tann's running out of goons. He needs to make it count soon otherwise it's just him and me.'

'You hope.'

'There is an element of that, I agree.'

'Everyone would feel a whole lot happier if I was with you.'

'Sudden girlfriend? Since when? They'd notice something was whiffy and scarper. Anyway, you're here for them,' I said, tilting my head at Tokuzo's apartment block. 'Let Mawker know what I'm up to. Tell him to get another car out here in case they split up. He won't like it, but then he doesn't like anything. And then come up to the flat.'

'I'll speak with him, but I'm walking up that road ahead of you first. I'd rather I was the human shield than some innocent bystander, just in case they do think fuck it and start firing.'

'Done.'

She moved off and I counted to ten and sauntered after her. She angled across the street and I followed, and then there was some more traffic turning in and a mother with a buggy and I was able to breathe easier. They were staying in the car. Unless they wanted tons of collateral and a shoot-out to the death, they were being careful. Which was nice to know. I could do with a break from legging it through construction sites.

I turned into the apartment block entrance and took the lift up to Lorraine's floor. I let myself in and they were sitting together on the sofa watching TV. Tokuzo had packed a case that stood by the door in case they had to bug out fast.

'Good thinking,' I said. I told them about Bradley, that she was nice and good. Much more professional than me, at least. I didn't hang about. I saw questions crystallising in their eyes and to talk was to instil doubt. The less they knew, the less they could fret. It wasn't ideal, but we were beyond that. Ideal was long gone, if it had ever even been here.

I got back to ground level and sneaked a peek. Car still there. Figures still seated in the front. Too long now for them to be waiting for a mate who just wanted to nip to the cashpoint or buy a paper.

In the unpopulated basement I walked to the Saab, head down, thinking about Romy. For some reason, by the time I was at the door, I was fantasising about her in a green and yellow bikini, beckoning to me from a sun lounger, loosening the ties at the back, asking me to rub sun cream on her.

When this was over I was dragging her off on holiday with me. I wouldn't take no for an answer. Tokuzo too, if she wanted to come and nobody thought it too weird. I went to grab the handle. And stopped. A spasm in the watch-it gland. Something. Not. Right.

I'd not believed a word of what I said to Bradley, about the people after me – the killers – and how they might not want to create a scene. I was trying to convince myself of something that they wouldn't think twice about. Why was that? Maybe they were innocents after all. There were any number of reasons a car would hang about on the street. Maybe it had broken down and they were waiting for help. They were picking up their mum to take her to the seaside and she was *still* getting ready. Hell, they could be undercover cops themselves and we'd all laugh about this later over pints at the Two Chairmen.

I looked behind me, hoping to see a shadow duck down behind another car, but as I'd already observed, there was nobody around. The car park was empty. Something wrong with the Saab then. But it looked fine. I walked its length, running my hand over its lines. What was itching at me?

I peered through the windows into the back seat. I'd seen enough horror films to warn me about unwanted visitors lurking in the rear footwell, ready to pop up and have their wicked way before third gear.

I took a breath and walked back to the lift. When I got down here I was fine. By the time I got to the car I was edgy. Re-enactment.

Romy in a bikini. More curves than a pure maths textbook. Green and yellow fabric. I'd never seen her in a bikini before, let alone one that looked like a lemon and lime confection. A bit like that tiny piece of earth wire sleeve lying on the floor. Hello.

I picked it up and returned to the car.

I got to my knees and had a look underneath. I went at it from every angle. Couldn't see anything attached. There was no obvious tampering going on there. I thought about the wheel arches and checked those, feeling softly with my fingertips. Passenger side front, nothing. Driver's side front... fuck.

Something metallic that wasn't meant to be there. Something that felt like magnets. Wires looping. I withdrew my hand and smelled my fingers. Oily, plasticky. I was put in mind of hot bitumen. But there was something sweet underneath it that reminded me of ripe plums. Whatever the fuck it was, it wasn't supposed to be in the wheel arch of a thirty-year-old Saab.

I don't know much about bombs, but I know they get very hot and very loud very quickly and tend to instantaneously shred anything meat-based within the immediate vicinity. I guessed the stooges in the car outside were waiting for some kind of evidence that their IED had me DOA. I guessed that the reason the bomb was on the driver's side as opposed to, say, under the fuel tank, was because it was a focused device meant to detonate in a localised area, i.e. pretty much right under my arse, in order to ensure I wouldn't survive the blast.

I called Mawker and told him my happy news. He swore for a while and I heard his muffled voice while he put the phone down and barked at Creamer, or someone on the other end of the police radio.

'I say we go in hard on those clowns in the Merc,' he said. 'Get them in solitary and sweat some info.'

I thought about that. It might work. It might not. If it worked it might not be instantly; it might take hours that we didn't have. And that was allowing for a peaceful capitulation. There was every chance an armed unit squealing on to the scene would be met with heavy resistance and possible injury to innocent bystanders. And at the end of it all I'd still be so far away from Sarah and so far away from Tann. I was in a perpetual state of running towards or running away. I was sick of running. I hated cross country at school and I didn't see why I should still be doing it now, when I was a grown-up able to make decisions for myself.

'Maybe I should die,' I said.

'Music to my ears,' Mawker said, 'but I don't follow.'

'Yes you do. Think about it. That bomb goes off, and we cart a body bag out to the ambulance. Let Laurel and Hardy think it's me. Maybe they'll go hurrying back to Master for their pat on the head.'

'We can't let the bomb go off,' Mawker said. 'People die when bombs go off. We have no idea how powerful it is.'

'It can't be that powerful otherwise they wouldn't be sitting fifty feet away in a tin box twiddling their fingers. If *they* have anything to do with it. We still don't know for sure.'

'Then we channel the blast somehow. Angle it so it's away from the street. Or time it so there's no passersby, so the fucking ceiling doesn't fall in.'

'But we have to do it soon while the car park's empty,' I said.

I heard him on the blower, summoning bodies. 'We'll meet you in the basement,' he said, and ended the call.

I was hopping about, unable to relax. I'd never been in close proximity to so many pounds of boom before, unless you counted the arse of Curryboy Caxton, who was an accident waiting to happen during my years at college. I tried to relax. Everything was in hand.

Presumably Mawker would get on to Bradley and have the concierge close off resident access to the car park and ensure the apartments above were cleared out. No vehicles to come in the front way unless IQs suddenly plummeted and helicopters swooped into the main drag carrying abseiling muppets wearing Bomb Squad T-shirts. Everything would arrive at the service bays to the rear.

The bomb couldn't be on a timer because there was no knowing when I'd return to it. Ditto a remote trigger because they couldn't see the car, unless they'd set up a camera or a microphone – and they hadn't because they'd have pressed the button as soon as they heard me on the phone to Mawker. Which meant it was primed to explode when the door was opened or the engine was started or maybe when the accelerator was depressed or a certain speed was attained. If it was the latter, then this little ruse would fail. Maybe they were in the car in order to follow me, waiting for that magic number to be reached. Otherwise they might as well sit on a roof, or watch from across the street, anonymous among the dozens of pedestrians buzzing around St Pancras.

I wiped sweat away from my forehead and waited.

Mawker was the first to arrive. 'You touched anything?'

'I had a fondle, yes.'

'And you're sure it's a bomb?'

'On second thoughts it could have been an armadillo holding some marzipan.'

'You touched it. Well that was fucking stupid. It could have gone off.'

He went on about various things, such as responsibility and keeping a cool head. I let him have his rant because he's one of those people who needs to fill space with his Ian-ness, whether it be gob or gabardine. He wasn't paying attention to me or what he was saying. His eyes were flicking all over the place as if he'd been given a thirty-second pass to the room of a hundred nude women.

Half a dozen EOD technicians in bomb suits filtered into the parking area. I was shepherded away with Mawker to the upper floor and told to wait while they were briefed with the plan. I watched various pieces of equipment disappearing through the doors including blasting initiators, protective blankets, bomb chambers, mirrors and detectors. A robot was wheeled in looking none too chuffed. A voice squawked on the radio that an ambulance was standing by. I saw a body bag stuffed to appear as if it was filled with a corpse dumped in the corridor, waiting to go on stage. A chill swept through me.

'Let's go,' Mawker said.

We went to the ground floor and moved through service areas to the rear of the building where Creamer was waiting across the street in the Volvo.

'What if there's a third man watching out?' I asked. 'It would make sense.'

'We have to assume not,' said Mawker. 'There's nothing we can do about it now.'

I recced the drag nevertheless, as we hurried over to the car and got in. We drove around to the west end of Caledonia Street. The black Merc was still positioned at the other end. Patience of saints, or more likely ultra-thick yes-men.

Another ten minutes and Mawker got a call from the EOD guys that the bomb had been identified. It wasn't a whopper. It wouldn't bring the building down. But it would take my legs off given half a chance. They had taken the necessary steps to channel the blast so that it caused minimal internal damage without stifling its effect. They were waiting for Mawker's signal to detonate.

'We have to wait for the street to clear,' Mawker said. 'We've got civvies dawdling with cups of coffee and a cyclist at the moment. Give us a sec.'

Each time it looked as though we could patch through a green light, a car or a van turned into the street. We couldn't create any kind of blockage or diversion because it was too risky. People stopped to look when that happened. Traffic started to build up elsewhere, which inevitably meant car horns. The moment a crowd gathered, the Merc men would notice and take off, no matter how thick they might be. Hence we'd evacuated people by dribs and drabs. They'd separate and scarper to one of any number of safe locations, well away from where we wanted them to go. So we sat on our hands, and we bit our tongues. And waited.

And then Mawker was on the radio, shouting '*GO! GO! GO!*' but before he'd finished there was a great lick of orange

243

fire that spurted from an underground grate, and a manhole cover came spinning out of the road like a coin toss by God, followed a split second later by the roar of the explosion.

'Fucking hell!' said Mawker, not unreasonably.

'That was *contained*?' I asked.

But he was on the radio, checking for casualties. Voices flooded back. Everyone fine. 'Sounded worse than it was... That was what you wanted, wasn't it?'

'Keep an eye on that Merc,' said Mawker to the driver. 'As soon as he leaves you give it some welly.'

The figures remained in the car, and in position. That, at least, erased any lingering doubts that they might not have any involvement in the bombing. Sirens and alarms were going off all over the place. People were screaming and running away. People were standing around filming the fire on their mobile phones.

The ambulance tore past us and parked obliquely across both lanes.

'The fuckholes,' Mawker said. He was on the radio barking orders but the ambulance crew were in emergency mode. A fire engine turned up. Police cars blocked the road behind us. At the other end of the road I could just see enough of the Merc to know they had a clear getaway should they be satisfied that I'd died in the blast.

'We have to move,' I said to Creamer. 'Get us out of this fucking jam.'

But he argued that if he took us on to the pavement we'd be right up the backside of the Merc and it might spook them.

'Everyone's fucking spooked,' I said. 'What does it matter? Do it!'

'Hang on,' Mawker said. 'We have to wait for the body bag. Otherwise they might not see it.'

We waited for an interminable time, but I guess they had to play the fake right. If they wheeled 'me' out too soon, it would look wonky and they might smell a rat.

Ten minutes. Fifteen. Sirens descending like holy hell.

Movement. My stunt double came rattling out of the doors.

'Shift it,' said Mawker as the Merc's exhaust trembled and breathed.

Creamer got the car on the pavement and we rounded the front of the ambulance just as another bunch of ambulance staff came rushing on to the pavement. Creamer stamped on the brakes. The Merc took off.

'Jesus fuck,' spat Mawker. 'Could this day fill up with any more shit?'

It could, because Creamer stalled the car the moment the path became clear again.

'You close that gap within twenty seconds,' said Mawker, 'or I'll have you out of the force before you know it. I'll make sure you have trouble getting a job cleaning cars, let alone driving the fuckers.'

Credit to him, Creamer sent the Volvo flying up the Caledonian Road.

'There they are,' said Mawker. 'The grievous little cunts. Do not lose them.'

Creamer eased back as we came within five hundred feet of the Merc, three cars between us. 'Shall I call a chopper in?' Creamer asked. 'Just in case?'

'No,' Mawker said. 'No excuses for them to abort whatever it is they're in the process of doing. You can atone for your sins, Mick.'

We followed them through Archway and Highgate towards Henlys Corner where the A1 meets the North Circular.

'Fuck's sake,' said Mawker. 'They're going for the motorway.'

'What did you expect?' I said. 'Tann in London? Hiding in plain sight? He'll be in some rancid little panic nest in Luton or Toddington.'

I was saying it but it didn't sound convincing to me. Part of me was kicking me in the pants telling me I knew exactly where he was, if I'd just cool my jets and apply cognitive reasoning. But I thought that about everything. My dumb brain gave me a kick in the pants to say Tokuzo could be tamed if I just gave her a back-rub and half a pound of Iberico ham.

'Come on, Creamer!' Mawker yelled. The Merc had scooted through the lights on red and we were stuck behind a conscientious driver with a green P sticker on the back of his Vauxhall. Mawker wound down the window. 'Oi, P for prick! Shift it. Now!' He sent out a few whoops on the police siren and the seas parted. By the time we got to Junction 1 the Merc was well gone.

'How about I put you on a charge?' Mawker blistered into Creamer's face from a distance of around one millimetre.

'How about I put you on your arse?' Creamer said.

Frost filled the car. Creamer turned the car around at Staples Corner and we shifted back through the diesel-stained streets of north London in a fine mist of rain. The wipers on the windscreen flailed occasionally and I found myself lulled by their infrequent rhythm, trying to anticipate when they'd swipe again. I slumped back in the seat and watched the windscreen load with moisture and the eventual
beat
of the wipers while Mawker and Creamer stewed in their juices like an old married couple who have bickered with

each other to the point of standstill and

beat

it became hypnotic, soporific, because the heat in the car had built from the tension and testosterone and I could go a five-minute nap, all things considered, despite

beat

losing the Merc and realising that my beautiful Saab was now nothing more than a ton of mangled memories. I closed my eyes and saw the shadow of the blade continue, left to right, then right to left. It reminded me of something and I was on a shingle beach and Becs was up ahead, hair whipping around her in the wind, her hand outstretched.

Come on, I'm fucking freezing.

The car's totalled.

Probably for the best. You'll have to make it up to Jimmy Two.

Shit. It was more his car than mine, really. He spent more time with it.

At the end of the day, it's just a tin box that takes you places. Slowly.

What are we doing here?

You tell me. This is your fantasy.

What if it was yours?

Bit Ed Al Poe, isn't it? Bit Twilight Zone?

My whole life is a bit *Twilight Zone.* How could it not be, with Mawker in it? I keep expecting his head to split open at any moment and some tentacled, many-mouthed thing to come slithering out.

You should go a bit easier on him.

See, this must be your fantasy. I wouldn't think that.

I think you'll end up together. Sitting in bed reading each other verses of erotic poetry.

Enough... We came here, didn't we, early on?

Your idea of a romantic day out.

Dungeness.

The tide was some distance off, a seam of pale grey that stitched the lead of the sky to the dun of the beach. Fishing boats trapped on the shingle faced the sea, their bows raised as if impatient to return. Collapsed light. The air was thick. It seemed to coat the beach in something you could tease back from the pebbles. We had photographs of all of this, in an album gathering dust and cat hairs back home, under the bed. And some things I couldn't collect. Explosions of static from the boats' radios. Her footsteps crunching through the shingle.

I remember the sea was affecting the light in some subtle way I had not recognised before, but my camera couldn't capture it. It erased an area above the horizon, a band of vague ochre that was perhaps full of rain, that shivered and crawled as if it might contain text, or the barest outline of it, some code to unpick. An explanation.

The beach was slowly burying its secrets. Great swathes of steel cable, an anchor that had lost its shape through the accretion of oxidant, cogs so large they might have something to do with the Earth's movement. All of it was slowly sinking into the endless shingle.

Us too if we don't keep moving.

Black flags whipping on the boats. They seemed too blasted by salt and wind to be up to the task of setting sail. White flecks on wave crests. It was getting rough out there. Small fishing boats tipped and waggled on the surf, bright and tiny against the huge expanses of blue-green pressing in all around them.

Rotting fish-heads and surgical gloves, thin, mateless

affairs flapping in the stones like translucent sea-creatures marooned by the tide. You notice how the shingle creeps over the toes of your boots; always the beach was in the process of sucking under, of burying.

I kissed you and I could taste salt on your mouth.

It's this way.

The strange, stunted vegetation like hunks of dried sponge or stained blotting paper trapped between the stones: sea campion, Babington's orache. Weatherboard cottages. A weird sizzle in the air, maybe from the power station or perhaps it was the taut lines of the night fishermen, buzzing with tension as lugworm and razor clam were cast into the creaming surf.

She moved ahead rising above another dune of pebbles. She waited for me, pointing. The moon was behind her. I couldn't see her face. And then I could. And then I couldn't. She was pointing at the lighthouse. When I got to her, she was still swaddled in dark but I could see the beam of the lighthouse coming again. Her voice, full of liquid: *Tōdai moto kurashi*. I didn't want to see her face this time. Because I knew it wouldn't be her standing next to me. I knew exactly who would be here in her stead.

I flew up out of that, swearing, sweating in the airless confines of the Volvo. Mawker and Creamer were gone. We were parked in a layby. I could see them up ahead standing in front of a caravan with a sign inviting motorists to try their *breakfast bap's, tea's and cofee's*. Mawker no doubt trying to wangle a free cuppa.

They came back and Mawker apologised, said he hadn't got me anything because I was sleepy bye-byes.

I waited until they stopped giggling about that, and then I said: 'I know where he is.'

21

Mawker was put out that he hadn't made the connection, I could see it in his furrowed brow and murmuring lips. That was the career copper in him. It didn't matter that we had some purpose, or that we might be an inch further along the road to saving Sarah's life. He was worried about the long game: the medals and citations that sparkled just beyond the finishing post. It hadn't gone unnoticed that when he got on the radio for backup, everything uttered was prefixed with 'I'.

'Of course,' he said now, as the car swept along the M1, somewhere north of Watford, 'there's no foundation to this. Just because some smart-dressed noodle-sucking doorman with nice hair signs off with some soppy platitude before he commits harry-carry, doesn't mean anything in my book.'

'That's because your book only ever has pictures in it,' I said. 'Of your mother with her tits out. And it's *harakiri*, you twannock.'

'Whatever,' he said. 'We're still pissing in the wind.'

'Fuck off, Ian,' I said. 'It's called following a lead.'

'It's called a waste of police resources.'

'If it's cold then blast me with both barrels. If there's something in it, then you'll take all the glory anyway. Win-win.'

'I'm not happy.'

'You're never happy. They say there's no such thing as bad pizza or bad sex. But I bet you've had both.'

'*Who* says?'

'Fuck knows,' I said. 'Your so-called parents.'

'That prison was razed to the ground,' he said. 'There's nothing left of it.'

'So why are there security guards on site?'

'I don't know. We didn't arrange it. NOMS set it up, maybe. It has to be watched, doesn't it? You don't want kiddies fannying around in there. Fucking death trap, isn't it?'

'Maybe,' I said. 'I think Henry wanted to help. At the last.'

'I think he wanted to put you off the scent.'

'Christ, Mawker. I'll go alone. Drop me here and go running back to your bosses at the Kremlin. See what they think about it.'

He went quiet but I could see he was still seething. He was going to get us into a sackful of trouble if he went in with his dander up. I wondered if I should risk arrest by knocking the fucker out. I'd rather take my chances just with Creamer than have Inspector Clouseau tagging along.

We got off the motorway at Aspley Guise and I directed Creamer to my bucolic parking spot. It was beginning to rain again. I wished I'd packed a hat and gloves. It was hellish cold after the heat of the Volvo.

'What have we got in here, weapon-wise?' I asked.

'This isn't an armed response vehicle, Sorrell,' Mawker said.

'Why not? We were responding. To people who are armed. Logic dictates—'

252

'Give it a rest,' he said. 'We've got handguns. And firepower is on its way.'

'What about me?'

'Talk them to death.'

So no gun safe. No carbines. No launcher. No fucking battering ram.

I led them through the trees to the area above the prison. It was gone four o'clock and the sky was heavily bruised. Lights were on in the Portakabin. We could see three or four figures in black moving around the grounds and the black Merc parked off road, on a swell of green a few feet away from where the cinders took over.

'Where's the backup?' I said.

'On its way,' said Mawker.

'So we what? We wait till they get here?'

'Looks like that,' said Creamer.

Both of their voices had lapsed into neutral police mode. Vapid faces. They could have been on duty at the reception of the local nick, filling out HORT/1 forms. I wanted them gone. Creamer waiting in the car and Mawker anywhere else, including up his own arsehole. I wanted time to think, to strategise. Company meant compromise, pressure and rushed decisions.

But really I wanted to be here alone, without any backup, because I didn't want anyone coming between me and Graeme Tann. I didn't want anybody to see what was going to happen to him.

'The place is fucked,' said Creamer. 'I can't see anywhere to hide.'

'That's just it,' I said. 'He's hiding in plain sight. Henry was right. The base of the lighthouse is dark. The light can't pick out anything below. And he's in its shadow.'

'How can you be sure?'

'We'd have had him by now,' Mawker said, which was a bit cocky of him, and not necessarily true, but at least it meant that he was coming around to agreeing with my hunch.

'When it's full dark,' I said, 'I'm going to nip down there and have a look around, see if I can find a prime spot to get in. You need to keep wat—'

'No you're not,' said Mawker. 'Creamer can do it.'

'But this is my play,' I said, hating the whine in my voice. 'My collar.'

'Your collar,' scoffed Mawker. 'You can't "collar" if you're not one of us. Be a good boy and sit tight. Otherwise I'll have you taken back to Broadway and you can wait for me there.'

'Ian. I have to see him.'

'Why?' he asked, his face darting into mine, searching my expression. 'I know exactly what you'll do, or try to do, and it's a good job we're here to pull on your leash.'

'Nobody need ever know,' I said.

'Need know what?' he said.

I looked at him and I looked at Creamer. I'd already said too much, but he wanted me to fall into the hole. I backed down. There was nothing to be gained by pushing Mawker's buttons, or suggesting he throw away the rule book and go rogue, apart from a couple of hours in a holding cell while they tidied up here, put Tann in a different cage and then I would be back to square one.

'Fuck it,' I said, and went into sulk mode.

They talked about possible ways forward, all of them unimaginative, suicidal. I couldn't hear anything in the way of backup and half an hour had gone by. No police helicopters. No TAU vans.

'What's going on, Mawker?' I asked. 'Where's the cavalry?'

'Shut it,' he said. And then a weird crack of sound. I saw red in his eyes, and then I saw red in Creamer's eyes. And then there was red in my eyes: Creamer's blood, because half his face had snapped off and he went down a second later, like an actor in a play who suddenly realises his death moment has arrived.

'Fuck!' Mawker yelled. And he kept yelling it. I got to him and shoved my hand over his face, but everything was slicked with Creamer's blood and I couldn't gain purchase. I dragged him back into the trees. He had the shakes, proper convulsions, and getting him to calm down, to focus, was becoming impossible. He was lashing out, crying, foaming at the mouth. I slapped him hard across the face and his head snapped back and connected with a tree trunk. Maybe he'd been knocked out but I wasn't so lucky. At least it shocked some calm into him. He sat there breathing hard and staring at me with a look that was either *Who the fuck are you?* or *Do that again and you're dead.*

'That was a sniper,' I said.

'A sniper?' His voice was all wrong, like something filtered through tons of cracked ice.

'Yes. Laser-guided. Creamer is dead. We need to move.'

'Move?'

'Yes, move. They know we're here. We have to do something right now or Tann will be away.'

'A sniper?'

I shared his bafflement – it was rare to come across sniper rifles of any kind in crime (organised or otherwise) in this country, let alone a marksman skilled enough to use one – but now was not the time to play Criminal Intelligence Analysts.

'Ian, they're coming.'

I grabbed him by the scruff of the neck and hauled him upright. Beams of light – I counted four before we shifted our arses – were sweeping across the grass, coming in our direction. Maybe half a mile off. I heard the bark of a dog. Christ.

We moved Creamer into the cover of the trees but it was pointless. The bubbles exploding from what was left of his face were death rattles. He was beyond help. I frisked him and took his Glock 17. He also had a Taser on him. I pocketed that too. On his leg he wore a sheathed knife, very much not standard police issue – a deep-bellied, drop point hunting blade with an ugly little gut hook. I heard my body singing its usual requiem at the sight of it, and was of a mind to leave it where it was, but they seemed to be carrying lots of interesting equipment so I reasoned that we needed to be as tooled up as possible. Finally I dragged his jacket off him and, much to Mawker's voluble disgust, mopped up a goodly amount of Creamer's blood with it.

'Let's go,' I told Mawker, and trailing the jacket behind us, we vanished into the trees.

22

Now I knew what it must have felt like for those prisoners on Red Row in the hours immediately after the prison fell. Fugitive life. Torchlight criss-crossed like duelling blades, bringing the limbs of the trees into eerie, dancing detail. It was too much for the wildlife. Owls and bats turned the night to ribbons. God knows what shuffled in the bracken. The dog – I thought, I hoped it was one dog – was barking as if at an audition for a reality show called *Shouty Animals*. It didn't seem any closer than before, but it didn't matter. It was an obstacle we would have to negotiate at some point; it wasn't just going to give up, or suddenly start behaving like something else, like a squirrel or a goldfish. I just wanted to put it off the scent for a while, to grant us some space in which to do what we had to do.

Mawker wasn't saying anything. I think he might have been in shock over the jacket versus face moment, which I'd executed with all the reverence with which a parent flannels a shitty toddler arse. More likely his silence was due to him being knackered. Ian Mawker is one of those coppers trapped in the 1970s. A career copper. In early, home late, if at all. If he'd married, he'd have been divorced by now, perhaps multiple times. A full English every morning and when dinner swung around it would invariably consist of something with chips. Bottle of whisky in the desk drawer. Give him his due, he didn't smoke, but he ate Rennies as if they were Jelly Tots and his temper oscillated somewhere between 'fucking furious' and 'bring me someone's head'. The only exercise I saw him partake of, other than lifting pints, was climbing in or out of the car or tonguing his superiors' perineums.

'Where are we going?' he managed to gasp.

'Away,' I said.

'I love... how you get... so chatty... under duress.'

'Do you need a piss?'

'What?'

I slowed to a jog. 'I said, do you need a piss?'

'What makes you think I haven't already? And shat myself. Fucking snipers. Fucking running around in the dark like kids at fucking Halloween.'

'Just go over there, will you? I'll go this way. Have a slash – jet it all over the place – and get back here, quick as.'

I didn't hang around to draw him a diagram or put up with any of his inevitable pulling rank shit, but moved off our trajectory and, dropping Creamer's jacket, unleashed the Kraken and urinated lustily. I hadn't been for a while and I hadn't imbibed my statutory eight glasses of water so what came out of me steamed like stewed leather. You could probably have picked it up and skipped with it.

Mawker was waiting for me, jogging on the spot. I started laughing and couldn't stop. No matter how indignant he became, or how many serious matters he invoked – Creamer's violent death chief among them – it only served to crease me

258

up even more. Only the sound of the dog (much closer now, I suspected it had been let off its leash) got me moving, but I still couldn't stop corpsing.

'What's so funny?' he asked.

'Nothing,' I said. 'Everything.'

'Creamer's not laughing.'

'No, but he's not listening to any more of your shit either. Swings and roundabouts, isn't it?' I stared at the trees. Boughs creaking. Branches tapping against each other. Leaf mould squelching underfoot.

'You hear anything?' I asked.

'Nothing relevant,' he said.

'What's the story about those guards?' I asked. 'When do security guards carry sniper rifles?'

'When they're not security guards.'

'You had a say in who took over here, right? After the investigation?'

'What investigation? We were here for six hours and then we got the call from above to piss off at speed. Money being wasted fannying around with magneta flake and squirrel brushes and photographs of broken windows. *How* not important. *Why* not important. Get out in the fields and find the fuckers. So you do. And you assume the site has been secured. It's what happens.'

'Not here.'

'Well, maybe it was. And then maybe Tann's men moved in and overpowered them. We'll find the bona fides tied up in the back of a Transit van when all the shit's been sieved out of this situation.'

'Tann's men.'

'I don't know for sure, but it looks that way.'

We moved. By my estimate we were roughly parallel with

the northernmost end of the prison grounds. If we dumped Creamer's jacket nearby we'd hopefully, in addition to the diversionary piss, have gained a little bit of time in which to remain maul-free and clean up this whole mess.

It didn't work out like that. Not quite. We were nearing the edge of the trees, cautious, watching out for that lethal red beam, when there was a horrible chopping sound and Mawker started screaming to wake the dead.

'Shut the fuck up,' I hissed, over and over, not realising that he couldn't hear me because he was in the depths of a pain so bad it made my bruised rib look like a luxury.

His ankle was a mess of red. I thought I could see bone when I shone a light into it, but I wasn't sure, and anyway, I killed the light to stop me from seeing too closely. He'd stepped in a fucking trap. A bear trap, a fox trap... whatever it was. It was designed to kill small things or incapacitate big things.

'What is it?' he yelped, his voice all strangled. I hunted around for a fallen branch, mainly to try to prise the jaws of the thing open, but more likely to beat him senseless if he didn't stop caterwauling.

'Fuck's sake, Ian,' I said. ''Tis but a flesh wound.'

He screamed at me and I had to cover his mouth with my hand. 'Okay,' I said. 'Okay. Breathe. Think of your happy place.'

I started trying to jam sticks into the jaws of the mechanism, but it quickly became clear that I needed something a bit more robust than the odd twig. And clearly Mawker didn't have a happy place, because he wouldn't stop mewling.

I could hear the thump of paws coming closer. The attempts to put the dog off the scent had failed miserably. Which was okay, I reckoned, as long as the handlers were still some distance behind.

I managed to wrench the jaws of the trap open sufficiently for Mawker to swing his foot free. He clenched it with his hands, which served only to increase his pain as far as I could see.

I checked the wound again. It was ugly and deep, but no major blood vessels had been damaged. The worst that might happen was infection if we didn't get it cleaned soon.

'I'll be back as soon as I can,' I said.

'Don't go,' he said. 'You can't leave me here.'

'You've got a gun, Ian,' I said. 'Point it at bad things.'

'Joel, please.'

'Stop it,' I said. 'You know I've got to go. You'll be okay. It might be fractured but you're not going to bleed out. And backup will be here s—'

'There's no backup.'

I could hear voices behind us, but they were far off and they seemed to be moving away. They'd followed the piss, it seemed. We had some time. Maybe enough for me to throttle this granite prick of a human being.

'We were going to do this without help?' I said.

His words were tight and shallow between teeth that kept gritting together. 'It's not going so well for me,' he said. 'At work... I've been overlooked on a couple of promotions. Brass have had me on the carpet over my conduct. Tardiness. And my drinking—'

I couldn't believe what I was hearing. We were sweating like pigs in the middle of the killing fields, one dead body already and a broken leg. Dogs and fuckers hot on our heels. And he was doing a career evaluation.

'You wanted to Rambo it and take all the glory,' I said. 'That's what it boils down to.'

'Come on, Sorrell,' he said. 'We can do this. Look at what

we've achieved so far. What has he got left? A couple of lifers sitting in their own shit?'

I stared at him. The man was mad. 'We don't know how many people are involved,' I said. 'He could have hostages—'

'No missing person reported. All prison guards accounted for. No demands made.'

'Yet,' I said. 'What about the kosher security? Sarah? He could have Sarah in chains.'

'Don't be fucking ridiculous,' he said. His face contorted; he wrapped his hand around his shattered ankle. I felt like treading on it. 'She visited him of her own volition.'

'It might look like that,' I said. 'But that manipulative cunt could have been employing any number of dirty tricks to get her here. He could have drugged her. Hypnotised her.'

'Listen to yourself,' he said.

'All right,' I said. 'Blackmail then. Bribery. Maybe he was teasing her with her mother's last words. Whatever it was. It must have been something. Why else would she visit her mother's killer?'

'Just give me your arm,' he said. 'Get me out of these fucking woods at least.'

'And into the sniper's sights? I'm sorely tempted,' I said.

'Leave me here and I'll die,' he said. 'It's cold. I'm wearing two layers. Both of them of shit quality. I'm in shock. You do the math.'

'Maths,' I said. 'It's maths. And the only maths I've got is you plus me equals eternities of fucking woe.'

I shrugged myself out of my jacket and hurled it at him. 'Get blood on that and I'll hold the fucking dog while it chews you a swathe of new arseholes,' I said. 'And if there isn't backup here ASAP there'll be arseholes upon arseholes. Do it, Ian. Do it fucking *now*.' Then I left, ignoring his pleas and threats.

I moved towards the wash of light rising from the sodium lamps that were arranged around the Portakabin. I could hear the rhythmic grunting of the generators again now. When the dog leapt for me I was slightly off balance, negotiating mud and a bank of earth and loose stones. I went down and the dog, perhaps unprepared for that, went scrabbling over the top of me. I felt a claw punch me in the jaw as it tried to gain purchase. I put out my hands to thrust it away and I hit a flank of solid muscle. Short hair. Heavier than a suitcase filled with bricks. This was no standard security animal – no German shepherd. This was a pit bull, nearly eighty pounds, a bullet of muscle and teeth. I'd given Mawker my leather jacket so now I no longer had anything I could use as an effective barrier between its teeth and my flesh.

It came for me, eyes rolled back in its head so I could see only white. Its massive jaws gaped open, revealing a calcium arsenal that could quite easily rip my face from my skull. I kicked out at it, but that only served to temporarily divert it: this beast was not going to give up. I was fucked unless I did something quick, incisive and permanently lethal.

It found its feet and set itself way quicker than I did. It came again. I slapped and kicked at its slavering chops, but one kick failed to meet its target and it sank its teeth into the meat of my calf. I was lucky. I'd understood that pit bulls lock their jaws when they've got hold of something savoury. Nothing will get it to let go, short of death and a pair of pliers. It seemed that this dog wasn't happy unless its teeth were in the optimum position, so it let go for a second. When it lurched to bite again, I rammed a branch between us. The dog growled; I guessed it wouldn't be up for a game of fetch.

I didn't know how to play this out. I'd heard other

stories about dogs. That if you could get them into a certain position and pull their forelegs apart, you could basically tear their hearts in two. I wasn't sure how likely this was. I didn't want to use the gun because it would serve only to attract the attention of people who were drifting away from the chase. And then I remembered Creamer's knife.

Please don't let me have stowed it in the pocket of my leather jacket... no, here it was, in its sheath, tucked into a back pocket of my jeans. The dog was at arm's length; I'd been able to lodge a spur of the branch into the leather collar around its neck. It wasn't coming any closer unless I dropped it, or its strength proved to be, as I suspected it might, supercanine.

I fiddled with the sheath, trying to get it away from the blade with my teeth without losing my grip on the branch or slicing my lips off. I managed it, finally, and I shut the dog up quick. I wiped the knife on my jeans and hung the dog from its collar on a tree so my pursuers could see the results of my ire and be sorely afraid.

No guards down in the grounds now; I suspected they were all in the woods, looking for us. I know what I'd do as soon as I saw Creamer's body, maybe checked the credentials in his wallet: I'd have been out of there like a shot, no matter what Tann was holding over my head.

But hang on. In the tower to the south-east, the only remaining structure from the riot fire. I saw a gleam of light off glass. A shadow shift position slightly. I wished for binoculars but I was sure they would only confirm what I suspected. The sniper. The lights would pick me out as soon as I broke from the cover of the trees. I'd be Joel mince within seconds, even if I zigzagged and used as much shelter as possible between me and him – the Portakabin, the car, the broken walls – I still had to expose myself in order to find Tann's retreat. I couldn't hide and seek at the same time.

Which meant I had to go around. The trees kept on north for another couple of hundred yards or so, and then suddenly stopped. Beyond that was exposed farmland and a stream. A copse coming back on the other side: shorn of many of its trees, but with enough limbs to keep me concealed until I got to the base of the tower. Then it would be all about how quiet I was.

I set off, keeping close to the edge of the woods without allowing myself to step where the fingers of light were able to reach. I couldn't hear any evidence of pursuit. I hoped they'd given up the chase as a bad idea and scarpered for a life of grime on the Costa del Kent.

At the top edge of the woods I waited, in case there were more sentries posted near the water. It was darker here, the light from the dip in the land where the prison was based failing to penetrate this far so I couldn't rely on what I could see. The stream cut through the land from east to west. It was narrow – I was pretty sure I could hop across it if needs be – but it was fast and the sound of the water deafened me to any movement through the grass, or the pebbled banks.

I shivered. The temperature was dropping fast. I watched a satellite fall smoothly across oblivion. *That was me*, I thought. Untethered, speeding, going round in fucking circles.

I nipped out from the trees, tensed against a cry or a barrage of gunfire, but none came. I hunkered down, jogging along the edge of the stream. I could smell the water, fresh and clean, but driven over the top of it from the fields was something thick and musky, maybe the natal den of a red fox.

I kept the diffuse halo of light to my right and angled towards the copse, keeping low, unsure as to when the tip of the tower would pop into view. And there it was, shockingly close now; I was convinced the sniper must have heard my footfalls in the grass. But he remained stationary, glassing the area to the south of the prison grounds, certain that our advance would be from that direction. Maybe he wasn't bothered by the thought of hordes of police arriving. This could be his Alamo, his Rorke's Drift. He'd take a few of the bastards with him. Well, not today, bucko.

I moved silently through the trees, alternating between keeping an eye on him and watching the ground for any sudden visitors. I took a few deep breaths and stepped out. I had about twenty feet to cover in which I was utterly susceptible. If he turned around, I was a goner.

And something came clattering out of the canopy – an owl or a crow, something big and spooked – and he *did* turn around, but his eye was drawn to the treetops. Once he realised it was only a bird, he'd relax, drop his gaze and there I'd be, right in his sights. Maybe I should wave. Start doing the Sand Dance, something to put him off guard for a second.

But I didn't need it because a gunshot went off in the woods opposite. *Fuck*, I thought, as the sniper swung around to peer into the trees to the east. Mawker. He'd been spotted. Either that or he'd had enough and topped himself. Worry about that later. I zipped across the remaining ten feet of no man's land and hugged the concrete base of the tower. I could hear the sniper's feet shuffle on the dusty floorboards high above. Part of the wall here was collapsed and I found an easy route into the tower without having to put myself in a dangerous position again. Metal steps ascended: a spiral staircase. The smell of cold carbon, cheated fire.

I took my boots off and left them at the foot of the stairs. Just my luck he'd be at the end of his shift and he'd meet me coming down. Or a chum would have taken pity on him and bring him up a cup of tea, sandwiching me. You have to risk it, though. Otherwise you'd still be sitting, shitting it in the dark with Mawker, jumping at shadows. Wondering how to proceed.

I padded up the steps and once I was level with his feet, swept my arm around them so he fell backwards. He hit his head on the metal skirting around the staircase access and tumbled arse over tit to the bottom. I followed him down and he was grey-faced, out cold. He was breathing shallowly and there was blood seeping from a huge knot on the back of his head.

I wondered whether I should retrieve the sniper rifle, but it would be no good at close quarters. I thought about manning his post and waiting for Tann to pop his head out, but there was no knowing where he'd appear from, and no guarantee that Bullseye here wouldn't come to and try to exact terrible revenge while I was waiting. I tossed the rifle into the trees.

I left the tower and entered the prison proper. Or rather, what was left of it. The walls were pretty much gone and the bars on the cells, the metal walkways that connected them were so much buckled scrap. I trudged down the central corridor, close to where the entrance had stood, trying to picture some of these rooms as they had been before the fire. It was difficult to do. Here would have been the spot where I had visited Tann earlier in the year – here were the swivel bolts in the floor that had secured the prisoners' chains – but everything else was incinerated, molten, black. Lengths of timber lay around, the moisture in them driven out by intense heat. All that remained were mackerel-striped chunks, filleted with huge gaps where the fibres had separated. Plastic chairs had become Dalí creations.

In a building with no rooms or walls, how could you hide?

I was beginning to think I'd got it wrong. Tann was no more here than I was in Barbados. He was hiding in some lackey's spare room, unable to go out during the day, a prisoner still, really.

I thought back to that day I'd come to visit him. I had been eager to get some kind of reaction out of him. I wanted to show him up as a petty, pathetic little man, and not the monster the tabloids would have people believe. But he rolled with my verbal blows, and when I lost my rag and tried to go for him, he brushed me aside as if I were nothing more than a troublesome gnat. Any dignity lost that day belonged to me. He had my measure. He knew I was weak.

Parking the car, walking across the car park. Security clearance. There'd been a delivery van, I remember. A white one, with a shining sun and jolly orange livery. Sunshine Laundry. Something like that. A blue hopper had been lowered on a hydraulic lift at the back of the van and the hopper had been trundled over to a delivery hatch. Towels and bedding, perhaps.

A utility area in a basement.

I wondered if the hatch might have opened on to a chute that ended in a cellar of some sort. Maybe the cellar had been spared any serious damage.

I stopped and stared at my feet and resisted the impulse to hop and dance away, as if I'd been walking on hot coals. It would make every sort of sense for Tann to be seeking refuge in the damp, black limbo of the cellar. A nothing man in a nowhere place.

I hunted around in the vicinity of the entrance for some remnants of the hatch, but a large portion of the forecourt was under tons of rubble. Instead I moved deeper into the prison, trying to fathom the logical location for a cellar entrance. It would be out of the way, a room within a room, perhaps. A storage room of some kind. Electrical or mechanical. The place where they kept the truncheons and tear gas. But I couldn't find anything like that and the one room that did show promise – what I guessed was some sort of mail sorting office – had no kind of door leading anywhere.

I didn't know what to do. What was also bothering me was the issue of the guards. I could see now that there were a number of additional cars parked nearby, along with the black Merc. I couldn't imagine anybody leaving behind a motor in favour of Shanks's pony, no matter how desperate the need to get away might be. Well, if I couldn't find Tann then I was going to make sure this lot were stuffed if they did come back.

I moved from car to car, slashing tyres. I finished with the Merc and took extra pleasure from ribboning his run-flats.

When that was done, my arm was burning with effort. I thought I heard the whoop of a siren, and began to relax. The cavalry was in the vicinity. It meant *Return to GO*. But at least there'd be no more deaths this night.

I headed over to the Portakabin. Empty, as I'd expected. A radio playing. The Carpenters. Who'd have thunk it? Tann's hard-bitten flunkies liked a bit of easy listening while they picked the blood from under their nails.

There were the remnants of some old meals. Pizza boxes in the main – somebody had been making a lot of meat feast runs – and a walkie-talkie battery charging dock. A copy of the *Daily Mirror*. A kettle and some tea-stained sugar solidifying in a bowl. A rug. And that was about it.

I went back outside and thought, *Hang on, who puts a rug down in a Portakabin?*

It was just a square patch of rubbish carpet – the kind of thing you'd find in a 1970s khazi. I lifted one corner and there was a hatch underneath it, crudely formed: the work of a box blade, maybe, and a couple of cheap hinges.

Soft fingers, I thought, slipping it open. Smells leapt out. Paraffin, hot metal, human waste.

Cigars.

I strained for voices but none came. Yellow metal rungs descended, cut off into fangs by the shadows. Maybe they had really been dismantled – I wouldn't put it past Tann – and I'd drop into a pit of fuel which he would then ignite.

I thought of Danny when my breath started to hitch. *Being scared is overrated.* I thought of Sarah and Becs. Whatever lay ahead of me wasn't what happened to her. Nothing could be like that. Which meant I could handle it. I swung my legs into the hatch and descended.

23

Pencil torch on: the beam revealed acres of crazy. It was a Health and Safety disaster zone. Washing machines disembowelled, parts strewn across the corridor. Strip lighting that hung from the ceiling, wires exposed. The heat from the fire had penetrated some areas. Plastic ducts and polystyrene ceiling tiles had melted and reformed into grotesque shapes. Water from the fire service hoses had deformed the walls; they were bellied and bowed. There was water underfoot still, in places up to a foot deep. A rat knifed through it, then darted into a metre-wide crack in the wall.

I wondered if this obstacle course had been designed as a primitive warning system, a way of alerting Tann to visitors, because it was impossible to advance without making any noise. *If he's here*, a voice said. And I had to go over again all the reasons why he would be here, why he couldn't fail to be here and—

So maybe he is here. But he could have watched you every step. It could have all been designed to get you to this spot, and even now he's starting up the bulldozer to push a thousand tons of fuck you on to your own and only escape route.

It's been a great emotional help to me, that fucking voice. I love how it's generated from within and yet only ever provides shit information. A bit of cheerleading wouldn't go amiss from time to time.

I waded through that evil-smelling water, slicked as it was with rainbows of oil and the contents of ruptured pipes. I thought I could hear music from up ahead but that could only be trickery. The beat of the rain on corrugated metal, the chuckle of water through the maze of shattered masonry. Mostly, though, I reckoned it was due to the exhausted lump of tissue at the top of my head. I was hungry and tired and, despite leaning heavily on what Danny Sweet had drummed into me, scared almost to a standstill.

But then I heard something different up ahead. It was less random than everything else. There was purpose in it: it sounded like the opening of a door – a door that no longer sat squarely in its frame and whose hinges were gritted and old. I heard it catch against a sodden, carpeted floor. The judder as it hit resistance and would swing no further. I heard footsteps, light and quick, splashing towards me.

I took out the gun and switched off the safety. It felt so tiny in my hand. I could have been holding a howitzer and I'd be convinced a shell from it would skid off Tann's body with all the destructive power of a raindrop.

My light picked out movement. Someone rapidly approaching. Someone else carrying a torch. The beams met and slashed across each other, finally pooling between us. My heart loud enough for her to hear.

'Joel,' she said.

I wanted to raise the torch, to train the beam of light on

her face. To touch it. To study it for hours. To make sure. But I didn't have to. Not really. Because she had spoken my name and her voice was the same as it had been the last time I heard it, when she was thirteen. Strong, confident, amused. Just like her mum.

I opened my mouth to say something but my tongue and lips had stiffened with shock. I'd imagined this moment so often, albeit in different surroundings, the beautiful tributes and apologies I would deliver, the wisdoms I would impart. Hopes and promises. But now it was here, my voice, if I could only find it, would not have been worthy of her or the situation. There was nothing I could say.

She passed her torch to her other hand and swept her fingers through her long hair. 'We're just through here,' she said, and turned and moved away.

I could smell the perfume in her wake, but although I recognised that, and her posture, and the playfulness and the edge in her voice, I was convincing myself that it was an astonishing imposter, that it was all a brilliant ruse to put me off guard. Up ahead was a trap, and she was complicit.

So, of course, I followed her through the doorway – how could I not? – my hand outstretched, aching to feel her warmth under my fingers once again, and her name trembled in my mouth.

24

There was power in this room. Portable LED lights hung from hooks in the walls. The music I thought I'd heard in the corridor was an album being played on a turntable. Old-time music. The Ink Spots. Sarah went over to it and returned the carriage to the first track.

'I didn't know you liked this kind of music,' I said.

'That person has changed, Joel,' she said.

She was my Sarah, but she was not my Sarah. Her eyes were glassy. Tann was sitting on a chair in the corner. She smiled at me, but it was filled with distance. She went to him and sat on the floor by his feet. I pointed the gun at his face. End it now. Nothing he can do or say can save him.

But Sarah got to her knees and positioned herself between us. 'Don't shoot him,' she said.

'Put your gun away, Joel,' Tann said. I realised what it was about Tann's voice that nagged at me. It wasn't just that it was oily and sly, more confident than he had any right to be. It was because there were no rough edges to his speech. No fillers, no pauses, no false starts. Every word was enunciated and no word was wasted. I don't know what that meant, if anything. Perhaps only that he was precise and economical.

'This will all be a lot smoother for you if you don't complicate matters with a weapon.'

'Fuck you,' I said. Ever the diplomat. 'There have been quite a number of people in my vicinity holding guns lately, and I don't want to feel left out.'

But my grip on the gun had already loosened. Sarah's words, not his, had seen to that. I felt the urge to ignore everyone and blow him to kingdom come when he placed a proprietorial hand on her shoulder, and began to stroke her skin.

'Get. Your. Fucking. Hands. Off. My. Daughter.'

'We need to talk,' they both said at the same time. They looked at each other and laughed. I felt I'd stumbled into a room being used by lovers just before or just after the act. I felt unwelcome, intrusive.

'Sarah,' I said. 'He killed your mother.'

She didn't seem to understand. She wore the smile of a person indulging in another's fantasies. Her eyes were preternaturally bright and intent. Her movement, though, was languid, as if she were encased in aspic. A table was littered with cups and plastic bottles of water. Twisted foil blister packs. Largactil. The liquid cosh. He was keeping her docile.

'What is this, Tann?' I said. 'You're drugging her? Why? You're working some kind of Stockholm Syndrome?'

Tann stood up. I could see that he too was armed. But whereas my Glock was subtle and understated, he was carrying a FAMAS. It didn't matter that his gun was louder than mine, or that it carried more ammunition and delivered it faster. One bullet was all you needed.

'Sarah suffers from anxiety and headaches. I'm helping her to get better,' he said.

'Bullshit,' I said. As if to underline his importance in her restoration, Sarah squeezed his hand and took another two tablets from the stash on the table. I resisted the urge to go over and slap them out of her hand. I had to play this with care.

'Why didn't you slip away when you had the chance?' I said. 'You could have made it to the coast, got a boat to the Continent... way before anyone realised you were out.'

'My life is here,' he said. 'Home is where the heart is.' He gave Sarah another tender, longing look.

'If you've touched her I'll kill you,' I said.

He turned his attention back to me and his face was twisted with disgust. 'I'm not a monster, Joel,' he said, without a hint of irony. The light slid around the neatly cut planes of his face as if it was something that had been applied, like lotion. 'But I'll tell you something that *is* monstrous.'

'Let me guess,' I said. 'Killing the wife of a man who couldn't really cope that well without her. Who subsequently lost touch with his daughter. And has suffered a couple of attempts on his life in the past week. On your orders.'

'That's not monstrous,' Tann said. 'That's bad luck. What's monstrous is seeing the woman you loved, the woman you devoted every minute to, cut you off in her prime, take everything from you. Leaving you to pick up the pieces.'

'What the fuck are you talking about?'

'We were to be married,' he said.

In my head I was shouldering closed a door to a room that was packed to the rafters with NO. But I didn't have the strength.

'I've had enough of this,' I said. 'You stand aside and let me take my daughter with me or I finish you right now.'

'I asked her. *Of course* I asked her. She was, after all, carrying our child.'

'Tann.' My voice was baby soft. I was finding it hard to breathe.

'But she said no. And she said she had taken the appropriate steps. She didn't like my... temper. She wished me well. She walked away.'

'I don't want to hear this shit.' But all I could think of was sitting on a sofa while Rebecca got ready for her visit to the doctor and the file containing her medical notes was right next to me. It only took a moment to nudge the cover open and see what was written inside.

How did I feel about that? I felt a little sneaky that I'd looked in the first place, because what was I expecting to find? Nothing good comes of that kind of curiosity. But there it had been. Evidence that Becs had been pregnant before she met me. Stark word: *termination*. But so what, really? We all make mistakes. She'd done what she felt was right. An abortion for someone who wasn't ready to be a mother. She'd have thought long and hard about it. I hadn't given it a second thought. An old boyfriend. A torn condom. A forgotten pill. Shit happens.

Tell me it wasn't him.

...

Becs. Tell me it wasn't him.

But Becs wasn't talking to me any more.

I wanted to say that it didn't matter. So what if he'd been on the scene one time, many, many years ago? Before he was a cunt, or as much of a cunt as he had become. We all learned by fucking up and Becs had fucked up, but had come back from it. She'd met me. We'd had Sarah.

'And so,' he said. 'I raped her. I raped Rebecca. I raped your wife. And this was after you two had got together. She never said a word. And I know why. Because she still loved me. She wanted to be with me and she was too fucked up to realise.'

'You're living in a fantasy world if you think my wife—'

'I WAS THERE FIRST!' he screamed. Sarah jumped, but the smile remained. She looked as if she couldn't fathom why she'd reacted.

The light twitched a little, as if affected by the ferocity of Tann's voice. I heard the buzz and grumble of loose ballast in the fluorescent tubes. I heard the trickle of soil as it repositioned itself in any number of cracks and chasms.

'You're a sick fuck,' I said. 'She'd have told me.'

'She was protecting you.'

'SHE'D HAVE TOLD ME!'

Sarah jumped again. Her gaze flickered between me and Tann. There was the slow collapse of the smile and panic building.

'Sarah is my child,' he said.

'She would have aborted again, if she suspected it was you.'

'You hear that, Sarah? Your so-called dad thinks you should have been vacuumed from the womb. There's familial love for you, right there.'

'Sarah, he's lying,' I said.

The lights went out and then came back on again. There was a deep groaning sound. Maybe the cellar was giving up the ghost after the damage caused by the fire and the subsequent tonnage of water. Call me strange, but I really didn't fancy being in here if the ceiling caved in. Tann and I looked at each other and there was a kind of amused irritation on his face, as if he was saying to me, *I didn't plan this, can't pin this on me.* And then the lights stuttered again. I saw Tann had taken a couple of steps towards the door.

279

He looked as if he'd been caught in a lewd act; the amused look remained, but there was a challenge in his eyes too. Sarah was no longer playing human shield. I didn't need asking twice. I loosed a couple of shots his way just as the darkness leapt back into the room. He responded in kind, already on the move, and the room filled with tracer, picking out snapshots of him and his creased eyes, his gritted teeth. Wood splintered and glass shattered as the shells from the FAMAS crashed into the surroundings. In my haste to get out of that hail of fire, I tripped over a chair leg but that pratfall saved me: bullets slammed into the walls above.

I returned fire but I was blind to some extent. I knew Sarah was to my right, still on her knees, and as yet she wasn't moving. I heard her, very clearly, scream out: 'Daddy! Please! No!'

If she did move she was liable to get her head blown off.

'Stay down,' I yelled.

The lights buzzed back on. Tann was at the doorway. He was leaving. I raised an arm to shoot but he was quicker. The lights went out. I felt a blow to my arm as if a silverback had taken a running jump at it while wearing steel toe-capped boots. I could no longer feel the Glock in my hand. I reached with my other, convinced I would touch only a splintered stump, but my arm was intact, albeit very hot and wet. It suddenly felt too heavy to keep upright and my shoulder failed, the arm hanging by my side, utterly useless. I felt fear creeping into me, while the blood pooled out.

The light flickered back on. Tann had given up on his escape plan, knowing that he had me at his mercy. He was standing a foot away from me. The muzzle of the FAMAS was five centimetres from my left eye. Close enough to smell the grease that the weapon had been packed in. But the dynamic in the room had all changed and I couldn't work out why. It wasn't just that Tann had the upper hand. Sarah was reaching out to pick up my gun. Her smile was so wide and liquid that I had the awful conviction that her entire jaw was going to slither out from her mouth and crack against the floor.

Christ, do it, I thought. *Kill me now rather than suffer any more thoughts like that.*

Light. Three figures. Dark.

Light. Four figures. Dark.

Tann said: 'Rest in hell. Writhe in agony. Bitch.' The light stuttered on again.

And Mawker shot him in the back.

Tann arched and the hand holding the FAMAS jerked wildly. It sprayed bullets. Several of them slammed through Mawker's jaw, snapping his head back, splintering bone through the rest of his face.

Darkness. Someone groaning. Someone gurgling. I heard someone shifting through the blood and glass, coming towards me. Tann at the last, finishing it. I was losing blood, but not at any great rate of knots. But I was kitten weak, undone by shock and fear.

I fished in my pocket and found the torch. I switched it on and Tann was looking at me. He was lying on the floor and looking at me. Blood ringed his mouth. He was dead. But no. He grinned and I saw the wash of blood on his teeth, like a vampire that has just fed. He shifted the muzzle of the gun so that it was trained on my heart. I'd given him enough light to finish his job. I'd authored my own demise. It might have been funny if it wasn't so fucking tragic.

'Thanks,' he said, but it was an effort. It was air. I could see the fight in him, the struggle to keep death away long enough for him to pull the trigger and take me with him.

'Why did you kill Rebecca?' I asked him. 'Why did you do what you did?'

'If I couldn't have her…'

I switched the torch off and there was a pop and I thought, *Is that it? What a pathetic sound to check out to. That's the noise that Death makes? Christ, someone lend Him an amp. And while we're at it, Death, what's with the continuous pain? My arm's giving me agony. Is this part of eternity's punishment? Is this—*

And then the room filled with an explosion of light so bright I had to shield my eyes and I thought, *Well sod me with a spatula: I made it to Heaven after all.*

Figures filled the light. Armed officers. Mawker was on his back, choking on blood. I got to him and rolled him on to his side. His eyes fastened on mine. I said all the right things, but they were all wrong. His lower jaw was gone. I gripped his hand and then I thought fuck that and I pulled him to me and held him tight and bollocks to the pain it caused me, and I held him until he stopped convulsing and he was gone.

Minutes later the paramedics arrived. I'd been shot clean through the arm. The shell had nutmegged the ulna and radius and politely avoided the artery before wiping its feet on the way out. They told me they had never seen a cleaner exit.

I was plugged and wrapped and I didn't keep my eyes off Sarah while they tended me. She'd been cloaked in one of those silver foil capes they give out to marathon runners. And they had magicked a drip from somewhere. Someone administered a shot. Something to combat the Largactil perhaps, or a sedative. A good sedative. I don't know. It seemed to do the trick though. She lost that manic look. For the first time since I'd lost her, she looked like my daughter. I could still see the child in her face.

25

I went looking for him.

My arm was in a sling, and I don't know if you've tried it, but climbing hundreds of steps with one arm is a sod of a job. It would probably be easier with one leg instead. I don't know what it is that makes it so knackering. Maybe it's to do with balance. Or maybe it's nothing to do with balance and all to do with posture. In any case, both things rate very low where I'm concerned.

I went up a couple of days before Christmas. There were festive lights on all the cranes. There was one guy on duty, the poor sap, a policeman because of what had happened. And he wasn't making an effort. He was sitting in a squad car with a radio playing Perry Como, sipping from a cup. 'Christmas Dream'. I hoped there was a nip of something other than coffee in that. I silently sent him best wishes and got myself up the damned skyscraper.

There were the leftovers of a party on the summit. There were windows too now, presumably put in especially so some pissed labourer didn't take a dive off the thirty-third floor. The wind howled outside as if complaining at its banishment. A skip full of empty Brew Dog bottles. Crumpled foil bags of dry roasted peanuts.

I found a candle, warm and soft at the business end; and there was the hot, plasticky odour of recently extinguished flame. I called out to him.

'That's not my name,' he said.

'But it's who you are.'

'According to some. To people who can't cope. Who think that giving a name to something they don't want to think about makes it more manageable.'

'It's the way we're hardwired,' I said. 'When you're a kid you fear what's underneath the bed if you don't know what it is. But as soon as you find out it's a zombie or a vampire, you have the upper hand. You can deal with it. You can prepare.'

'So, fifty storeys high, how do you prepare for me?'

'You saved my life,' I said. 'I wanted to thank you.'

'We did all that,' he said. 'You're here to turn me in.'

'To ask you to give yourself up,' I said.

'I did,' he said. 'I stopped. Years ago.'

'And that's supposed to mean anything? The passage of years? People forget, scars heal, that kind of thing?'

'Something like that.'

'You said you were the architect.'

'I was an architect. Of sorts.'

'Of death.'

He smiled and walked to the window. Teeming lights everywhere. Traffic surged across London Bridge like something molten.

'What *is* your name?'

'Whittaker,' he said. 'Struan Whittaker.'

'Why did you stop, Struan?' I asked. 'Jesus, why did you start?'

He rubbed his face and I heard the hiss of stubble in the open space like water thrown on a hot plate.

'I was young and angry,' he said. 'I used to be able to see things from my bedroom window. Tower block on the High Street in Stratford. I used to be able to see park space. A view down the river. And then the skyscrapers came and started blocking out life. I could no longer see the river. Or the parks. Just sheets of steel and glass. Shining columns of money.'

'You lived in a tower block.'

'Yes. And well loved, it was. Well used. The residential blocks being thrown up now in London... who can afford to live in them, other than the stratospherically rich?'

'The people building them... the people you pushed off the upper floors... they weren't stratospherically rich. They were construction workers. They were dads and brothers and sons. Why did they deserve to die?'

'You're right,' he snapped. His voice quivered with some kind of emotion I couldn't discern. Anger, guilt? It seemed defensive and belligerent in equal measure. 'And that's why I quit. I took a step back. It was a protest but I couldn't see what it was I was really doing. When I understood, when I saw the newspapers and the faces of the people who died – not just shadows in hard hats – I stopped. That and the birth of my son. I recognised the monster I'd become.'

'You recognised it but you did nothing about it. You can make up for that now. You can give yourself up.'

'Or?'

'I won't grass. Not tonight. But tomorrow the police will be here. And I'll give them your name. I'll give them a description.'

'If you walk away from here.'

'You're an old man now, Struan.'

'I kept myself fit.'

'Maybe. But the truth is, I don't want another fight.'

'My son died, you know.'

'I'm sorry to hear that. Really, I am.'

'He was killed on a train track. Dicking about with his mates. Playing chicken with InterCity 125s. One of his mates told me later that he never looked like leaving the tracks. He wasn't poised, ready to jump out the way. He just stood there. He was thirteen.'

'Why did you come back to these buildings?' I asked. I was getting cold. The ache in my arm was intensifying. I needed some co-codamol and a glass – one glass – of something warming.

'I don't know,' he said.

'You weren't going to—'

'What? Reignite my reign of terror?'

'Jump. You weren't going to jump, were you?'

He looked at me thoughtfully, but he didn't say anything.

'Your life falls apart when you lose a child,' he said.

'Tell me about it.'

'My wife walked away. I lost my job. Drink, you know. But I made some progress. Maybe I come up here because, ironically… the view…'

'It is spectacular.'

'To fly above this,' he said. 'To soar over the city. Imagine that.'

'Imagine.'

'Give me this evening,' he said.

I didn't say anything else. I didn't know how to phrase what I should have said next.

I left him, remembering the fire in his eyes when he saw Henry Herschell step across the threshold, and I went home.

In the morning it was on the news.

26

Ian Mawker was cremated at Mortlake the next day. There was a thin mist tangled in the treetops, but you could tell the sky was bright beyond it. Everyone was wondering whether the sun would be strong enough to chase it all away.

A couple of people spoke at the service. One of them was a sweet old guy who had been in the police back in the 1960s. A more civilised time, according to him. The villains were polite, apparently. Called you sir. Mawker used to go to him for advice. And to gain a sense of perspective.

After the curtain had slipped open to receive his coffin and the organ had gone quiet, I headed off. I didn't want to listen to the stories over sandwiches and warm beer. I'd been a part of them. I also didn't want to lock horns with some of the Mawkerites who'd been giving me the beady while the hymns were being sung. I hadn't always seen eye to eye with Mawker, but I'd be damned if I buggered his funeral up by brawling with his bum-polishers.

Someone collared me, nevertheless, as I was getting into the car Jimmy Two was letting me use (a Ford Mondeo, if you're interested, with an automatic gearbox to help me with my gammy arm) while I went about finding a replacement for the Saab. It was the sweet old guy, as it happened. He introduced himself as Stuart Frobisher and shook my hand. His skin was soft and yielding, but his grip was firmer than you'd expect. He gave me an envelope.

'I'm executor of Ian's estate,' he said. 'That was in his drawer. Sealed. Addressed to you.'

'Thank you,' I said.

'I doubt it's money,' he said. 'And I doubt it's a card of any sort. Because you're a cunt and a half, son. He used to tell me all about you. He could have filled a pint pot with stomach acid on a daily basis because of you. If there's any justice in the world it will be an invitation to join him in the fucking furnace.'

There wasn't an awful lot I could have said to that. I watched him walk back, the sweet old man. Stuart Frobisher in his cardigan, with his candy-floss hair. He was received by a gaggle of old dears who cooed and laughed at something he said.

I got in the car and opened the envelope. There was a photograph of Mawker standing in his kitchen, a glass of whisky in one hand. The other hand was outstretched towards the lens, and he was sticking the Vs up at me. I started laughing and couldn't stop. The laughter turned to tears and returned to laughter. People walked by and gave me funny looks.

I got myself under control, drove home and attached the photograph to the fridge door.

27

Sarah was staying with me. She had the bed, I had the sofa. Mengele went to sleep with her every night. I heard him through the wall, purring his nuts off. Maybe it was because she'd renamed him. Was it that easy? I don't know. Does the deed poll count where cats are concerned? Anyway, she was calling him Deano because he was cool, like Dean Martin, like James Dean, but also because... sardines. I'd never fed him sardines, but I got where she was coming from. It didn't stop him behaving like a Nazi overlord with me, mind.

She was hungry but there was nothing in the kitchen. I said I'd take her out for dinner. She suggested I contact Romy and invite her too. I said I would. But not tonight. Soon.

'She likes you,' she said.

'And I like her.'

'So do something about it. Mum would want you to.'

'I know. I know.'

I watched her slip into her suede jacket and tie the laces of her sixteen-hole oxblood DMs. No make-up. She was pale and beautiful. She was tired and beautiful. We traipsed downstairs to the ground floor and I thought of the gift I'd bought her, wrapped as best as I could, hidden in my underwear drawer. I hoped she'd like it. It had cost a lot of money, but I reckoned all these Christmases I'd been unable to get her anything, well, this was payback for those.

We stepped out on to Homer Street and the air was brittle and fresh and good. I wanted to ask her so many questions. I wanted to talk to her about her mum. I wanted to grill her about Tann. I wanted to tell her how much I was sorry and I wanted to show her too. I wanted to hug her. My God, I desperately wanted to hug her.

But there was plenty of time for all of that. Whenever she was ready.

'I fancy moussaka,' she said.

'You're kidding,' I said. 'I hate Greek food.'

'I know,' she said. 'And, insult to injury, you're paying for the bastard.'

It was drugs, I'd told her, at the hospital later that night. She was tired. Drifting. *Drugs and duplicity. That's all. He's good at that. He's a puppeteer. A string puller. He wanted to get at me through you. But I know your mum. And I know you. And I know me. You are me. Of me. I'll take any test. I know your mum. Sarah. Sarah. Sarah.*

We headed towards Edgware Road. As we crossed Crawford Street, she slipped her hand into mine.

ACKNOWLEDGMENTS

Thanks again to Mum and Dad, Rhonda, Ethan, Ripley and Zac, and all the readers and writers I'm lucky to call friends. Thanks to Mary and Tim for good food and company in a series of interesting houses. Thanks also to Paul and Helen Lomax for excellent karate tuition over the past couple of years – Joel wouldn't be alive today if it weren't for you. I'm grateful to David Carrier for risqué jokes and for looking after my stuff for too many years: RIP, sir. Thanks to Adèle Fielding for her medical prowess, and for introducing me to London. I'm grateful too to Miranda Jewess for kicks up the arse and arms around the shoulder, to Cat Camacho, and to Julia Lloyd for stunning covers.

ABOUT THE AUTHOR

Conrad Williams is the author of nine novels, four novellas and a collection of short stories. *One* was the winner of the August Derleth award for Best Novel (British Fantasy Awards 2010), while *The Unblemished* won the International Horror Guild Award for Best Novel in 2007 (he beat the shortlisted Stephen King on both occasions). He won the British Fantasy Award for Best Newcomer in 1993, and another British Fantasy Award for Best Novella (*The Scalding Rooms*) in 2008. His first crime novel, and the first Joel Sorrell thriller, *Dust and Desire*, was published in 2015, with *Sonata of the Dead* following in 2016. He lives in Manchester.

ALSO AVAILABLE FROM TITAN BOOKS

THE JOEL SORRELL THRILLERS
CONRAD WILLIAMS

DUST AND DESIRE

Joel Sorrell, a bruised, bad-mouthed PI, is a sucker for missing person cases. And not just because he's searching for his daughter, who vanished after his wife was murdered. Joel feels a kinship with the desperate and the damned. So when the mysterious Kara Geenan begs him to find her missing brother, Joel agrees. Then an attempt is made on his life, and Kara vanishes… A vicious serial killer is on the hunt, and Joel suspects that answers may lie in his own hellish past.

SONATA OF THE DEAD

Even as he recovers from his encounter with an unhinged killer, PI Joel Sorrell cannot forget his search for Sarah. He receives a tip that photographs of her have been found at a murder scene, where a young man whom Sarah knew when they were children has been killed. Finding a link between the victim and a writers' group, Joel follows the thread, but every lead ends in another body. Someone is targeting the group, and it is only a matter of time before Joel's daughter is run to ground.

PRAISE FOR THE SERIES
"Gritty and compelling"
Mark Billingham, bestselling author of *Rush of Blood*

TITANBOOKS.COM

ALSO AVAILABLE FROM TITAN BOOKS

THE BLOOD STRAND
A FAROES NOVEL

CHRIS OULD

Having left the Faroes as a child, Jan Reyna is now a British police detective, and the islands are foreign to him. But he is drawn back when his estranged father is found unconscious with a shotgun by his side and someone else's blood at the scene. Then a man's body is washed up on an isolated beach. Is Reyna's father responsible? Looking for answers, Reyna falls in with local detective Hjalti Hentze. But as the stakes get higher and Reyna learns more about his family and the truth behind his mother's flight from the Faroes, he must decide whether to stay, or to forsake the strange, windswept islands for good.

"This one is a winner… For fans of Henning Mankell and Elizabeth George"
Booklist (starred review)

"An absorbing new mystery"
Library Journal

"The plot takes many unexpected twists en route to the satisfying ending"
Publishers Weekly

TITANBOOKS.COM

ALSO AVAILABLE FROM TITAN BOOKS

HACK
AN F.X. SHEPHERD NOVEL

KIERAN CROWLEY

It's a dog-eat-dog world at the infamous tabloid the *New York Mail*, where brand new pet columnist F.X. Shepherd accidentally finds himself on the trail of The Hacker, a serial killer targeting unpleasant celebrities in inventive—and often decorative—ways. And it's only his second day on the job. Luckily Shepherd has hidden talents, not to mention a hidden agenda. But as bodies and suspects accumulate, he finds himself running afoul of cutthroat office politics, the NYPD, and Ginny Mac, an attractive but ruthless reporter for a competing newspaper. And when Shepherd himself is contacted by The Hacker, he realizes he may be next on the killer's list…

"A rollicking, sharp-witted crime novel"
Kirkus Reviews

"Laugh out loud funny and suspenseful—it's like Jack Reacher meets Jack Black"
Rebecca Cantrell, New York Times bestselling author of *The Blood Gospel*

"A joy to read and captures the imagination from the start"
Long Island Press

TITANBOOKS.COM

ALSO AVAILABLE FROM TITAN BOOKS

THE AGE OF TREACHERY
A DUNCAN FORRESTER NOVEL

GAVIN SCOTT

It is the winter of 1946, and after years of war, ex-Special Operations Executive agent Duncan Forrester is back at his Oxford college as a junior Ancient History Fellow. But his peace is shattered when a hated colleague is found dead, and his closest friend is arrested for the murder. Convinced that the police have the wrong man, and hearing rumours that the victim was in possession of a mysterious Viking saga, Forrester follows the trail of the manuscript from the ruins of Berlin to the forests of Norway, hoping that it is the key to the man's death. But he is not alone in his search, and he soon discovers that old adversaries are still at war...

"A wonderful historical setting, brilliantly captured"
Maureen Jennings, bestselling author of
The Murdoch Mysteries

"A suspenseful murder mystery that holds the reader's interest to the last page"
Michael Kurland, award-winning author of
The Infernal Device

TITANBOOKS.COM

ALSO AVAILABLE FROM TITAN BOOKS

IMPURE BLOOD
A CAPTAIN DARAC NOVEL

PETER MORFOOT

In the heat of a French summer, Captain Paul Darac of the Nice Brigade Criminelle is called to a highly sensitive crime scene. A man has been murdered in the midst of a prayer group, but no one saw how it was done. And the more Darac and his team learn about the victim, the longer their list of suspects grows. Darac's hunt for the murderer will uncover a desire for revenge years in the making, and put the life of one of his own at risk...

"A delightful example of the disenchanted French boulevardier"
Library Journal (starred review)

"Engrossing... An auspicious debut for Darac"
Publishers Weekly

"A sprawling, ambitious series debut"
Kirkus Reviews

TITANBOOKS.COM

ALSO AVAILABLE FROM TITAN BOOKS

WRITTEN IN DEAD WAX
A VINYL DETECTIVE NOVEL

ANDREW CARTMEL

He is a record collector – a connoisseur of vinyl, hunting out rare and elusive LPs. His business card describes him as the 'Vinyl Detective' and some people take this more literally than others. Like the beautiful, mysterious woman who wants to pay him a large sum of money to find a priceless lost recording – on behalf of an extremely wealthy (and rather sinister) shadowy client. Given that he's just about to run out of cat biscuits, this gets our hero's full attention. So begins a painful and dangerous odyssey in search of the rarest jazz record of them all…

"This charming mystery feels as companionable as a leisurely afternoon trawling the vintage shops with a good friend"
Kirkus Reviews

"Marvelously inventive and endlessly fascinating"
Publishers Weekly

"Vinyl fans, this one's for you"
Booklist

TITANBOOKS.COM

ALSO AVAILABLE FROM TITAN BOOKS

THE BURSAR'S WIFE
A GEORGE KOCHARYAN NOVEL

E.G. RODFORD

Meet George Kocharyan, Cambridge Confidential Services' one and only private investigator. Amidst the usual jobs following unfaithful spouses, he is approached by the glamorous Sylvia Booker, who fears that her daughter Lucy has fallen in with the wrong crowd. Aided by his assistant Sandra and her teenage son, George soon discovers that Sylvia has good reason to be concerned. Then an unfaithful wife he had been following is found dead. As his investigation continues—enlivened by a mild stabbing and the unwanted attention of Detective Inspector Vicky Stubbing—George begins to wonder if all the threads are connected...

"Funny and engaging, a promising debut"
The Sunday Times

"A quirky and persuasive new entry in the ranks of crime fiction"
Barry Forshaw, *Crime Time*

"An absolute delight—a gumshoe thriller that reminded me of Raymond Chandler"
Steven Dunne, author of *A Killing Moon*

TITANBOOKS.COM

For more fantastic fiction, author events, exclusive excerpts,
competitions, limited editions and more

VISIT OUR WEBSITE
titanbooks.com

LIKE US ON FACEBOOK
facebook.com/titanbooks

FOLLOW US ON TWITTER
@TitanBooks

EMAIL US
readerfeedback@titanemail.com